CARVED IN BLOOD

MICHAEL BENNETT
CARVED IN BLOOD

A Hana Westerman Thriller

Atlantic Monthly Press
New York

Copyright © 2025 by Michael Bennett

All rights reserved. No part of this book may be reproduced in any form or by any electronic or mechanical means, including information storage and retrieval systems, without permission in writing from the publisher, except by a reviewer, who may quote brief passages in a review. Scanning, uploading, and electronic distribution of this book or the facilitation of such without the permission of the publisher is prohibited. Please purchase only authorized electronic editions, and do not participate in or encourage electronic piracy of copyrighted materials. Your support of the author's rights is appreciated. Any member of educational institutions wishing to photocopy part or all of the work for classroom use, or anthology, should send inquiries to Grove Atlantic, 154 West 14th Street, New York, NY 10011 or permissions@groveatlantic.com.

Any use of this publication to train generative artificial intelligence ("AI") technologies is expressly prohibited. The author and publisher reserve all rights to license uses of this work for generative AI training and development of machine learning language models.

Original characters created and developed by Michael Bennett and Jane Holland
'Little Boxes' written and composed by Malvina Reynolds © 1962
'Lose My Breath' written by Shawn Carter, Sean Garrett, LaShawn Daniels, Beyoncé, Michelle Williams, Rodney Jerkins, Kelly Rowland and Fred Jerkins III
(from Destiny Fulfilled © Destiny's Child 2004)
'Thunderstruck' written and composed by Angus Young and Malcolm Young
(from The Razors Edge © AC/DC 1990)
'Te Aroha' – traditional Māori waiata
Textbook of Abnormal Psychology by Roy Melvin Dorcus and George Wilson Shaffer
(first publication Baltimore: Williams and Wilkins Co., 1934)
My Little Pony toys and media © Hasbro
Māori design by Māhina Rose Holland Bennett

First published in Great Britain in 2025 by Simon & Schuster UK Ltd

Printed in the United States of America

First Grove Atlantic hardcover editon: July 2025

Typeset in Sabon MT Std by Palimpsest Book Production Limited, Falkirk, Stirlingshire

Library of Congress Cataloging-in-Publication data is available for this title.

ISBN 978-0-8021-6454-4
eISBN 978-0-8021-6455-1

Atlantic Monthly Press
an imprint of Grove Atlantic
154 West 14th Street
New York, NY 10011

Distributed by Publishers Group West

groveatlantic.com

25 26 27 28   10 9 8 7 6 5 4 3 2 1

For Mark Bennett
(2nd April 1950 – 20th October 2024).

For Bruce Bennett
(20th March 1953 – 1st February 2025).

Shine bright among the stars, big brothers.

1

YEE-HA

After Hana came face to face with one, she got a little obsessed with mako sharks.

It happened late summer, some months ago. She was out swimming, as part of her usual routine: a 10.13-km run before dawn, then into the ocean as the sun comes up over the black sand dunes of Tātā Bay. She was fifty metres offshore when she saw something flash past underneath her. She knew straight away it was a mako, with its distinctive short fins. Later, having spent far too much time googling the creature, she learned that they are very curious. This one sure was. It must have clocked her, just as she clocked it. It came back, circled her. Hana ducked underwater, eyes open in the stinging salt, deciding that if it was going to attack, she wanted to see it coming.

Turning with the shark, Hana stayed focused on the creature. Watching it, as it watched her.

The eyes. Cold. Emotionless.

She'd find out later that a mako, if it decides to attack, can almost instantly hit speeds of fifty miles an hour or more. Coming at you so fast, there's not much you can do, even if you're watching its every move. It was probably good she wasn't aware of any of that at the time, she thought. The shark circled twice. Three times. Its eyes never leaving her. Then it left, disappearing into the shadows of the ocean.

Hana swam in to shore.

It's six months later. Summer is long gone. June is the depths of the southern hemisphere winter, but Hana is still swimming every morning, unfazed by the chilly waters or the close encounter. This morning, walking up the sands as the sun rises, she looks at the nearby headland beyond the dunes. She finds herself lost in a very different memory – one from nineteen years earlier. Going down to this headland, at this same time of year, to watch the rising of the sacred stars. Matariki is the constellation that guided the waka* across the mapless oceans to New Zealand; metaphorically, the stars are the sacred celestial beings which help us chart our own lives down here on earth. When Matariki rises, it is a time for remembering the dead; a time for saying goodbye. And it is also a time for starting anew.

---

* Waka – the ocean-going canoes that carried the Māori tribes to New Zealand one thousand years ago.

Hana's daughter Addison is a Matariki baby, born near the end of June. When Addison was just a few days old, Hana brought her down from Auckland to Tātā Bay to meet her grandparents, Hana's mum and dad. Eru and Jos wrapped their granddaughter up in every blanket they had in the house, and they all went down to the headland, where Eru blessed the newborn as the sacred stars looked down.

'All babies are special,' he said in te reo Māori.* 'But I have a feeling this one might be even more special.'

Drying herself on the sands, Hana breathes deep. Ten days to go until the rising of Matariki. There's something about this time of year, even if you're not someone who lives by the stars and the traditional calendar. Rising in the darkest days of winter, always close to the shortest day of the year, somehow the energy from that twinkling constellation over four hundred light years away seems to change the way you walk on the face of this world. The return of the stars makes it just that little bit easier to get through the frosts and rains and storms of an unpredictable New Zealand winter.

The weather is behaving today. It's looking like it will be a fine mid-winter morning.

Hana heads for her house. It's going to be a big day for Tātā Bay.

---

* Te reo Māori (or just 'te reo') – the Māori language.

The police car drives around the perimeter of the rugby field. The siren is wailing, the lights are flashing. Behind the steering wheel is Tīmoti, eighteen years old, grinning like crazy. His mum, Eyes, is watching with her cousin Hana. Tīmoti has reason to smile, and it's not just because he's behind the steering wheel of a police car with all the emergency lights flashing. Today is driver's licence testing day. When Hana quit the Auckland police force and moved back to Tātā Bay, she set up a scheme with her dad; a training programme to help a group of young locals earn their driver's licences. Tātā Bay is a small place, with little work and zero educational opportunities after you leave high school. A driver's licence is a passport to a future most young people won't be able to get in their tiny hometown.

When Hana and Eru were sure the students were as ready as they'd ever be, she applied for funding from the local council to get a testing officer from Auckland to come to Tātā Bay, so the nervous young drivers could do their practical driving tests on roads they were comfortable with. Hana and Eru are proud as hell of the students and the programme, and so is the rest of their family. Addison and her partner PLUS 1 are down for the day and are prepping the celebration sausage sizzle over the fence at the marae,* even though Addison hasn't actually eaten anything with legs since she figured out at five years old that sausages were the result of lambs dying.

---

* Marae – the communal buildings and meeting place of a tribe.

Addison has also sweet-talked her dad Jaye, Hana's ex, into driving down from the big city with his second wife, Marissa, and her two pre-teen daughters, Vita and Sammie. Understanding how important the day was to Hana and Eru, Jaye brought a surprise with him. He'd signed out a uniform car from Auckland's Central Police Station, where he works. Jaye is a detective inspector, so he'd never normally be in a patrol car, but he figured that bringing the police vehicle would be a good public relations gesture. A bit of goodwill for a local community trying to do the right thing by their youth. Now each driver who successfully passes the test gets to make a couple of laps of the rugby field, sirens blaring and red and blue lights flashing.

The police car pulls up by the rugby goalposts and Tīmoti gets out. He does a little celebration hip swivel. Flicks his carefully shaved mullet, grinning. *Oh yeah.* Tīmoti was the second-to-last driver tested. He passed, as everyone else before him had, and the others gather around to congratulate him.

Hana watches as the testing car appears at the end of the road leading to the marae. The last driver indicates carefully, heading into the car park. She's the same age as Tīmoti, a young woman named Maia. She's missed quite a few lessons, and Hana's cousin Eyes told her it's because Maia's grandmother is unwell, and she's been helping care for her. When she has managed to turn up for classes, Maia has always worked hard. But of all the students, she is the one Hana is most worried about.

The car pulls up and Maia goes to join the others. 'How'd you go?' one of them asks.

'I dunno. He didn't say anything the whole way. Is that good or bad?'

No one's quite sure.

The testing officer gets out, and as he carefully completes his checklist and heads across to where she and Eru are waiting with Maia, Hana doesn't miss the serious look on his face.

'I'm not quite sure how to tell you this,' he says. Maia's face falls, fearing the worst. 'I can't remember the last time I tested six people in a row and passed all of them without a single fail. Congratulations.'

He gives Maia her certificate. Eru throws his battered felt cowboy hat in the air, Maia jumps behind the steering wheel of the cop car, Jaye flicks the sirens and lights on, and the rest of the students all run around the field after the patrol vehicle, yelling and whooping.

Next to Hana, her cousin Eyes grins.

'Nice to see a bunch of Māori kids chasing the cops instead of the other way around.'

The day before, Hana was at the local Tātā Bay dairy* picking up tomato sauce, BBQ sausages and sliced bread for the sausage sizzle, when she heard the sound of a

---

* Dairy – convenience store.

big throaty engine. Outside the shop window, a pale-blue Mark III Zephyr was pulling up. She knew the car. It belongs to Erwin Rendall, a tough guy with a long criminal record, who arrived in the area a couple of years earlier. Rendall has a reputation for running a car-theft operation, stealing cars and farm vehicles, cutting them down in the compound he bought cheap in a neighbouring town and selling on the parts.

Hana's had run-ins with him before, and when he came into the dairy, he saw her straight away. He was wearing his usual: a cut-off denim jacket that showed the big 'FTW' tatt on his bicep. Straggly, lank hair and a thick black-grey beard. He raised his eyebrows at her.

'Sheriff.'

The name he's always mocked Hana with, since he found out she's an ex-cop. Rendall held her gaze, and for a moment it occurred to Hana that his eyes weren't that different to the mako's. Emotionless. Cold.

As he went around the shelves, Hana went slo-mo on her own shopping. Her radar is always up when the Mark III Zephyr turns up. Rendall has form in luring vulnerable young people into his gang, with the promise of easy bucks and a gangster lifestyle. The last thing Hana wants is him trying to recruit any of the young locals like Maia and the other kids she and Eru are working with.

She watched as Rendall approached the counter with an armful of pet food.

'My bloody dog. She's gonna eat me out of house and home.'

The nervous shop owner rang up the sale. Rendall put down a couple of bills. He waited for the change and headed for the door, pausing near Hana.

'I know we've had our moments,' he said. 'We're not ever gonna sit down and have a beer. But we live in the same postcode. Doesn't have to be unpleasant.'

Hana watched as he headed out to the Mark III and drove away.

He's a bully and a thief and Hana doesn't trust him, not for a moment. Certainly no more than she'd trust the mako. If Rendall *has* decided to be less of a pain in the arse for the locals, that's not at all unwelcome, but she's still going to keep a close eye on him.

'So that's your dad's girlfriend?' Jaye asks.

It's a couple of hours after Maia finished her siren-wailing victory lap of the rugby field. In the marae, the driver's licence group have devoured the sausage sizzle, and they're all being polite and respectful enough to hang around in the wharekai* for a while, although Hana's pretty sure they've already lined up their six-packs of pre-mixed bourbon and coke and are just dying to head down to the sand dunes to celebrate properly.

There's a microphone set up at one end of the dining hall, where Eru gave a little speech to congratulate them

---

* Wharekai – dining hall.

all. Now he's at the mic with a woman his age, her face all smiles behind a mass of curly silver-blonde hair. They're singing an old Dolly Parton and Kenny Rogers number, and it's clear this isn't the first time they've performed it together. Eru has always had a gorgeous voice, and the woman is playing her guitar and harmonizing effortlessly.

'Yep. That's her,' Hana tells Jaye and Marissa. 'That's Daisy.'

Finding out that her seventy-four-year-old widowed father has a girlfriend she knew nothing about hasn't been easy for Hana. That's an understatement. Her mum passed away fifteen years earlier, and as far as Hana was aware, Eru was planning on flying solo for the rest of his life. It never entered her mind that there might be someone else. All of that changed a couple of months ago. Hana had just got back from a pre-dawn run. 10.13 km, as always. She'd jumped in the ocean, headed home and put the coffee on, before realizing she was out of milk. She'd pulled her running shoes back on and jogged the half-mile to her dad's place, gone inside, not even bothering to knock, assuming he'd be asleep. As she opened the door of the fridge she heard a voice.

'You must be Hana.'

She looked up to see a mass of silver-blonde curls. Daisy was wrapped up in her dad's old dressing gown. Seeing the look on Hana's face, she burst out with a shimmering laugh that was a little like the sound a wind chime makes on a summer day.

'I told the old man to talk to you about me. He just keeps saying, she can find out when she finds out. Guess you found out.' Daisy smiled, easy and warm.

After Daisy drove back to her home in Auckland later that day, Eru came across to Hana's place with a tray of cheese-and-onion scones she had made.

'She said she thought you'd got a bit of a jolt. She asked me to say she hopes these help.'

As Eru halved and buttered a couple of scones, Hana became aware of an unusual awkwardness between her and her dad. But actually, the awkwardness was all on her side.

'Go on, e kō.* I know you have pātai,'† Eru said. 'Ask away.'

'Okay then. Who's Daisy?'

'An ex-accountant. Retired now and living in a nice place in West Auckland. She has two grown kids, both in finance. And in case you're worried, we're not up to any skullduggery, we're not going behind anyone's back. She got divorced twenty years ago.'

Eru handed Hana a scone, as usual with way too much butter, as usual forgetting she doesn't like butter. Hana didn't bother reminding him.

'How'd you meet?' she asked, aware of how unimaginative the question was.

Eru took a big mouthful of his own scone. 'Online.'

'You hooked up on *Tinder*?'

---

* E kō – my daughter.
† Pātai – questions.

'For an ex-cop you're surprisingly unaware of the world. There's a site called Glow. Much more age appropriate. Fifties plus. Old people's Tinder. We matched on pretty much every box. Hobbies, politics, music. Kai.* These are good, eh?'

Hana wasn't the least bit interested in the scones.

'So the last few months, all those weekends you've been going to Auckland, when you said you were going to see old friends . . . You were seeing her?'

'In my defence. She's a wee bit old. And she's a friend,' Eru said with a smile. 'Oh my God, girl. The look on your face. It's parents who are meant to be all red-faced when they find out the kid is seeing someone they don't know about.'

Hana had no idea how to reply. What Eru was saying was true. But that didn't change how she was feeling.

'We were seeing if things were going to work out. They worked out.' He shrugged, starting in on buttering the other half of his scone. 'She's a hell of a singer. We do open mic nights at the pub just down the road from her place. We won a meat pack one time.'

'You could have told me, Dad.'

Eru paused. 'I meant to. Daisy asked me, like fifty times. I just knew it'd be – well . . . how it is now. Difficult. The only woman you've ever known me to be close to is your mum. And Daisy's not your mum.'

Eru brushed scone crumbs from the table.

---

* Kai – food.

'I love your māmā as much as I did the day she passed. That won't ever change. Loving her doesn't stop me loving Daisy too. I hope maybe you'll relax enough to love her too.'

'I'm not unrelaxed. I'm just confused.'

'Actually, you're kind of the definition of unrelaxed. But that's okay. That's just how you are, my girl.'

A smile came to Eru's face.

'Anything else you want to know? Just to get it out there – we're physically intimate.'

'Oh my God, Dad, please, *shut up.*'

Maybe Eru was right. Maybe Hana was just being uptight and unrelaxed, though she'd never thought of herself that way, and it had been a bit confronting when he'd said it. But there's another reason Hana is struggling with the idea of Daisy.

A few months earlier, while helping Eru fill out a form on his computer, Hana had accidentally come across his search engine history. She'd found multiple searches about symptoms of dementia and early-onset Alzheimer's. A sick feeling had threatened to overwhelm her at the realization that Eru had found reason to believe he might be becoming unwell. But he'd never said anything about it, and she knew she had to allow him the dignity of making up his own mind about when to tell her. She had to let him have control over his own decisions, and over his own health.

But somehow, Daisy made everything different. Did she know? Was this really the right time to start a new relationship, if Hana's dad was facing an uncertain future?

Now, in the dining hall, Jaye and Marissa watch as Eru and Daisy finish their duet.

'She looks so lovely,' Marissa says.

Jaye nods, smiling. 'I hope we have their energy when we get to their age.'

Addison and PLUS 1 have already met Daisy a few times, and they'd both fallen in love with her warmth, her ready laugh, how much she clearly adores Addison's grandpa. Hana, more and more, has the feeling she's the odd one out.

As the song ends, Daisy and Eru pass the microphone to Addison, who takes the stage, her half-sisters alongside her. 'We've got a special performance,' Addison says. She nods at Vita, who starts playing a song on her phone, holding it up to the microphone. It's a goofy country slash hip-hop number about cowboys and roping steers and riding across the prairies. Everyone in the room knows it; it went viral a few months prior as a TikTok dance challenge.

The moment the music starts, Marissa shoots a look at Jaye.

'Don't. Don't you dare. You've embarrassed me enough with this thing.'

But there's already a big smile on Jaye's face, his toes tapping on the floor beneath his chair.

When the song was at the peak of its TikTok thing, Sammie and Vita made Addison practise with them for hour after hour. Getting all the moves. There's no rhyme or reason to why something explodes on social media, and it was the same with this song, which seemed the absolute least likely reason for tweens and teens and young twenty-somethings across the globe to suddenly decide to video themselves doing a routine that occupied an indefinable space between kind-of-geeky and kind-of-cool.

But it happened.

Sammie and Vita desperately wanted to record their version of the dance moves. The *chase-the-runaway-horse*. The *hoe-down*. The *lasso-twirl*. The *bow-legged-gallop*. The *heel-tap* to *toe-tap* and back to *heel-tap* again. What Addison and Vita and Sammie didn't know was that, having heard it so many times, Jaye had got as addicted to the song as they had. He'd watched the girls practising, he'd scrolled TikTok looking at hundreds of other versions. When the girls finally decided they were good enough to make their own video, Jaye got in on the act. He had the routine down pat. He even added in his own move at the end, a *cowboy-hat-tilt* with a drawling baritone 'Yee-ha'. The girls posted the video, with Jaye centre stage, and he's shared the clip with pretty much everyone he and Marissa knows, to her ongoing mortification.

'Detective Inspector Hamilton,' Addison calls into the microphone, trying not to giggle. 'We need you onstage to investigate a crime against dance.'

Vita and Sammie gesture to Jaye, *come on.* All the driver's licence graduates are chanting his name.

'I can't say no!' Jaye grins at Marissa. 'Can I borrow your hat?' he asks Eru.

The music starts in earnest. Jaye, Addison and the two young girls line up, side by side. All of the driver's licence kids are laughing their arses off, and before long they're all on their feet mirroring the moves. It's a chaotic mix of *hoe-downs* and *lassos* and *gallops*. And in the middle of it all, Jaye, beaming and unabashed, at least twenty years too old for any of this, but not giving a toss. The song ends, Jaye does the *cowboy-hat-tilt*. Leans in to the microphone.

'Yee-ha.'

The whole dining room falls apart laughing.

Marissa looks at Hana.

'Good decision, divorcing that man.'

'Good decision, marrying him,' Hana replies, smiling.

Before Maia headed down to the dunes with the others, she introduced Hana to her grandmother. 'This is my Nanny Niki.'

Hana could see how full of pride the older woman was at her granddaughter earning her driver's licence. But she could also see the great difficulty she had moving. As Maia walked her nanny out to the car, Hana asked Eyes what was wrong with her. Eyes explained that

Nanny Niki had needed a hip replacement for years, but she didn't want to cause any fuss, not when there were so many others more in need of hospital care than her. Her family had finally made her get on the waiting list, but it was going to be a long time before she would have the surgery she now badly needed. In the meantime, the pain was becoming increasingly debilitating.

'The pain meds don't do much, and Nan doesn't qualify for medicinal cannabis,' Eyes told Hana. 'So we do what we can to help her get through.'

'What does that mean?'

Eyes looked long and hard at Hana before replying.

'Am I talking to my cuz? Or an ex-cop?'

In Tātā Bay, even though Hana is becoming more and more a part of the tapestry of the community, no one's forgotten that she's ex-police. Around the marae she's still sometimes referred to as 'Kermit's friend'. As in, Miss Piggy. But at least now this is said to her face, with a teasing smile, not as an insult whispered behind her back.

'Weed works for Nanny Niki,' Eyes explained quietly. 'Helps with the pain, helps her sleep. But money's tight, eh. I buy her a joint or two when I can afford it. Others do the same. It helps. But it's not easy for the old girl.'

Out in the car park, as Jaye and Marissa and the girls get ready to leave for the drive back to Auckland, Addison is a bag of nerves, and Hana's not sure why.

Addison has been dealing with some big decisions lately. She and PLUS 1 are taking their music more and more seriously; they've recorded a new song that their label can't stop raving about. 'They think it's going to be our break-out,' Addison told Hana when she played it for her, and Hana was so excited after she'd heard it that she didn't sleep that night. Addison's also recently started volunteer work at Gen Helpline, an anonymous call-in service for teens and early twenties, putting her activism into practice, and Hana couldn't be prouder. But she can't quite figure out why Addison and PLUS 1 suddenly seem so nervous.

'You okay, love?'

'Not really.'

Addison clears her throat.

'Mum. Dad. Marissa. Grandpa and Daisy. Before everyone goes . . .'

Hana has seen Addison perform dozens of times now. She's incredible on stage, in her element, no nerves at all. But here in the car park, surrounded by all the people who love her most, she's suddenly like a painfully shy ten-year-old.

'What's up?' Eru asks in te reo. Hana glances at Jaye. Neither has any idea what's going on.

'When I was little, Grandpa,' Addison says, 'you used

to talk about the rising of Matariki. How special it was. And I remember saying goodbye to Grandma Jos, down at the beach, when Matariki rose that year.'

'And we said hello to you at Matariki, down there on the headland. But you were five days old, so it's okay you don't remember,' Eru says.

Addison glances at PLUS 1. 'It's Matariki soon. We're planning a bit of a celebration,' she says. She puts out her hand, laces her fingers between PLUS 1's.

Hana blinks. She looks at Jaye again. An unspoken communication between the two parents. *Is this actually happening? Surely not? Maybe?*

'We're not sure how to do this . . .' PLUS 1 starts. They turn towards Eru. 'I mean, do we have to ask permission? And who do we ask? You, Grandpa? Or Hana, or Jaye?'

Hana starts to smile. 'Oh my God.' She covers her mouth. 'Did I say that aloud?'

'Yeah, you did, Mum.'

Now Eru is smiling too, ear to ear.

'No one's asked me permission for anything for a long time,' he says. 'That'd be a nice change.'

'Okay then.' Addison nods. She squeezes PLUS 1's hand, so tight they wince a little.

'We want to get married,' Addison says. 'And we want to have our engagement party the night Matariki rises.'

'Is that okay with you guys?' PLUS 1 asks.

'Yes!' Vita shrieks, Sammie too, both of them jumping

up and down, throwing themselves over PLUS 1. Jaye hugs Marissa. Daisy's tinkling laughter fills the air as Eru spins her around in a circle.

Hana starts crying, wrapping her daughter in a huge, all-encompassing hug.

'God yes, it's okay,' she whispers in Addison's ear.

It was a two-hour drive back to Auckland, and the smile never left Jaye's face the whole way. It's getting dark now as he walks home from returning the cop car to the Central Police Station and dropping back the keys.

He's got a ciggie in his hand.

It's a habit he's had from back in the old days. When he was an undercover cop, he had to get into a lot of stuff. It comes with the territory. The booze and the ciggies are the least of it. You have to do drugs, sometimes serious drugs; you need to fully blend into the landscape, play the role and walk the walk. For some cops, re-entry is made more complicated because of drug dependencies developed while undercover. But for Jaye, coming back into the real world, it was really only the ciggies he missed. He'd got a bit of a taste for them.

He takes a long drag. When he bought the packet after dropping Riss and the girls off home, he also picked up breath freshener. Marissa knows nothing about the ciggies, and Jaye is pretty sure she'd kill him if she found out.

Turning the corner into their street, he finishes his smoke. Don't want a neighbour to notice and say something indiscreet. He pauses at the gate of their house. The engagement party is in a couple of weeks. He wants to get something special to toast Addison and PLUS 1 with. *Champagne.* He actually has lots of time to organize it. Then again, it's only a five-minute walk to the liquor store. A chance for one more ciggie on the way. Another on the way back, after he's bought the champagne.

No time like the present.

Jaye turns and heads back down the street. When he's out of sight of the house, he lights up again. Takes a deep drag.

He walks across the road towards the liquor store, taking a last pull on the ciggie, stubbing it out against his shoe heel. The habit he'd got into all those years before. He slips the half-finished cigarette into his back pocket to finish afterwards, and heads into the store.

As the door closes behind Jaye, across the road, a car pulls up.

It's steel grey. A Toyota Corolla.

Behind the steering wheel, the driver pulls on a balaclava with gloved hands.

On the passenger seat, there's a bag. The driver opens it, looks in.

Inside, there's a revolver.

The driver takes out the gun. Checks the chamber is loaded. Slips it back into the bag.

Adjusts the balaclava.

Then the driver gets out of the car, closes the door and walks towards the liquor store.

2

2 MINUTES 24 SECONDS

The digital timestamp on the security footage reads 17:41:20 as Detective Inspector Jaye Hamilton enters the liquor store.

Two wide-angle cameras are mounted above the door inside, both black and white and low res, no sound. The first camera covers the entryway and the front of the store, including the till, where the store manager, the only other person in the shop, is working on the computer. In the footage, Hamilton nods to the young manager, a guy he knows named Mickey.

17:41:31 – Hamilton passes from the first camera into the feed from the second camera, which covers the rear of the premises. He walks towards the refrigerators at the back of the store.

Jaye's never had reason to hands-on purchase a bottle of champagne before. When he and Hana got married, they were just out of police college and couldn't afford anything fancy. At Marissa and Jaye's wedding, they left the arrangements to the caterers. He has a vague idea that to be actual champagne, the grapes should be grown and bottled in a particular region of France.

Prosecco won't cut it. This is special.

Jaye's not much for flowery language; that's not cop-speak. But there's no other way to put it than flowery. His heart is soaring. The look on Addison's face when she and PLUS 1 asked Eru's permission, it nearly killed him. She was always one of those kids who could look at you with such seriousness that it felt like you were facing a judge, and you'd wonder what you'd done wrong. Then the next minute she'd explode into shrieks of giggles. Jaye has never met anyone like Addison, and he's pretty sure he doesn't feel that way just because she's his kid. It took him a little while to fully get his head around the gender non-binary thing with PLUS 1, but he could see straight away what a great fit they were together: both of them smart, caring, tough as iron, vulnerable as tissue paper.

'Anything in particular you're after, Mr Hamilton?' Mickey calls out from the counter.

'Actually, yeah. Champagne.'

He pronounces the word with a bit of a self-mocking attempt at a French accent.

'Woah. Flash guy, eh? The top shelf of the right-hand-side fridge. Scream out if you need a hand.'

Jaye finds the shelf, opens the fridge door. He picks up a bottle. French. But not from the Champagne region.

That won't do.

17:41:54 – on the store's second camera, Hamilton stands in front of an open refrigerator door at the rear of the shop. Over the following twenty-five seconds, he takes out a couple of bottles, closely reading the labels before replacing each in the fridge.

17:42:30 – in footage from a CCTV camera mounted on a lamp post opposite the store, the door of the steel-grey 2005 Toyota Corolla that pulled in half a minute earlier opens.

Jaye has narrowed it down to three bottles. They're all from the Champagne region in France, and he's pleasantly surprised that his local place runs to that many choices. All three say 'non-vintage' on the label. He's getting a bit of an education. 'Vintage' is probably more desirable than 'non-vintage', Jaye figures, but looking at the prices, he's happy that the store doesn't actually stock the vintage option.

It'll come down to how the label looks. Lined up with the other contenders behind the glass of the fridge door, the one with the bright-red stripe running diagonally from the neck like a sash feels like it's the front runner.

What happened with Addison and PLUS 1 earlier that day makes Jaye think about when he'd asked Marissa to marry him. He'd had no idea what she'd say. All he'd known was he wanted to grow old with her. Jaye's best friend Tony, Marissa's former husband, had been an AOS* officer who'd been killed in the line of duty. Mourning Tony together, Marissa and Jaye had slowly grown closer, until, at a certain point, Jaye had realized that it was so much more than grief that tied them to each other. He'd hoped that was how she felt too, but there'd been only one way to find out. After Sammie and Vita were settled in front of the telly one evening, Jaye asked the question. He didn't know what her response would be, but what he hadn't expected was the look on her face. What seemed to be anger.

'Riss?'

She stared at him for a good half-minute. It felt like a half-year.

'I didn't want to fall in love with you,' she said finally, her voice shaky. 'I really didn't. Why couldn't you do anything other than what you do? *Anything*.'

Jaye knew exactly what she was saying, and why.

'I'll quit the cops. I'll retrain. I dunno, I'll become a vet, we can set up a practice together.' He meant every

---

* AOS – Armed Offenders Squad.

word he was saying. 'I don't care. I'll be an accountant for you.'

'*Fuck you.*'

She pushed him in the chest, so hard and unexpected that he nearly lost his footing. The girls hurried in from the television room.

'Mummy? Why did you say a bad word?'

'What's wrong?'

Marissa picked up her daughters, held them close. Kissed them both.

'Me and Jaye are getting married.'

Looking at the three bottles in the fridge, Jaye smiles. Definitely the one with the red diagonal sash.

Elegant.

17:42:34 – on the external CCTV footage, the offender gets out of the car, closes the door, glances both ways up and down the street. He has an embossed plastic bag in his hand, black with a bright orange circle, the trademark of a popular video game brand. He walks directly across the road towards the store, getting larger in the frame with every step.

17:42:34 – at the same timestamp, on the security footage from the first camera inside the shop, the manager remains absorbed in the invoices he is processing at the counter.

On the second camera's feed, DI Hamilton is still in

front of the fridge at the rear of the store, where he has been for nearly a full minute, studying the champagne bottles on the top shelf.

Six should do it, Jaye thinks. *We probably won't drink them all, but what's left can go in a box for the wedding itself.*

The wedding. His little girl. Getting married.

Another memory comes to Jaye. The moment when Hana told him she was pregnant.

They were a half-year out from graduating police college, both just starting their careers. A baby wasn't remotely on their radar. They'd never even discussed the idea. If they'd talked it through and made a decision, if they'd worked out the right time for one or the other of them to take a year or two off to be the primary caregiver, if they'd actually had a plan . . . well, that would have been something. But there was no plan.

'What do we do?' she asked. It was early days, but her periods were like clockwork, and Hana was sure.

It felt like a hell of a problem. The universe intervening, without warning, turning everything completely upside down.

Jaye took a moment.

'Here's what we do. We close our eyes.'

'What?'

He looked at her, reassuring. Then he closed his eyes.

'I can't do this on my own,' he said, knowing she hadn't closed hers.

Hana closed her eyes.

'We're going to hold our hands out in front of us.'

They both held their hands out.

'We'll count to three. If we want to go with this thing, all good, palms up. If it's too scary and impossible and just wrong right now, that's all good too. Palms down. Okay?'

She nodded *okay*.

'My eyes are closed, Hana,' he said. 'I can't tell if you're nodding.'

'I'm nodding.'

They counted together.

'One. Two. Three.'

They opened their eyes.

They both had their palms facing upwards, towards the sky.

As the shop's front-door buzzer goes, Jaye makes his decision.

Six bottles. The one with the red-sash label.

He opens the fridge door.

17:42:38 – in the feed from the first camera, the front door of the liquor store opens. The manager doesn't look up from what he is doing. He doesn't see that the person who has just entered the shop is wearing a balaclava; he doesn't see the offender take the revolver from the plastic bag with the orange circle.

17:42:39 – on the footage from the second camera, at the rear of the shop, DI Hamilton takes a bottle of champagne from the refrigerator.

17:42:40 – the offender rushes the counter, the revolver in his hand. The young manager only looks up a half-second before the offender grabs him by the back of the neck and slams his face down hard against the counter.

Jaye grabs the red-sash bottle, the last one on the shelf. As he closes the refrigerator door, there's a noise from the front of the store. *Maybe Mickey knocked something over*, Jaye thinks, as he heads towards the front.

'Got any more GH Mumm out the back?' he calls out, keeping a firm grip on the bottle. Ninety bucks a pop, he really doesn't want to drop the thing, vintage or non-vintage. No answer, but there's another sharp sound, then another, followed by what sounds like a muffled grunt.

'Mickey? You right, mate?'

Walking out from behind the shelves that hold the gin, vodka and rum, Jaye finally sees what's happening at the counter.

17:42:44 – on the feed from the first security camera, the offender slams the manager's head down onto the counter a second time, then a third. The manager will later say he remembers nothing of what happened.

17:42:48 – on the feed from the second security camera, DI Hamilton appears to have heard the sounds of the assault. He walks at pace, pausing as he reaches the point where he can see the counter.

17:42:49 – the offender slams the manager's head down a final time, leaving a pool of blood on the counter. In all, the manager's head is smashed against the counter four times in less than five seconds.

17:42:50 – DI Hamilton takes several steps towards the counter, appearing to call out as he does. Without audio, it's unclear what was said; if it was a warning to stop the assault, or if Hamilton identified himself as a police officer. Clearly believing the young manager was in danger of serious injury, Hamilton raised the bottle in his hand – his only available weapon.

17:42:52 – the offender releases his grip on the manager, who falls to the floor, unconscious. He turns to face Hamilton, who is now only a few steps away. As Hamilton gets to within a metre of the counter, the offender discharges his weapon twice. Hamilton falls.

17:42:54 to 17:43:38 – as Hamilton lies unmoving on the ground, the offender pauses long enough to make sure he is not getting up. He opens the till, takes all the notes. Lifts up the internal tray, pulls out the cash float hidden beneath. Avoiding the growing circle of blood around DI Hamilton, he pushes the money into the pocket of his hoodie, puts the revolver back into the bag and heads for the door.

I never saw a gun, Jaye thinks, lying on the floor.

The first bullet had been like a hammer blow to his chest, so completely shocking and unexpected that for a moment he'd wondered if he'd been hit by an actual hammer. Maybe the guy assaulting Mickey with such intent had an equally vicious mate who Jaye had failed to see. When the second bullet hit him, only a half-second later, his body was already detaching from the physical experience of pain. He could feel, in a removed kind of way, the bullet entering the side of his face, splintering his cheek bones. He was aware of falling, in the sense that he could feel the physics of his body dropping through space, but it was like he was a puppet who'd had all its strings sliced, and the severing of those strings had also cut off his ability to feel the physical sensation of impact.

After he hit the floor, the pain stopped altogether.

Jaye is kind of happy about that.

In the position he's fallen, he is facing the till. The legs of the guy who shot him are standing above where Mickey is lying on the ground. Jaye's cop instincts kick in, realizing it would be a good thing if he could lift his head, get a glimpse of the guy at the counter, look for any distinguishing marks under the balaclava, or a watch maybe, or any jewellery he might be wearing. But the damn puppet strings are cut, and now he can't move his head.

The guy at the counter finishes rifling through the till. Jaye vaguely registers legs walking over him and disappearing from sight. Off in the distance, like it's coming from somewhere on the other side of town, he hears the door buzzer. He heard the buzzer when the guy came in, Jaye remembers now. *If only I'd turned at that moment, seen he was in a balaclava*, he thinks. *I might have had time to react in a way that was a bit more organized than rushing the counter with the stupid champagne bottle raised like a club, yelling, 'I'm a cop!'*

If I'd turned when the buzzer went, Jaye thinks, *I might have seen the gun.*

Jaye's field of view is narrowing fast, a whiteness gathering around the periphery of his vision, like clouds filling the sky from all points of the compass. He can see Mickey groaning and starting to move, which he is relieved about. *That young guy's going to have a hell of a headache from the beating he was given*, Jaye thinks, *but it looks like he'll be all right. Thank God.*

As the white clouds keep closing in, Jaye realizes it's his brain shutting down, his body giving itself the best chance to get through. In the last seconds before the sea of clouds takes over, he moves his eyes down towards his legs. One is sprawled out beneath him in what looks like an unusual and agonizing angle, although Jaye has no sensation of the pain.

He has no idea of the trajectory of the two bullets after they entered his body. *Did either hit my spine?* he wonders.

Knowing he's about to lose consciousness, he gathers everything he has, willing his broken puppet body to make one last effort. Telling his foot, *Please, move for me. Show me you can do it.* In the moment before the cloud cover closes completely, the last thing he sees is his left shoe moving slightly. It's just a half inch or so. But that's enough. That's good.

I'm not paralysed, Jaye thinks, as the last of the clouds fill his vision.

Whew. Small mercies.

17:43:39 – on the exterior CCTV camera footage, the offender appears from the direction of the liquor store's entrance, pausing for a moment to check the street is empty. He hurries across to the steel-grey Corolla, the bag with the bright orange circle in his hand, and gets in.

17:43:44 – the Corolla indicates. It pulls away, driving carefully, and disappears from the CCTV frame.

A total of two minutes twenty-four seconds have passed since DI Hamilton walked into the store.

3

I'M INVESTED

'The width of a pencil lead. This much.'

Marissa holds up the tips of her thumb and her index finger, the tiniest sliver of space between them. 'A couple of millimetres. The bullet went in his cheek and came out behind his ear. It didn't actually damage his skull. Thank God. Fragments of bone in the brain would have made everything a hundred times worse.'

Hana and Addison are in one of the whānau* rooms of the intensive care department of Auckland City Hospital with Marissa and her daughters. Hana drove up far too fast from Tātā Bay the moment she got the news. She wanted to be the one to tell Addison, and they went straight to the hospital to be with Marissa during the eleven long

---

* Whānau – family.

hours that Jaye was in emergency surgery. The operation was complex: a vascular team repairing the arteries and veins in his shoulder and chest where the first bullet hit; an orthopaedic surgeon working on the bones in his shoulder and cheek area; and a neurological team on standby, monitoring brain swelling from the trauma of the impact of the second bullet. It was a long, hard night, but the medical teams kept the family informed as they worked, and just before dawn Hana could sense a level of cautious optimism in the updates.

There's another person in the room, someone who's not a member of Jaye's family. Elisa Williams is a senior cop from the Counties Manukau policing district. She's the same rank as Jaye, a detective inspector. Within an hour of the hold-up, Williams was urgently transferred to Auckland Central CIB,* to lead the investigation into the armed robbery and shooting.

'The doctors said it's a miracle,' Marissa continues, and Hana gets the sense that she is avoiding the painful emotions she is feeling by focusing on these medical details. 'I mean, they didn't use those words. What they said was, if the bullet had hit Jaye by just the difference of the width of a pencil lead, things would be very different.'

'If anyone deserves a miracle, it's Jaye,' Williams says gently.

'He's in a medically induced coma. There's the risk

---

* CIB – Criminal Investigation Branch.

of swelling in the brain, or post-op infection. They're keeping him switched off, while his body works on putting itself back together.'

Marissa glances over to where her girls are sitting with Addison. She smiles, wanting to do all she can to ensure that none of them are feeling the same terror she is.

'I got the staff to go through the whole protocol: the anaesthetics and muscle relaxants and pain meds they've got him on. I asked for a rundown of all the drugs, the doses. I guess the last person you want waiting in one of these rooms is a veterinarian who knows her drugs. But they were amazing. They gave me the whole list, the exact doses, everything . . .'

Marissa trails away, realizing how she must sound.

'I'm sorry. I must seem like some kind of medical chat-bot,' she pre-empts. 'Coping mechanism. But you do what you do to get through, right?'

Williams puts a hand on Marissa's arm. 'I'm going to find the person who did this,' she says.

Hana watches. She's always been impressed by Elisa Williams, and this feeling has only strengthened in the few minutes the senior cop has been here. The warmth with which Williams is treating Jaye's family; how she hugged everyone when she arrived, an embrace that was genuine and heartfelt and tearful. She'd taken the time to pick up muffins and croissants, a symbolic koha* that is naturally part of Williams' Pasifika cultural tradition

---

* Koha – gift, offering.

in the face of such a tectonic family upheaval. It's the kind of gesture that makes a huge difference.

Willliams is of first-generation Samoan descent, the daughter of parents who came to New Zealand from the Pacific Islands when she was still a baby. She made her way to the police via an unusual route: she is ex-army, having enrolled in the forces as soon as she could, when she turned eighteen. She quickly proved to be a rising star, becoming the first woman accepted into the SAS, the special operations branch of the New Zealand army. After serving in Afghanistan, she left the armed services, and the New Zealand police accepted her application with open arms, fast-tracking her into a senior role. Williams was a major in the SAS at age thirty, now she's a DI at thirty-eight. In terms of career trajectories, it's not a record, but it's deeply impressive.

When Williams was made detective inspector, Hana went to the ceremony, and she and Jaye had a drink with her afterwards. Williams told them she'd left the SAS because she'd come to see what she was doing overseas as being less about service to global peace, and more a painful and soul-destroying process of witnessing warring nations implode.

'My parents came to New Zealand to give us the best life we could have,' she said. 'I wanted to come home. Give back to the land that gave us so much. Make my own country a better place. Not watch another one tear itself apart.'

In Elisa Williams, Hana sees the kind of cop that can

make true systemic change. Brown, young, smart. Brave as hell. Not wedded to the old ways of doing things. Williams has had nothing to do with the old ways – she's been a cop for less than a decade.

'I'm looking forward to maybe working with you one day,' Williams said to Hana at the end of the celebrations. But a few months later Hana quit the cops, and they never got the chance.

Hana remembers that at one point during the evening someone asked Williams if she'd ever killed anyone. Hana saw the slightly pained expression on her face. It's the kind of question that must be continually asked of anyone who's served in a war zone, especially in an elite force like the SAS. Williams politely changed the subject. As they were leaving, Jaye said, 'I have no idea what she did in Afghanistan. But nothing would surprise me. I can't think of anyone I'd rather have watching my back.'

Ironically, now, that's pretty much exactly what Williams is doing.

'We'll do our job. We'll find the guy. Your energy needs to be here, with Jaye, with your family, getting him through the next hours and days. I'll tell you as much or as little as you want. I'll be guided by you, by what you and your whānau need.'

Marissa looks to where the girls are sitting with Addison. The family room is full of things that are meant to help give the people who end up here half a shot at forgetting, even for a minute or two, that this is the last place in the world they want to be, that someone somewhere rolled the dice, and they came up with losing numbers. There are boxes of toys, board games, a television, books and magazines. Addison has been playing Go Fish with the girls, but it's been half-hearted at best. Now Vita and Sammie are both watching their mother. Seeing her fighting to hold it together, but, as the two people on earth who know her best, knowing she really isn't holding it together, not in the least.

Marissa looks back to Williams.

'Why?' she finally asks the cop. 'Why did this happen?'

Williams has spent the last few hours watching and rewatching the CCTV footage from the liquor store. It wasn't easy viewing. She tries to frame the awful things she saw in a way that will be manageable for everyone in the room to digest.

'Money was taken. The till was emptied. The aggravated robbery was particularly violent. I believe Jaye feared that the manager was about to be badly injured or killed. So, he stepped in. He tried to intervene. He could well have saved the young man's life.'

Marissa's fingers slowly turn her wedding ring.

'They gave me the things that were on him when he went into surgery,' she says quietly, after a moment. 'There was a packet of cigarettes in his pocket.'

'What?' Addison says. 'Dad doesn't smoke.'

Marissa has to smile.

'Don't get the wrong idea,' she says. 'Your dad's not a nicotine addict. He sneaks a smoke when something big happens. If he's just come out on the right side of an important case, or there's been a big arrest. He uses breath freshener before he gets home. He thinks I don't know. I guess he was having a celebration ciggie, for you and PLUS 1.'

Sitting at the table, Addison holds on to the younger girls just a little tighter.

Williams knows it's time to leave. She gets her bag and goes around the room, hugging everyone again.

She pauses at the door. 'You do what Jaye needs you to do for him. I promise you, we will too.'

Williams is waiting at the elevator from the ICU down to the entrance level when Hana hurries from the family room.

'Elisa. Mind if I ride down with you?'

As the elevator arrives and the two women get in, Hana comes straight to the point.

'I want to help.'

'Thank you,' Williams says. 'I know you do.'

'No, I mean, I want to be part of this, Elisa. I want to be hands-on. I want to actually be in there, working with you and your team.'

In the elevator, Williams presses the down button.

'They've put me in Jaye's office,' she says as the doors close. 'I felt a bit funny at first, but I guess it's just being pragmatic. It'll be at least a few months before he's back at his desk and for the investigation I need to be there on the eighth floor, with the team.'

As the elevator descends, Williams looks long and hard at Hana.

'This morning,' she continues, 'I was looking for somewhere to leave my laptop. I found your ID badge in a drawer. Jaye clearly hasn't given up hope that you'll change your mind. Is that what you're saying? Do you want your job back?'

Hana considers the question.

'I quit,' she answers. 'It was the right decision. I'm not changing my mind. But for this bloody thing that's happened, you're going to need all the help you can get. And I'm a good set of eyes.'

'That's an understatement.'

'I know it's bending the rules, someone with a family connection being part of the team. But if you want me, I think I can help. I'm invested.'

The elevator reaches the ground level. The doors open. Williams doesn't even pause to consider her answer.

'See you in the office.'

4

DIFFERENT

He knew from a young age that he was different.

The first time he saw a dead body, it was the woman who lived a couple of miles down the road. She was old and couldn't drive anymore, and he made a few bucks every week biking to the shops to buy her groceries. This particular day he'd picked up her order and come in the back door to find her body on the kitchen floor. He could see straight away she was gone. He made himself a cup of tea and a sandwich, because that was part of the deal, and it had been a long ride in the hot sun and he was starving. The old woman had collapsed, inconveniently, in the middle of the kitchen, and he had to step over her several times to get from where the bread was kept in the pantry, to the refrigerator, where the butter and the luncheon sausage lived, then back again to fetch a plate.

He made his food and leaned against the table, chewing as he stared down at her.

He'd eaten half the sandwich before he thought about the effects of rigor mortis. He touched the woman's face. Gripped a fold of wrinkled flesh between a thumb and forefinger and moved it to and fro. She was cold, and he could feel the muscles stiffening beneath her papery old skin. He found the relevant volume of the *Encyclopaedia Britannica* on her shelves, and as he ate the other half of the sandwich, he worked out that given the state of her body, she had likely been dead for two to four hours. He finished the sandwich. It was good. But he was still hungry. And between making the sandwich and working out when the old woman had breathed her last, he'd remembered the new mustard that he'd picked up for her as part of her order.

It was wholegrain. An unusually fancy choice.

Perhaps she knew she was about to die.

He had to step back and forth over the body several more times, returning the encyclopaedia to the bookshelf, making himself another luncheon sausage sandwich. This time with the wholegrain mustard. As he ate the second sandwich, he opened her purse, which was clutched in her hand, to retrieve the payment for his work that day. He pocketed an extra $10 as an end-of-services fee. As he reclasped the purse in her hand, he could feel that the muscles of her fingers were stiffening too, which he'd just read happens a little while after the muscles of the face.

Perhaps his calculation was off. Perhaps her elderly heart had stopped an hour or more earlier than he'd first reckoned.

He finished the sandwich and washed the plate and the knife he'd used, knowing it might seem odd to the ambulance officer or the undertaker that he'd eaten two sandwiches next to a dead body before bothering to call anyone. He rubbed his eyes briskly, reddening them. He had a feeling that when people started arriving, he should seem to be in some way upset by what had happened.

Then he picked up the phone and called the emergency services.

It's not entirely clear to him why the memory of the old woman dead on the kitchen floor surfaces at this particular moment.

There were so many memories that could have come to him. He'd read once about a Belgian woman, one of only a few dozen people in the world with something called 'superior autobiographical memory'. The woman could remember exactly what she'd been doing on every day of her life. Every maths lesson she'd had at school, the day and date she'd had it. The shoes she'd been wearing or the colour of her hair tie that day. She could recite every Lord of the Rings book from memory. None of this seemed at all extraordinary. Memories come easily to him; they always have. It's as though the pathways of the neurons in his brain are less like interconnected wires, and more like the rolls of glue paper you unravel and hang from the ceiling to trap flies when they make the mistake of walking on them.

His mind is a sticky place that traps stuff and doesn't let it go.

In his early years at school it was spelling, maths and reading. Later on, algebra and chemistry, geography and computing. The seven times table would take all the other six-year-old kids weeks to memorize. He mastered it in fifteen minutes. All of that was easy. So easy, it didn't even feel like learning. It was the other things that were mysterious.

Why the water kept falling from a primary school classmate's eyes when she lost her favourite toy. Why the boys and girls in his class would smile shyly when they greeted each other in the morning. Why the smiles would become much wider, and their eyes would shine, when they sang 'Happy Birthday' for one of the other kids.

These things were endlessly perplexing. An infinitely more complex skill to master than reciting pi to twenty decimal places. But he understood, instinctively, and early, that he had to work this stuff out.

He taught himself how to smile, and when it was appropriate to smile, and how broad that smile should be depending on the nuance of the moment. He taught himself when and how much to cry. And he learned the other emotions. Loneliness. Amusement. Affection. Because he was good at reading when he was very young, he could look up the emotions in a dictionary or encyclopaedia, find out what they signified and work out how those feelings might be represented in a person's face, in their posture, in the sound of their voice.

There was one emotion he didn't have to learn from a book.

Anger.

Out in the garden shed, where the uncle who came to stay with his family once or twice a year would take him when everyone else was at work or asleep; the things that happened in that garden shed taught him what that particular emotion meant.

As he walks quickly to the car, another unexpected memory arrives. Being at the graveyard, watching the old woman's casket being lowered into the ground.

Tears blurred his vision as the box entered the earth. He'd been practising in front of the mirror. He knew what needed doing, so there'd be no sideways glances, so that no one would notice his lack of emotion and label him as odd. Point him out as someone who should be watched.

Different.

But even as the well-rehearsed tears filled his eyes, what he was really feeling was a strong sense of curiosity. After he'd made the phone call and before the ambulance had arrived, he'd gone back to the encyclopaedia. He'd looked up everything he could about what happens to the human body after death: the rate of decay, the various kinds of necrophagous species like beetles and flies that consume dead flesh. Later, he'd thought a lot about the effects of the embalming process: how would the presence of formaldehyde and methanol and sodium borate affect the decomposition of her body? Would it discourage the flesh-eating insects, and, if so, how long before the chemicals would have dispersed enough for the bugs to gather and claim their meal?

He thought, *If only I could ask them not to fill in the dirt. If only I could unscrew the top of the box, leave the old woman exposed to the elements and the insect life*. Then he could come back every morning and night, count the number of flesh-eating organisms, watch nature do the things that nature does.

But he couldn't ask that, he knew.

Such a wasted opportunity.

Getting into the car, he realizes why he thought at that particular moment of the old woman who'd lived down the road. It was so blindingly obvious.

When he pulled the trigger, twice; when the bottle of expensive champagne hit the concrete floor and smashed; when the guy crumpled, his blood already mingling with the pool of spilled alcohol – he ended up on his side, his right arm underneath him, his left arm twisted behind him on the floor.

It was the exact same position he'd found the old woman in.

He starts the engine. He nods to himself, relieved to have worked out where the nagging memory echo came from.

His mind is a sticky place. Nothing escapes.

5

WATER

What Hana remembers most is the man's eyes.

It was the closest she's ever been to pulling the trigger. The closest she's ever come to killing someone.

It was a few months after she'd been promoted to detective sergeant. It happened on K Road, outside a second-hand clothes shop near a little side alley where, back in the day before there were more street patrols, drugs were sold and sex workers would agree terms before getting into their clients' cars and disappearing to a deserted parking building somewhere. On this particular day, Hana was heading back towards Central Police Station from a call-out when an alert came over the comms. A violent confrontation on K Road. A young woman being held at knifepoint. Hana and the uniformed cop she was with were the closest car to the scene. They pulled in, and Hana could see even before she got out, the situation was bad. A guy, big and burly and wearing just a pair of jeans, no top, was holding a terrified young woman backed up against the plate glass of the shopfront. It was a broken bottle in his hands, not a knife, but if anything that just made the situation shittier and scarier. He'd used the bottle to slash his own skin, blood all over his chest, and now one of his lacerated arms was around the young woman's torso, restraining her, while his other held the broken bottleneck against the soft flesh of her neck.

They found out later that the young woman was a shop assistant from the second-hand clothes store. She'd been nice to the burly guy that morning, when she'd passed him on his square of cardboard, a cup in front of him for coins. She hadn't given him money, but she'd bought him coffee and a muffin. There was no way she could have known that she'd chosen a day when his inner chemistry was caught in an increasingly frenetic whirling dervish; an internal series of chaotic somersaults and pirouettes fuelled by a new cheap cut of methamphetamine he'd bought and consumed way too much of, way too fast. He'd sipped the coffee she'd bought him. His world, already pinwheeling, chose that moment to fly completely out of orbit. The girl had given him the coffee because she wanted to poison him; he was suddenly quite certain of this fact. He spat out the coffee, ripped off his shirt, smashed the beer bottle he'd finished an hour earlier. He tested the broken glass against his own skin, but it did nothing to bring his twisting, turning universe under control. So, he went into the second-hand shop and grabbed the young woman who'd put poison into his veins, hauling her out, screaming, onto the street.

That's where Hana found them, a half-minute later.

New Zealand cops don't carry weapons, but arms can be locked in a gun-safe in the boot of most police cars. Because of the nature of the earlier call-out, there was a Glock revolver in the vehicle Hana was in. She got the gun from the safe, telling the uniformed cop to call for urgent back-up, then she ran across the street, towards the second-hand shop, weapon drawn, calling to the guy, trying to talk him down, to get him to drop the broken bottle.

'Let her go. We can talk. I can help you.'

He didn't let her go.

His eyes are what she remembers.

The complete absence of colour in the irises. His pupils were fully dilated by adrenaline, by anger, by fury, by the nasty chemicals he'd ingested. He stared at Hana as she closed the distance between them, step by cautious step. She kept talking the whole way, looking for a non-lethal outcome to the situation. But she could see he wasn't about to release the young woman. He wasn't processing anything in any logical way. She got to a point on the footpath where she was ninety-nine per cent certain she could successfully take a fatal shot, put the guy dead on the ground without injuring his hostage.

Hana knew, that's what had to happen. There was no option two. If your life, the life of another officer or the life of a member of the public is in imminent danger, lethal force is justified. And necessary.

Her finger tightened on the trigger.

Then, unexpectedly, a noise, from the other side of the road. A truckie had found himself caught up in the row of traffic that had completely stalled because of what was happening on the footpath. The driver couldn't see the cause of the deadlock; all he knew was he had a delivery deadline, his truck wasn't moving and he'd had enough. Airhorns on the open road are loud. In a built-up area like K Road, an echo-chamber of two-storey shops facing each other across a narrow street, the sound is ear-splitting.

The truckie leaned on his airhorn.

Thank God.

For a moment, the shirtless, bleeding guy's eyes turned in the direction of the sound. Hana reacted instantly, her finger slipping off the trigger less than a millimetre from the point at which the bullet would have exploded from the gun. She threw herself forward, changing her grip on the Glock. The guy's colourless eyes didn't even have time to look back in her direction before she brought the sidearm down hard across his temple, and he fell, unconscious, the broken bottle released from his hand.

His lucky day. If not for a pissed-off, impatient truck driver, he would have been dead before he hit the pavement, a bullet in his brain.

And, in a way, it was Hana's lucky day too, she thought later.

If not for that airhorn, she would have lived the rest of her days knowing she had killed another human being, the memory returning to her again and again in the dead of night when the thoughts won't stop racing. It would have been entirely justified, of course; that's not the issue. The point is, if she'd pulled that trigger, from that day on she would forever have been a member of a very select group of humanity. She would always be someone who had taken a life.

Hana is looking at her reflection in the same K Road shopfront window. The store has changed hands and function in the years since the incident, and now it's a vape shop, one of a half dozen along the mile of this street. She's been in a daze in the hours since leaving the hospital, on autopilot, and she's not really sure how she found her way back to this spot.

In her mind she's been running over what happened to Jaye at the liquor shop again and again. As a cop, Hana was trained to kill. But you do everything you possibly can to never pull the trigger. The guy in the liquor store pulled the trigger. Twice.

Hana stands very still. Looking at her reflection.

Then she turns and walks across the road, heading two hundred metres down the street, until she gets to an unmarked doorway by a wholefoods café. She knocks on the door. Waits a moment or two, then knocks again, louder, above the ever-noisy K Road. Footsteps come down the stairs. Sebastian Kang opens the door. A smile, as he realizes who it is. But the smile fades, as he clocks the look on her face.

'Hana. What's wrong?'

'Can I come in?'

'Of course.'

Hana pushes past him, into the little entranceway that leads to the staircase up to his apartment. Sebastian closes the door behind them.

'Did you hear?' she asks. 'The shooting in the booze shop?'

Sebastian nods, *of course*.

'It was Jaye.'

'Oh God. Oh Hana.'

He goes to hug her, but Hana holds up her hands. She doesn't want to be held, not at this moment, not the way she's feeling.

'I'm so angry, I can't think straight. This shitty job. This city. Jaye has Marissa, there's those two little girls who love him. There's Addison.'

Hana slams the palm of her hand into the wall and sinks onto the bottom step of the narrow stairwell. Sebastian leans against the door, giving her space. Silent. In the face of her pain, he knows there's nothing he can say that will help.

But perhaps there's something he can do.

The sun is going down as two dark shapes enter the water, heading away from the inner-city beach and out into the growing darkness of Auckland harbour. They're swimming hard. It's how Hana and Sebastian first came to know each other: they used to do the same open-water swims when they were still cops, before they left the force, each at different times, for different reasons. When Sebastian quit and set up his private investigation business, they'd still meet up for an occasional swim. Then after Hana took early retirement, he started to offer her casual investigation jobs when he had more work than he could handle.

Sebastian's always been the slightly faster swimmer, but as the sun goes down out to the west, he's having to push hard to keep up with Hana.

Watching her at the bottom of the stairs up to his inner-city office slash flat, after an explosion of emotion the like of which he'd never seen from her before, Sebastian knew that sitting down and having a cup of tea wasn't what she needed. He grabbed his wetsuit, and a spare. 'Come with me,' he said.

Hana was silent in the passenger seat as he drove them down to the beach.

Out in the darkening harbour, they skirt close to the stony shore of Rat Island, Hana still leading the way. The tiny rocky outcrop isn't much of an island; it could easily fit into an Olympic-size swimming pool. It's named 'Rat' because its silhouette looks like a rat hunched on all fours, not because rodents actually live there. Swimming in the wash of Hana's feet, Sebastian listens for boat engines, keeping an eye out for any vessels that might not see two swimmers in grey wetsuits in the growing dark. As she leads the way through the handful of yachts moored just beyond the island, he can feel the kicking of her feet slowing a little. The rhythm of her breathing, at first sharp and irregular gasps of air, her lungs rebelling as they hit the cold winter waters, is starting to become more even. Another couple of hundred yards beyond the yachts, Hana slows to a stop. She treads water.

Ahead, a few hundred yards away, and towering above where they are down at water level, the lights of the harbour bridge are coming to life.

Sebastian stays beside her.

He knows she'll talk when she's ready.

A month or so earlier, Sebastian asked Hana to come with him to a family event. He'd tried to couch it as an off-hand invitation. His dad and mum are pastors of a Korean Presbyterian church on the north shore of Auckland city, and they were having a fundraising event – a bingo evening and cake stall to raise money for some renovations for the church hall.

'My folks don't speak a whole lot of English,' Sebastian warned. 'I'll translate the bingo numbers for you.'

'What do I take? For your parents?'

'You don't have to bring anything.'

'I was brought up right,' Hana said with a smile.

Sebastian suggested she bring a few persimmons and nashi pears.

Hana had a sense that the invitation meant something. Even when they were both still in the cops, she had enjoyed the calm ease between them. Sebastian is a guy you notice, with a ready smile and a good sense of humour, but he was never the alpha male type so often drawn to the police. When she did investigative jobs for him, they'd meet at a fish taco joint for Sebastian to give Hana her fee. The evenings in the noisy restaurant were fun, and she'd noticed that they'd started to extend quite a bit beyond what might be expected to complete a simple business transaction.

Hana was okay with that.

More than okay.

Occasionally they'd meet for fish tacos even if there wasn't a job for her, or they'd arrange to swim together if she was in Auckland visiting Addison and PLUS 1. Neither of them called these meetings dates. But it was getting harder to pretend it was a purely work relationship. An invitation to meet Sebastian's family felt like another small step onwards from friends and workmates towards something else. But what that something else was, neither was completely sure.

Bingo in the Korean Presbyterian Church hall was a surprisingly fun evening. Everyone was polite as hell, and Sebastian's parents were warm and welcoming. Using Sebastian to translate, they thanked Hana for the persimmons and nashis. They told her how proud they were of their son.

'They want me to tell you that I'm fluent in three languages.'

'Tell them I know already,' Hana said with a laugh. Sebastian had told her that as well as Korean and English, his parents had made him learn Mandarin, hoping he'd go into business.

'I'm going to say you had no idea, and you are very impressed. Trust me. You don't want them to think I've been bragging.'

At the end of the night, while Sebastian was saying goodbye to his parents, one of the older congregation members took a moment with Hana. The woman was a senior member of the church; she'd called the numbers for bingo, and Hana had noticed that most of the congregation deferred to her.

'You're very beautiful,' the woman told Hana. She was in her late sixties, with piercing eyes that held Hana's in a way that Sebastian's parents' – both naturally shy – hadn't.

'Thank you,' Hana replied, smiling.

'It's so good divorce is acceptable in New Zealand,' the woman continued. 'We Koreans, we're very old-fashioned. Ending a marriage is a source of such shame for us. Especially when there's a child. Among religious families, it's unheard of.'

The woman's gaze turned towards Sebastian's parents, meaningfully.

Hana kept a polite smile on her face.

'And your beautiful skin. In Korea, we try hard to stay pale. Dark skin is a sign you work in the fields. You're so lucky you don't have that kind of small-mindedness in your country.'

Later, as Hana drove them over the harbour bridge, back towards the city, she told Sebastian about the conversation. He was mortified.

'I'm so sorry.'

'Don't be. I was trying not to laugh,' Hana admitted, smiling.

'That woman. She's always been like that – a rude, bossy battleaxe. That's not how we Koreans are. My parents can't stand her.'

'Honestly, it's okay,' Hana said.

'You're not offended?'

'Why would I be? As long as you don't have a problem hanging out with someone who works in the fields.'

Sebastian buried his head in his hand, half blushing from the embarrassment, half giggling. Hana kept driving, a big smile on her face.

Out in the water beyond Rat Island and the yachts, it's almost completely dark now. On the far side of the harbour, a mile away, there's a big sugar factory. A container ship is moored at the jetty, being loaded with refined sugar products, the whole area lit up bright as day as cranes haul containers onto the boat. But there are no lights on this side of the harbour, and with the sun gone, the winter waters that were already cold when they got in are getting icy.

'We should probably head back in,' Sebastian says.

'Yeah.' Hana's voice is tight.

'Are you okay?'

'No.'

To their left, far off to the west, in the sky over the distant mountain ranges, the last glow of the pink sunset fades.

'Jaye is a good man,' she says. 'It's not fucking fair.'

Upstairs in the small flat behind the office, Hana spends a good quarter-hour in Sebastian's shower, getting some warmth back into her bones. After Sebastian gets through the shower, they sit together in silence, sharing the only thing he has in the fridge: a round of Camembert and some crackers. They both eat quickly, ravenous.

'That really helped,' Hana says. 'Thanks.'

'You told me once it's something your dad always says. Water heals. Koreans believe the same.'

Hana looks at the last slice of Camembert on the plate. 'Want it?'

'It's yours.'

Hana slides the cheese onto a cracker. She chews slowly this time. Swallows. She undoes the towel wrapped around her wet hair. She folds it up carefully and places it beside her.

'Can I stay?' she asks.

Making love was surprising.

It hadn't been planned, it hadn't been expected. But at the same time, it seemed somehow very familiar. Normal and easy, in a way that neither Hana nor Sebastian could have anticipated. *We share so much*, Hana thought afterwards, lying in the dark, her arms cradling Sebastian's head. Both had left one of the most intense careers in existence. They each knew and understood what the other had gone through; the culture shock of re-emerging from cop-world back into real life. Of starting again. But more than that. They knew each other's bodies, from swimming kilometre after kilometre together. Gently running her hands along Sebastian's shoulders as he slept, Hana felt the muscle that stretched from his neck to his shoulder blade: the trapezius, the hard little triangle that marked him out as a serious swimmer. Her fingers traced the outline of his trap, then drifted to the corresponding area on her own body.

We share the same muscle, she thought, as she fell asleep.

The sun isn't quite rising when she has the dream.

Hana is inside the liquor store. She has a Glock, as she had on K Road when she confronted the drug-fucked guy with the bleeding torso. In the dream, the man in the balaclava raises his gun and points it towards Jaye. Hana has her weapon aimed right between his eyes. But this time, unlike on K Road, there's no distraction, no blasting airhorn. Hana can see he's going to shoot. He's going to kill Jaye.

She doesn't hesitate. She pulls the trigger.

Hana wakes. An acid taste in her mouth, like she's about to be sick. She looks over at Sebastian, still asleep beside her. A shaft of street light is hitting the triangular muscle between his neck and his shoulder. Now is the time when she could make coffee for them both, she thinks. Come back to bed and be there with him as he wakes. They could be together as the sun comes up.

She could cry with him again, as she did out in the water just before they swam to shore.

But instead, Hana quietly pulls on her clothes.

She slips down the stairs and out the front door, as Sebastian sleeps.

6

THE CAR ON TELLY

'Talofa lava.* Tēnā koutou katoa.† Good morning.'

The press conference takes place in the media room of Auckland's Central Police Station. Interest in the shooting is intense; the room is full, cameras from all major news outlets filming DI Elisa Williams' first public statement on the case. Something about this feels different to the acts of violence that usually make the news. Walking into a shop is something all of us do most days, without a moment's thought, and that this could change the course of a life in an instant feels somehow frighteningly personal.

As Hana watches from the rear of the room, images are projected onto the AV screens either side of where

---
* Talofa lava – greetings (Samoan).
† Tēnā koutou katoa – greetings to all (te reo Māori, formal greeting).

Williams stands at the lectern, beginning with screenshots from the camera on the street outside the liquor store, of the gunman's car driving away after the shooting.

'The vehicle we are seeking is a Toyota Corolla, a 2005 model. The number plates are FUR947, but these are stolen plates. If you think you recognize this vehicle, please contact us urgently. Do not approach the car or the driver, but dial 111 immediately.'

A series of screenshots of the gunman from the security cameras scroll on the screens as Williams continues.

'Someone knows who this person is. Someone knows who did this. If he is your partner or if he is your son, if he is your father or your brother, I understand what you are going through. I understand the pain you are feeling, I understand your confusion. You love him. But I need you to know this. It is no act of love to protect him. He is a danger to himself. To the community. And although I know you do not want to believe this, he is a danger to you and your family. Please. If you love him. Call us. Tell us where he is, so we can bring him in safely. So we can make sure neither he nor anyone else is hurt.'

Another photo follows, filling the screens. It's Jaye, smiling, in full dress uniform. Victims are not necessarily immediately identified in cases of life-threatening violence, but the decision was made together with Marissa and Addison that putting his face out there might encourage people with information to speak up.

'An honoured and respected cop bravely intervened in

a violent crime. Jaye Hamilton tried to do the right thing, to protect an innocent member of the public, and for this action, he was shot. He is in Auckland City Hospital on life support. The person who shot him is walking free. Please help us identify who did this.'

Within hours the images of the car, the balaclava-clad gunman and the victim become the most clicked-on news stories in the country.

On the eighth floor, after the press conference, Hana is sworn in by the district commander as a temporary constable of the New Zealand Police, a legal prerequisite to her being able to work as part of the investigation. She recites an oath of allegiance to the king, and swears that as a temporary constable she will perform all the duties of the office of constable according to law.

'It's good to have you back,' the district commander tells Hana after he issues her certificate of affirmation. 'Let's find this guy.'

Hana is given a desk at the rear of the CIB area. When she was last officially here, she was a detective senior sergeant, one of the most senior cops in the division. There weren't many steps up the ladder for her still to climb. Now, she's at the opposite end of the hierarchy: the rank she was twenty years earlier when she was a fresh-faced newbie straight out of police college. A constable, and a temporary constable at that.

It might be a big step backwards from where she was before, but, looking around the office, Hana is glad she's there. Even with several dozen detectives transferred in from other precincts for the investigation, the CIB have their hands full. Based on the liquor store's security footage, the Firearms Investigation Team have identified the weapon as an Alfa Carbine; a type of long-barrelled firearm that is frighteningly easy to cut down into a more readily concealed handgun. Equally scary is the fact that in recent years several hundred Alfa Carbines imported into the country have found their way into the black market, a place that keeps no receipts or records of sales. It's impossible to track who bought the weapon that shot Jaye, or where it could have been purchased from, so Elisa Williams has had to cast the net wide. Anyone with prior convictions for weapons offences or aggravated robbery is being questioned, their movements scrutinized, alibis checked. Any guns found that match the type seen on the CCTV footage are being seized for ballistics testing.

It's a huge job. A time-consuming numbers game.

Then there's the other evidential strand the cops have. The steel-grey Toyota Corolla. Since the media conference, there have been many reported sightings of cars that match the description, all immediately followed up by the CIB. Nothing has checked out. Hana has been assigned to a big team of sworn and non-sworn staff given the painstaking job of working their way through the feeds from thousands of CCTV cameras from around the city, trying to establish where the vehicle went. The team has pieced together the Corolla's movements for the first mile or so after it left the liquor store. Then the trail runs out. The farther out from the central city area, the sparser the CCTV coverage becomes. After a certain point, it becomes a case of searching ever more sporadic video footage frame by frame, looking for a vehicle that's neither a particularly distinctive colour, nor a particularly unusual make.

'It's not exactly looking for a needle in a haystack,' Stan Riordan tells Hana, as he sets her up with a police-issue laptop to access the CCTV files. 'But it's pretty close.'

Stan and Hana are tight. They worked together in the CIB in the months before Hana left the cops – Stan was her offsider.* He was badly injured in the course of her final investigation, losing his lower left leg when a booby-trapped vehicle exploded. The accident invalidated him from active duty as a detective. Since then, as Stan has recuperated, he's been confined to desk-duty work, all the while desperate to make it back to being a detective. Since she left the cops Hana has kept in touch with him, and he has a close relationship with Addison.

'You've lost weight,' Hana says, as Stan finishes setting up her laptop.

'Not really. I've just redistributed. Feel.'

Stan takes her hand, puts it on his arm. He flexes the

---

* Offsider – a junior detective in the same team.

tricep under his shirt sleeve, grinning. Hana raises her eyebrows. The muscle is like rock.

'I don't know which is harder. My arms or my leg,' Stan says, tapping his titanium artificial limb.

'When's the physical test?' Hana asks.

'Next month.'

To earn his detective badge back, along with the procedural and investigative assessments – which Hana knows Stan will easily pass – there's the standard physical assessment for cops, the PCT. A particularly challenging obstacle course that needs to be completed in under two minutes. It's going to be Stan's biggest hurdle.

'I've been training my arse off. My hundred metres time is within half a second of what it was when I had two legs. I'll be the first amputee in the history of the Auckland CIB. I'm gonna do it, boss.'

Hana smiles. Stan has never been able to stop calling her 'boss', and while she tried for the first year after she retired to make him use her actual name, she knows now he's never going to.

'This is your login name and password,' Stan says, entering them on the laptop. 'The CCTV downloads are all being collated on the mainframe and I've loaded the link for your first set of video files.' Stan hands the laptop over, the familiar ready-to-please smile on his face.

'Any questions, call out. Good to see you, boss.'

'You too,' Hana says.

As he starts to turn away, Stan hesitates. The smile on his face fades. He lowers his voice.

'What happened with Jaye,' he starts. 'It makes me want to punch something.'

'I feel the same. But I'm not sure breaking our knuckles will help, Stan.'

'All the same. The *bastard*.'

As Stan heads away, Hana opens the first of the CCTV files.

She starts the video feed rolling, settling in to do the hard yards.

'You don't have to be here, Addison.'

'Yes, I do. I really do.'

Addison is in the tearoom at Gen Helpline. She'd been rostered on for an evening shift, but no one had expected her to actually turn up, and when she did, her supervisor made her a cup of tea and sat her down.

'They let us in to see Dad this afternoon. Just for a few minutes. We had to wear masks, those blue gown things,' Addison says, everything tumbling out. 'He had a big tube down his throat. All this bruising on his face. His head and throat wrapped in bandages. It didn't look like my dad. I just kept crying and crying. God. I'm doing it again.'

The supervisor puts a box of tissues in front of Addison. She dries her eyes.

'I watched Marissa, Dad's wife. How she handled it. She just held his hand. Firm. Steady. And she talked to him, so calm. She kept saying, "We're in this together. We're going to get out the other side, together. You're the strongest human being I know, and I'm going to be even stronger. You're not on your own."'

'She sounds amazing.'

'She is. I never really realized. All I could do was cry.'

'No daughter should have to go through this.'

'Well, it's not like I've got a choice,' Addison says. 'But Marissa being there is the best thing on earth for Dad right now. Me being useless and falling apart, he doesn't need.'

Addison gestures towards the phone room.

'In here, taking calls. It gives me something to focus on that's not Dad. I can be some kind of useful, to someone else.'

The supervisor nods, understanding.

'Next time you see him, you'll be strong, I know you will. But I understand why you can't be there right now.'

The supervisor reaches out, takes Addison's hand.

'Finish your cup of tea. Get your crying done in here. Then get out to the phones.'

Hana stares at the low-res feed from her next tranche of CCTV footage. She blinks, takes a few deep breaths, refocusing. You don't want to miss the vital two-second window when a steel-grey vehicle might happen to pass through the frame.

Every time she spots what looks like the right colour and model of car, she sends the timestamp of the clip through to the IT section. The clip is put through a video enhancement process, to compare the vehicle with the one outside the liquor store and confirm the number plate. Hana has sent through a dozen clips in the last few hours; none have turned out to be the car. It's been the same for the many other sworn and non-sworn staff working on the process.

The uniformed and plainclothes car patrols out on the streets looking for the vehicle have had no more luck.

By early evening, the camera feeds from streets in a seven-kilometre radius of the liquor store have been completed. One sighting of the car is confirmed, on video footage from a back street leading towards the eastern suburbs of the city. It's a much needed breakthrough. Now they know the car was heading east, at least when it passed this camera.

A new database of files is collated, pulling together all the downloads from the cameras in the direction the car was heading. As Hana receives her next set of video feeds, she gets a text.

Hope you're okay x I'm here

It's from Sebastian. Hana thinks about replying. She's not sure how. It's been a disorienting forty-eight hours in every way. Finding out about Jaye. Feeling an indefinable need to see Sebastian. His knowing, somehow, that getting into the freezing saltwater of the harbour was going to help.

And it did.

But then, afterwards. Back in his apartment. What happened, happened so fast. Too fast, really, looking back, even though it was she who suggested she stay the night. If she's being honest, she's not at all sure how she's feeling. She's not sure what happens next. The only thing she knows is, right now, she doesn't have the headspace to line up her thoughts and her feelings or make much sense of anything.

She turns back to the camera footage.

She doesn't reply to the text.

A few hours into her shift, Addison heads back into the tearoom. She's lost track of how many cups of tea she's had. She'd like nothing more than a joint, and she might have one with PLUS 1 when she gets home. Although it's a coin toss as to whether weed would help right now, or if it would just make her weepier.

As she comes into the tearoom, one of the other volunteers is on her phone, watching Elisa Williams at the press conference.

'I'm so sorry,' she says, hurriedly switching it off.

'It's okay. You don't have to pretend you're not watching,' Addison says as she pours hot water over a teabag. 'I'm really glad everyone is seeing that video. Someone's going to recognize the car. The sooner they find it, the better.'

She's looked at the clip a number of times herself. If she wasn't so tired, she'd suggest to PLUS 1 that they go drive the streets later, themselves, looking for the steel-grey Toyota Corolla.

She takes her cup, heads back to her cubicle, settling in for the last hour.

On a busy night, a Gen Helpline volunteer might get two calls an hour. Friday and Saturday evenings you expect more – the nights when solitariness makes itself felt most acutely. But sometimes it's entirely random. You can go a whole night without the phone going, or you can go for a shift where calls come in back to back.

As Addison sips her tea, the red light in front of her blinks on. She pulls on her headphones.

'Kia ora,* Gen Helpline.'

Silence on the other end.

'Gen Helpline, thank you for calling. Can I help you?'

'You're that Addison chick, eh.'

The voice on the other end of the phone is female. Whoever it is, she sounds young.

When she'd started at Gen Helpline, Addison had posted on all her socials about volunteering, to get her increasing numbers of followers to support the service, to donate, to maybe think about volunteering too. But she'd especially wanted to use her profile to encourage other people her age to use the counselling service if they needed it. Gen Helpline had pushed Addison's messaging

---

* Kia ora – hello.

out to as much of the media as possible, and there'd been quite a bit of uptake. A less welcome outcome was that an occasional fanboy or girl would call to talk to Addison. Or people just pranking, wanting to have bragging rights that they'd talked to the bald rapper girl who played Thursday nights at Sailor Bar.

'Yes, this is Addison. Nice to meet you. How can I help?'

On the other end of the line, silence.

There's a routine you get taught at training. If you have a caller who stops responding, it doesn't mean they're not there. It might just be that they're not ready to talk. Give them space, but also keep gently trying to get them to open up, letting them know you're there.

'I'm glad you called. How are you tonight?'

Still silence. She's about to try again when the other person speaks.

'What happened to your dad. I'm sorry.'

Several news stories had identified the connection between Jaye and upcoming local musician Addison. Still, she hadn't been expecting a caller to have registered this, still less to offer sympathies. It takes her a moment to know how to respond. Stay on script. You're there for the other person.

'Thank you. I appreciate it. What would you like to talk about?'

'I saw the news. I saw the photo of the car they're saying belongs to the shooter. It's a fucking set-up.'

Addison has no idea what to make of this. She can

hear anger in the young woman's voice, and something else. Something that sounds like real fear.

'I don't understand. Do you know who owns the car? Do you know where it is?'

Silence again. From the other end, Addison can hear a vague buzzing, like it's a bad connection. And something else in the distance: a faint sound, like a car alarm ringing.

'Tell them. Tell the pigs,' the young woman says. Addison has noticed that she has a particular way of speaking. It's as if she takes a moment to decide what to say, then when she knows, it comes out quickfire, a sudden burst of words. 'Tell them it's a fucking set-up.'

'What do you know? Please tell me.'

In the silence that follows, the distant ringing sound in the background of the call stops.

'What happened to your dad is fucked,' the young woman says.

The red light in front of Addison dies, the call ended.

She sits there alone, shaking.

There's a framed photo that Addison keeps by her bed.

It's Jaye as a young man, with five-year-old Addison. It was taken a couple of years after Hana and Jaye split up, when he was working in an undercover unit. Jaye's hair is long and greasy, and he's got a straggly beard.

He looks a complete freak, the photo-negative of the dad that she's known the entire rest of her life.

Addison loves the photo.

'Maybe that's when he started smoking?' she says to Hana.

'Maybe.'

Hana is staying with Addison and PLUS 1, arriving home from the station about the same time that Addison finished her shift at Gen Helpline. Addison decided she really didn't want the joint she'd been thinking about, and not just because her mum was staying the night.

They are all sitting on Hana's bed with yet another cup of tea. Boca the puppy is nestled in PLUS 1's lap, though she isn't really a puppy anymore, and she's almost at the stage where she's too big to sit on anyone's lap. As Boca happily snuffles in her sleep, Addison tells Hana about the strange call she got from the young woman.

'What did she say about the car, exactly?' Hana asks.

'Nothing really. She just kept saying, "it's a set-up".'

'The gunman drove to the liquor store in the vehicle. Afterwards he drove away in it. I'm not sure what the cops could be getting wrong in any of that.'

Addison has no idea what to make of the call either. Hana thinks it through.

'Gen Helpline doesn't track or record calls, right?' she asks.

'We're not allowed to.'

'Then there's no way to find out who the caller was.

But in any case, you've had a bit of trolling since you've been there. Sounds like someone being a dick. Wanting to get a reaction out of you. Maybe just let it go, love.'

As they finish their cups of tea, Hana has something else on her mind. She explains to Addison and PLUS 1 about the older woman back in Tātā Bay. Nanny Niki, who needs a hip replacement. How she's on a waiting list and the operation isn't going to happen any time soon, and in the meantime she's suffering from the increasingly debilitating pain, which is only really eased by marijuana. Hana especially doesn't want Niki's granddaughter Maia getting caught up in anything potentially compromising by going to someone like Erwin Rendall and his gang to find drugs for her nanny.

'I know I give you a hard time, about smoking dope. But I can't stop thinking about that poor woman. I was wondering, since you know where to find that kind of thing . . .'

PLUS 1 and Addison share a look.

'Mum. You want us to score weed for you?'

'It's not actually for me.'

Addison is trying hard not to smile.

'What's so funny?'

'Nothing. Nothing at all, Mum.'

Boca is starting to snore now. PLUS 1 lifts the dog up, gives Hana a kiss and heads to the room they share with Addison. Addison finishes her cup of tea, moving into Hana's arms. She looks again at the photo of greasy-haired twenty-something Jaye.

'Is Dad going to be all right?'

Hana can't answer the question.

As Addison rests her head against her mother's shoulder, Hana holds her daughter tight.

7

SELFIE

As soon as the doors of the elevator open on the eighth floor, Hana knows something has changed.

The day before, through the long hours she spent scrolling through CCTV footage, there was constant movement in and out of the open office area. The team leaders and DI Williams circulating among the personnel; sworn staff heading out to follow up on reported sightings of the gunman's vehicle; CIB officers bringing in people with criminal histories that potentially fitted the circumstances of the hold-up. Perpetual movement and focused energy, underlaid with the continual buzz of phone calls and hushed, urgent conversations.

This morning there's almost complete silence.

Everyone is gathered around one workstation. It's the desk of a young non-sworn officer working as part of the CCTV analysis team. She'd been given a series of red light camera feeds from the east Auckland suburbs to review, covering a three-hour period after the hold-up.

Hana joins the others. DI Williams is next to the non-sworn officer. Hana's pretty sure Elisa hasn't been home in the last twenty-four hours, or anywhere near a bed for that matter, but if she's as exhausted as she has every right to be, she's showing no sign. Her face is alive as she watches the laptop screen.

On the computer, there's a still image of a vehicle that set off a red light camera at an intersection beside an East Auckland shopping mall. The timestamp is just over half an hour after the shooting. Red light cameras are angled to capture the offending vehicles' number-plates, so unlike much of the other CCTV coverage, this shot doesn't need any digital enhancement. The numberplate is centre of frame, completely clear.

FUR947

It's the gunman's car.

There are dozens of people gathered around the small table, elbow to elbow. Hana can sense electricity in the air; she's feeling it herself. But no one makes a sound.

'The violation video record?' Williams asks.

With new models of these cameras, a photo being taken triggers an accompanying thirty-second video of the offence, to be used as subsidiary evidence or to document the circumstances of any accident at the intersection that might result from a vehicle running the red light.

The non-sworn officer brings up the video file, presses play.

Hana watches the jumpy black-and-white footage. The Corolla accelerates through the intersection. Thirty metres on, it makes a right-hand turn, into a parking area at the rear of the shopping mall. The vehicle can be seen pulling in at the very rear of the car park, near a large dumpster. The driver gets out. It's after sunset, so the figure is hard to distinguish in the shadows, but it's just possible to see them throwing something into the dumpster. As the driver walks away, the thirty-second video ends.

Williams takes down the details of the intersection. She pulls together two teams of detectives to go with her to the car park. 'Good work,' she says to the non-sworn officer, then, looking around at the faces of everyone gathered, 'Thank you, everyone.'

As Williams heads for the elevator, she shoots a look at Hana.

'Come on then.'

Three unmarked police cars speed east, lights flashing. In the front car, as Williams is on the phone co-ordinating forensics teams to meet them at the shopping mall car park, Hana has time to think about what happened earlier that morning.

As she was leaving the house to head to the station,

a car pulled up. It was Sebastian. He had takeaway coffees and pastries for Hana, Addison and PLUS 1.

'I figure you don't have time for cooking.' Sebastian also held a bunch of flowers in his hands. Seeing Hana's gaze on them, he explained, 'To take to the hospital.'

Hana took the coffee and food inside, leaving them on the table for the others. Then she came back to where Sebastian was waiting on the doorstep. He'd texted a couple more times, and she hadn't returned the messages, or called him. She knew it wasn't fair. But she hadn't known what to say.

'I'm sorry I haven't been in touch.'

'It's a hell of a time.'

'It's not just that,' Hana said, closing the front door of the house behind her. 'The other night. When I came to your place. I don't know how to feel about it.'

'I don't understand,' he said, a perplexed look in his eyes.

Face to face with Sebastian, Hana wished she'd worked through what it was she was actually feeling; how she'd explain why she hadn't returned his texts. Now she had to stumble her way through.

'I guess it's not how I thought it would happen,' she said, awkwardly.

She knows how Sebastian communicates. He listens, intensely. He lets her speak, and he only ever talks when he knows exactly what he wants to say. He's not someone who fills every space. It was up to Hana to keep talking.

'I was angry. Hurting. I still am. It was me – I don't know – being vulnerable. More vulnerable than I've been in a very long time.'

She paused, trying to read Sebastian's body language. If he was upset or angry, he was hiding it very well.

'I don't know what I'm saying, Seb. It's just . . . I feel like that's not how a relationship should start.'

Sebastian waited, making sure she had nothing more to say. Then, to her surprise, he smiled.

'That wasn't the start of a relationship, Hana. I've known exactly how I feel about you since that swim when I couldn't breathe. Since you told me it was okay for me not to be a cop anymore.'

A few years earlier, in the middle of a cross-harbour swim that they'd both been competing in, Hana had stopped to help Sebastian when he'd had a panic attack in deep water. It had been triggered by a particularly traumatic event he'd witnessed at work: the heartbreaking aftermath of a murder-suicide – a young, depressed mother and her baby girl. It had completely derailed him, but he hadn't spoken to anyone about it until Hana stopped in the middle of the race, floated with him, made him tell her what was happening. She could see he wanted out of the cops. She'd told him if that's what he needed, that's what he had to do. He'd quit a week later.

On the doorstep, Sebastian continued, gently.

'It's the worst time. I don't want to make things harder for you.' Hana could see his sympathy was genuine and without rancour. 'Let's catch up when things are settled. Send my love to Jaye.'

He handed her the flowers.

'I love you. I thought you felt the same. I thought that's what the other night was about. Guess I got that wrong. That's okay. Doesn't change how I feel.'

As Sebastian headed back to his car, Hana blinked. Having stumbled around in her own confused emotions for some time, it was a jolt to hear the easy, simple clarity of his feelings.

The unmarked police car slows.

'Here we go,' Williams says, bringing Hana back to the present.

They stop at traffic lights; the same intersection they'd been looking at on the laptop screen just thirty minutes earlier. Beyond it, the shopping centre. The lights turn from red to green, and Williams indicates to take the same turn into the car park that the Corolla took on the video, heading for the rear of the shopping centre.

She pulls to a halt, the other two unmarked vehicles stopping behind her.

Ahead, next to the orange dumpster they'd seen on the video, is the steel-grey Toyota Corolla.

After the rear section of the car park is secured, a forensics team arrives with a tow truck to remove the Corolla for testing at the forensic garage at Central Police

Station. An initial search of the vehicle has come up empty. No sign of the weapon, or anything that might identify the gunman.

As the car is winched onto the deck of the truck, Hana grabs a paper suit and latex gloves from one of the police vehicles and pulls them on. Before she can head for the skip to start searching for whatever the gunman threw in there, she notices DI Williams is also pulling a forensics suit over her clothes.

'I got this,' Hana says. 'I'm the constable, remember. Newbie cops get all the shit jobs. Besides, you have to be spick and span for the media.'

'I've got a change of clothes at the office,' Williams says, pulling on gloves.

She gives Hana a boost up the side of the skip, quickly slipping in beside her as Hana carefully moves aside some crushed cardboard boxes. They work methodically, starting on one side of the dumpster and lifting out discarded shop fittings and empty packing cases, handing them out to a waiting uniformed cop, trying to ignore the smell.

'Whatever he threw in here, it's been a couple of days,' Hana says as they lift a heavy section of broken metal shelving. 'Hope the bin hasn't been emptied in the meantime.'

Williams murmurs in agreement. Having hoisted the shelving out of the dumpster, she moves towards the back, pulling aside a bulging black plastic rubbish bag as she goes. Instantly, her posture stiffens.

'Hana.'

On the metal floor of the dumpster lies a plastic tote bag. Black, with a big orange circle. The bag the gunman carried the weapon in. Williams carefully looks inside. There's no gun. But there's something that might be of at least as much use.

A cell phone.

Hana finds herself holding her breath as Williams tries the 'on' button. Nothing. The battery's dead.

Neither of them speak as they clamber out of the skip and head back over to the unmarked CIB cars. Williams plugs the phone into a charge cord, presses 'on' again. This time it kicks into life. She tries to swipe it open and a keypad pops up; the phone is password protected.

But there's a home-screen image. Williams shows Hana.

It's a selfie. A young man in a back-to-front baseball cap, staring out from the screen.

Hana studies the picture. The guy is Māori. He looks about Addison's age. His face is serious, like he's trying hard in the selfie to come off as a tough guy, but not quite succeeding. There's an openness and gentleness in his eyes that no amount of gangster posturing can hide. Looking at the young man's face, a sick feeling builds in Hana's stomach.

Why the hell did this kid go and get a gun, walk into a shop and do the awful thing he did?

8

SAME

He knew he was different.

But for a long time he tried so hard to be the same as everyone else.

There was a girl with long wavy hair and braces on her top teeth. This was in his first year of high school, at the age when he could see all around him that girls were looking at boys and boys were looking at girls, in ways he didn't understand. At a certain point, the girl with the wavy hair and the braces started looking at him in those same ways.

By observing, he could see how it went, so he looked harder, and he learned.

He watched as his classmates showed off, doing things that weren't in the least impressive, laughing at things that weren't in the least funny, sending each other signals he came to understand as flirting. From a distance he learned all he could about these odd rituals. In the mirror he practised making the smiles he was meant to make. Then, when he felt he understood enough, he gave the girl with the wavy hair and the braces the kind of smile he'd seen other boys give girls.

She smiled back. The same as he'd seen other girls smile at boys.

Maybe there was a chance.

Maybe he could be the same as the others.

About this time, the magpie flew into the glass pane of his bedroom window.

It made a hell of a noise, and when he went out into the garden, the bird was lying in the weeds below his window. It was alive, it was breathing, but its eyes were wild with terror, and its head was at an angle that, it seemed to him, it really shouldn't be. *Its neck is broken*, he thought. But when he got closer, the bird managed to lift its head a little, looking at him. The complexities of human body language were impenetrable to him, like trying to understand alien Morse code, but what happened in an animal's eyes was a much simpler text to read. He could see the bird wasn't afraid of him. Rather, it was pleading.

Help me.

So, he did.

He carefully picked the magpie up. He carried it into the garden shed where his uncle took him when he came to visit. He gathered some clean, dry grass and put it in a box. He fetched honey from the kitchen, and a teaspoon and a cup of water. As the magpie lay on the bed of dry grass, he fed it water and honey in spoonfuls.

This is what it means to care for something, he thought.

He was intrigued by this idea. If he cared for this bird, gave it tenderness and succour, the way he'd seen people care for animals or little babies in films and TV shows and read about in books, perhaps he would feel the things the characters in those stories felt.

If he smiled and flirted with the girl with wavy hair and braces, maybe he'd feel the things other boys felt.

He finished feeding the wounded bird, and surrounded it with dry straw, to keep it warm.

He was interested to see how this would go.

As the magpie healed in the garden shed, he and the wavy-haired girl with the braces did the things he'd seen others their age doing. She suggested they go to the movies. They swam in the river. One lunchtime they went to the trees at the very back of the school and she lit a cigarette she'd stolen from her father. He tried it, but it wasn't exciting. It made him cough and feel foggy.

One afternoon, walking home from school, she took him to climb a hill near her house. There was a stand of forest there that was ready to be milled, the trees grown tall and dense. There was so much foliage that they couldn't see the views out over the town.

Which meant the town couldn't see them.

There, hidden among the trees, she squeezed the front of his trousers. She pressed her mouth against his and did something with her tongue. She looked at him in a new way, a way that he didn't understand any more clearly than the other ways she'd looked at him.

He could tell, though, that his reaction wasn't what she had hoped for.

What's wrong? the girl with the wavy hair asked. Don't you like me?

He went home. At school the next day, when he saw her, he didn't use the smile he'd practised in the mirror. He looked straight past her.

And he walked away.

After a few days of honey and water, he came into the toolshed after school to find the magpie standing on its own in the box full of dried grass.

He could see in the bird's eyes: it wasn't afraid. What the girl wanted when she squeezed him or put her mouth on his was a mystery to him. But the things the magpie was feeling, these he understood.

With the magpie, it was simple.

He'd healed the bird. He'd cared for it. He'd fed it. He'd

made it well. It trusted him. This meant the bird loved him, he thought.

He carefully picked the magpie up from the box. It stood in his hand. It was surprisingly light, and he realized then that this was a young bird, still learning the dangers of the world, which was probably why it had flown at full speed into his window. He held out his hand, encouraging the bird to fly. It spread its wings, flew once around the shed, then came back down to land in the box with the dried grass.

He crouched down next to it. He gently stroked the inky black feathers, fascinated by their soft outer tips, the strength of each feather's shaft where it met the bird's body. He'd never heard of a magpie allowing itself to be touched in this way.

Yeah. He was pretty sure. The bird loved him.

At that moment, as he petted the bird, he remembered another time he'd been in this shed. As his uncle did what he did, he saw a dark shape moving in the corner. *A rat*, he thought. He concentrated on the rat's movements in the shadows; a way of ignoring what was happening. A way of ignoring the sounds his uncle was making. The sounds he was making himself.

He picked the magpie up again. Its body warm and trembling in one hand, caressing its head with the other. He quickly twisted the bird's head a full 360 degrees. There was a satisfying crunching sound, like a branch breaking when you stand on it in the forest.

He put the magpie back in the box, closed the door of the shed and left the dead bird for the rats.

9

THE GOOD SON

It's lunch service at Moon Lake Bistro and Lounge, and the main dining area is almost full. The restaurant is a source of endless joy for the owner Bo, more usually known by his friends and employees as Gold Brother. Bo's favoured nickname comes from the delicate gold chain he always wears, hanging casually in the neckline of his signature designer tracksuits. In his thirties now, he first arrived from China when hip-hop was hitting big in New Zealand, and he likes to think the look he has styled for himself is a bit LA rap, but with a more understated style than the rappers, with their chunky, showy silver chains.

Bo's taste for the elegance of gold extends to the private dining lounge at the very back of Moon Lake, in front of his office. There's a gold braided cord blocking entry to the lounge, and the wallpaper inside is embossed in red and gold. It was the proudest day of his life when he bought business class tickets to fly his parents to Auckland from the city where he was raised, and he was able to host them for a celebration dinner in the lounge. Back home, Bo's family own a moderately successful printing business, which did well enough for them to be able to send their son to New Zealand to learn English, with the goal that when he returned home and entered the business world, his fluency would make him far more successful than his parents had been.

In the speech he made to his parents that night, he paid tribute to their foresight. He again told the story he'd told them so many times, and which they in turn had retold to all their friends and family. After arriving in New Zealand, he'd worked hard at his studies, his English becoming so accomplished that he was offered work as a tutor at the English language school he'd studied at. He'd worked and saved hard, and eventually bought a share in the school. He'd made good investments, including establishing the restaurant, two plastering businesses and a small printing company, continuing the family tradition. *This country is like a promised land for our people*, Bo had often said in emails to his parents, and it was true. Chinese and other Asian populations now make up fifteen per cent of the New Zealand population, and Chinese immigration has lastingly enriched the culture and the diversity of the country. Chinese-born New Zealanders are business leaders, city councillors, mayors, members of parliament, Bo told his parents. *Maybe one day I could be the first Chinese Prime Minister of New Zealand!* he wrote in a particularly effusive email.

At the end of his speech to his parents in the private lounge, Bo raised his glass.

'You made me who I am. All this is because of you. I pray I have proved myself a son worthy of your love.'

His mother and father looked around at the red-and-gold finery with tears in their eyes.

Some of what Bo had told his parents was true enough. He'd certainly made canny investments and, as a legitimate businessman, he was doing very well. But he'd left quite a lot of his actual history out of the story, and he'd reimagined much of the rest. Bo had never gone on to work at the language school his parents had sent him to, nor had he ever become a business partner in it. He was certainly a very good student, studying long and hard in his first months in New Zealand. Like so many language school students though, he acutely felt the lack of connections, so far from family and friends, so far from his own culture. After many months sitting alone at night in the cheap city-fringe apartment his parents had rented for him, he ended up going with the other students to the city's only casino, socializing there, putting the occasional coin into the slot machines and watching in awe as the wealthiest gamblers at the baccarat and roulette tables placed their jaw-dropping bets.

Imagine if I had even half the money those men have, Bo would think, watching the high rollers. *Imagine the life I could give my parents, if I had just a little of that money. They could sell their business, retire somewhere warm and comfortable.*

If Bo was ever asked to pinpoint the driving motivation of his life, he could honestly reply, his hand on his heart: 'To be a good son.'

After he'd been going to the casino for a few months, one of the high rollers asked Bo to join him for a drink up at the VIP room. It was a thrilling experience. The man who had invited him was from an area near Bo's hometown, and he had an offer for his compatriot. He needed someone to do contract work. Bo would be given a quantity of cash, which he'd change into tokens to play the slot machines, collecting whatever winnings accrued. It was a common enough way to launder money and, spending so much time in the casino, Bo was well aware of how it worked. The machines had a payout rate of around ninety per cent, so the ten per cent lost to the machines and the fee paid to the person playing them was a relatively cost-efficient tax. The casino was full of others doing the same job, and Bo quickly joined their ranks. As his English got better, he spent less and less time going to the language school, and more time at the slot machines. Soon enough, he was made another offer. Another member of the VIP lounge crowd, who had heard that he was reliable and trustworthy, had a package coming, for a friend. They needed an address to send it to. The money Bo was offered for that one delivery to his meagre city-fringe apartment was more than the allowance his parents sent him to live on for three whole months.

It was the first package of many.

Bo started making serious money as a 'catcher', receiving packages at his apartment and handing them over to his employer in the underground casino car park. He stopped going to the language school, though, in any case, by now his English was nearly perfect. He saved his profits wisely, and made his first investment in a legitimate business. Ever the fast learner, at a certain point Bo started to ask himself why he was risking it all as a catcher and getting so little of the rewards. He asked the right questions and learned about the supply chain; how the packages moved from mainland Asia, or more often now from South America, down to New Zealand, bypassing Australia with its far more effective border controls. When his employer felt he was getting too old for the business and decided to retire and take his considerable wealth home, Bo made him an offer. Within a year of first sitting down with a bag of someone else's money at a slot machine, he was employing other newly arrived language students to do the same. He started wearing the gold chain that he has since never been without, and began to encourage others to call him by his preferred nickname. In another six months he had opened Moon Lake Bistro and Lounge, and by then he was importing the packages himself.

But his parents were aware of none of this.

All they knew was that their son owned a beautiful restaurant, an expensive car, an apartment on the glamorous waterfront of Auckland city. It was beyond the wildest hopes they'd ever dared hold for him. After he toasted them that Sunday night, Bo gave them each gold designer watches. When they flew home, the first thing they did was to send him a WeChat photo of them standing outside the family printing business, proudly displaying their gleaming presents.

Bo cried, long into the night, looking at the beaming faces of his parents in that picture.

He'd done it. He had given them the greatest of all gifts.

Gold Brother had made his parents proud.

He was a good son.

Sitting in his office now, Bo hears a knock at the door. It opens.

'Gold Brother, come and see what you think,' Hàoyǔ says. On the books for Inland Revenue, Hàoyǔ is the manager of Moon Lake Bistro and Lounge, although he has absolutely no knowledge of or interest in the hospitality business. His real value to Gold Brother is in areas that would be challenging to classify for taxation purposes.

Gold Brother follows Hàoyǔ into the private lounge. It has been lavishly decorated with tinsel and balloons for Hàoyǔ's wife's fiftieth birthday celebration in a couple of days' time, keeping true to the red-and-gold palette of the room.

'I think your wife will love this,' Gold Brother tells the older man, and he means it.

Hàoyǔ beams. But his smile fades as he sees two new arrivals walking through the restaurant, heading for the private lounge. The man and the woman are both in suits, and neither Hàoyǔ nor Gold Brother need to look closely at the nametags hanging from their necks to know they are CIB detectives.

'Can I help you, officers?' Gold Brother asks, in his perfect English, unfastening the cord blocking the way to the private lounge and gesturing for the cops to enter. Hàoyǔ shoots a look towards a couple of staff members, and they approach the lounge, watching the newcomers warily.

The male detective places a photo on the nearest table. It's a printed image of the selfie from the screensaver on the phone found in the dumpster.

Gold Brother studies the photo. 'Who is this young man?' he asks.

'We were hoping you could tell us.'

Back at police headquarters, some of the pieces of the puzzle are coming together.

Several partial and full fingerprints were lifted from the steel-grey Toyota Corolla. They were matched to someone with a police record: a young man who'd been arrested a couple of years earlier for car conversion. Now the cops had a name for the guy in the selfie with the backwards cap.

Toa Davis.

When Digital Forensics broke into the phone, they found that one particular number had been called repeatedly over the last several months, sometimes two or three times a day.

It was the number for the front desk of Moon Lake Bistro and Lounge.

The National Organised Crime Group is a division of the New Zealand Police. Within NOCG there are a number of separate divisions, including, among others, specialist surveillance teams, a motorcycle gang unit and the Asian Organised Crime squad. When the connection between Toa Davis and Moon Lake Bistro and Lounge was established, DI Williams brought the members of the AOC up to the eighth floor. The head of the squad, Detective Sergeant Truong, told the assembled officers that Moon Lake was well known to his unit as one of the organized crime groups operating at the end of a long, multi-tiered chain through which narcotics were funnelled from the northern hemisphere into New Zealand.

'The product comes from Asia and, more often now, from Mexico,' Truong explained. 'The offshore cartels get a good return for their efforts. New Zealand has the highest per gram street prices in the world for methamphetamine and cocaine. And with the amount of unmonitored coastline we have, it's way easier to get product into this country than Australia.'

Hana knew the chain of distribution well enough from her time in the CIB, as did pretty much all of the officers present, but she respected DS Truong making absolutely sure everyone was working from the same set of underlying facts.

'The local organized crime groups act like supermarket warehouses, receiving the incoming goods and distributing them on, most often via low-paid locals on the ground. Which is where your guy most likely fits in,' he continued, indicating the selfie from the phone, projected onto one of the big screens on the CIB walls. 'We know Moon Lake is involved in the trade. We think they're big players. Toa Davis is exactly the kind of person a syndicate would employ as a courier. A donkey, moving the product around to the street-level suppliers. From the warehouse to the shop door, so to speak.'

He studied the selfie, the face of the young man they now know to be Toa Davis.

'You think this guy's the shooter?' he asked.

'His fingerprints and DNA are all through the vehicle,' Williams said.

Truong looked around his team. 'We'll give you everything we have. I just don't know how much that will help. We had someone on the inside of Moon Lake: an informant we'd been developing in their rank and file. He was answerable to Hàoyǔ, an older guy. Gold Brother is the top of the tree, but he keeps the shady stuff at arm's length. Hàoyǔ is his 2IC, the hands-on enforcer. A big shipment was about to arrive and we were ready to set up the bust, with the idea that we'd have our inside contact on a plane and out of the country before we made the arrests.'

'What happened?' Williams asked.

'The informant got cold feet. When we pressed him, he told us he thought maybe Hàoyǔ was onto him. He started pulling back. Then he disappeared.'

'What does that mean, disappeared?'

'Just that. Gone. Never turned up to the next meeting. Never heard from him again. Maybe he got himself a false passport, found his own way home. Or maybe he was taken for a visit to the Desert Road.'

Looks pass between the cops. Everyone knows what a visit to the Desert Road means.

The Desert Road is an area in the central plateau of the North Island that's as bleak and barren as the name suggests. Covered in tussock grassland, the area is surrounded by some of the most spectacular mountains in the country, and its hundreds of square miles of land can disappear under a layer of snow and ice for long periods of the winter. A number of victims of organized crime have been found buried off the main state highway that runs through the Desert Road. It's widely believed there could be many more shallow graves, waiting to be found.

'Hàoyǔ looks like someone's good-natured uncle. But don't be fooled,' Truong continued. 'If he takes you to the Desert Road, it's a one-way trip.'

'You know these guys,' Williams said. 'If you were me, what's the next step?'

'We don't have anyone on the inside of Moon Lake now. We have their phone lines monitored, of course. But Hàoyǔ is nobody's fool. You call the front desk, identify yourself, and if they want to talk to you, you're given another number. It's a burner. Each day the burner SIM card is tossed, replaced by a new one before we can establish a tap.'

DS Truong looked again at the projected image of Toa Davis.

'If this guy's connected to Moon Lake, and he's still involved with them? You don't have too many options, except going in the front door.'

DI Williams and Hana watch the interviews with Gold Brother and Hàoyǔ through the video feeds from the interview rooms, where they are spoken to separately.

Gold Brother is unfailingly polite, but his answer to every question is essentially the same, his body language dismissive.

'I don't know this person with the baseball cap. I've never met him in my life.'

In the second room, Hàoyǔ answers with the assistance of a Mandarin translator. His responses are identical to those of his boss. When asked why the number of Moon Lake Bistro and Lounge was logged so many times on Toa Davis' phone, Hàoyǔ smiles coldly.

'Perhaps the young man likes Chinese food. People do, you know.'

The night before, after Toa Davis' fingerprints were identified, Hana drove with DI Williams to speak to the young man's estranged family. The whānau lives in a tiny town several hours north of Auckland. They asked Hana and Williams to meet them at their marae.

The meeting house is in a beautiful location, on top of a hill that looks out over a windswept coastline. Some wharenui* are covered in elaborate wooden carvings that tell the history of the tribes, how they journeyed to Aotearoa,† the stories of their tūpuna.‡ For tribes with a strong history of carving and weaving, the buildings can be spectacular – living, breathing works of art. This little meeting house was well kept and maintained, Hana could see, but humble. Simply painted walls and ceilings; plain, unadorned panels; nothing carved or woven.

'Toa was sixteen years old when the cops first came knocking at our door.'

Toa's mother was in the meeting house, along with his

---

* Wharenui – meeting house/meeting houses.
† Aotearoa – New Zealand (literally, the Land of the Long White Cloud).
‡ Tūpuna – ancestors.

grandmother and grandfather, and a number of other locals there to support them. Hana knew from Toa's records that his father had passed away when he was still in primary school, which had hit the boy hard. When they had been welcomed into the wharenui, they had been introduced to Toa's older brother. Hana noticed that the brother stayed out the front of the marae, unwilling to come in and be part of the discussion.

'He was always a bit of a loner,' Toa's mother continued. 'Never had many mates. Then at a certain point he fell in with some kids from the next town. Me and Kura, his big brother, we tried to get him to stay away from them. But he wouldn't listen. They nicked a car one night. Took it for a joyride, trashed it. They got away with it. So, a couple of nights later they did the same again. This time they got caught.'

Hana could see, outside the wharenui, the brother was close enough to hear the conversation. He was tense, his shoulders rigid.

'The other kids denied everything. Their parents made up bullshit excuses to protect them. And the cops listened, 'cos they were white and Toa wasn't.'

The mother had a blanket around her shoulders. She wrapped it tighter about herself, against the winter cold. Her eyes went out to where Toa's brother was standing.

'Afterwards, when he came back here. After he'd been released from the remand home. It was his grandmother's birthday party, here in the marae. Her seventieth.' Her voice broke a little. One of the older women put her hand on her arm. 'Kura was out the front waiting. Pretty much where he is now. With his dad gone, Kura thought it was his job to be the man of the family. He told Toa he wasn't welcome back here. He said, "You're not part of this family no more."'

She wiped her eyes.

'Toa tried to push past his big brother. Kura took to him. Gave him a hiding. In front of everyone. I didn't know what to do. Didn't know how to stop what was happening.'

It took her a minute to gather herself. Hana and Williams waited, feeling for her.

'When his brother was finished, Toa picked himself up,' the mother finally said. 'He walked out the gate. He didn't look back. That was a year and a half ago. We haven't seen or heard from him since.'

As they were leaving, Williams handed out her card to everyone in the meeting house.

'If you hear anything from Toa, please call me straight away.'

At the front of the meeting house, she held out one of her cards to the older brother. He didn't take it.

'The little prick knows he's not welcome,' he said, his arms folded. 'He won't try and come back here.'

The sun is going down as Hana runs up Maungawhau, one of the dozens of volcanic peaks that circle central

Auckland. Maungawhau used to be a pā,* designed to withstand the onslaughts of enemy tribes seeking to claim the rich soils and the commanding defensive positions for themselves.

She keeps running up past the carved terraces that circled the summit, where high wooden stockades once stood, topped with points carved down to razor sharpness, to prevent enemies scaling the walls. She reaches the top of the maunga.† Looks out, as darkness falls over the city.

After going to meet Toa's family, Hana is pretty sure that he's not going to end up back in his hometown. The CIB team are working around the clock, searching the streets, questioning others in the criminal underworld that Toa seems to have become a part of since his brother sent him on his way. But all of the enquiries so far have suggested that he doesn't seem to be affiliated to any other organized crime groups or gangs.

Toa Davis is a lone operator.

From the top of Maungawhau, there's a 360-degree view of the city. Auckland has a population of nearly two million people, spread over a massive area of land, almost the footprint of greater Los Angeles. So many dark corners. So many places to hide. There's only one known point of connection to Toa. The number on his phone.

Moon Lake Bistro and Lounge.

---

* Pā – fortress.
† Maunga – mountain.

But the place is a closed book. No way in. No way to know if they are harbouring him; if he did the hold-up for them, and they're protecting him now. Moon Lake is a fortress, as impenetrable as Maungawhau was, with walls just as impossible to pass.

We've got to find a way in, Hana thinks.

10

TELL ME WHERE YOU ARE

Addison watches herself in one of the floor-to-ceiling mirrors that line the walls. She's working hard as she pounds one of the big seventy-kilogram bags. It's something she and PLUS 1 have been doing for a few months now. They're in the gym where Dax works, a guy their age who Addison got to know; he was the boyfriend of a young woman who'd been murdered and whose bones Addison stumbled upon in the sand dunes near her mother's place. They stayed in touch, and Addison and PLUS 1 started coming to the gym to have personal training sessions with him.

A bit of a germophobe, Addison splashed out on boxing gloves for her and PLUS 1, so they don't have to borrow the very well-worn loaners at the gym.

'You two are good. Must be the music stuff,' Dax

says, impressed, as PLUS 1 and Addison punch the big bags. Dax often says that boxing's about rhythm. He also says boxing is ninety per cent mental, ten per cent physical. That bit Addison doesn't get. Her brain is fine after one of Dax's sessions; what hurts is her body. Every inch of her body.

'There's amateur sparring nights, every couple of months,' Dax says. 'You should try it out.'

'Seriously?' Addison says, chuffed at the compliment.

'Actually, I meant PLUS 1.'

PLUS 1 beams. They throw a show-offy flurry of punches.

'No offence, Addison,' Dax hurriedly adds. 'You should give it a go too. It's just, PLUS 1 was born for this.'

'I'm so hurt,' Addison says with a grin. 'Beating people to a pulp has always been a major life goal.'

PLUS 1 used to be a competitive diver when they were in their early teens. They're flexible, with fast reactions and the kind of spatial awareness you need when you're exploding off a diving board and somersaulting through the air. Addison has seen how, when she and PLUS 1 are sparring, PLUS 1's eyes are continually dancing, watching Addison's eyeline, her hands. Anticipating what's coming. It's like PLUS 1 can see every flex in Addison's hand, the smallest change in angle before she's about to throw a jab, and they're already moving, stepping away, sliding out of the trajectory of her glove. Addison never seems quite able to connect with PLUS 1's head guard.

As she keeps pounding the heavy bag, Addison sucks in big gulps of oxygen.

She's been trying to turn the regular rhythm into a kind of mantra – left-right, left-right. A way to just be in her body. A way not to think about her dad lying in the hospital bed. It works for a while. But then the same thoughts come flooding back.

The rhythm of her gloves slows and stops. Her head falls. PLUS 1 knows why.

'It's okay, babe. It's gonna be okay.'

'I can't do the show. I can't face it. Can we cancel?'

The regular Thursday-night gig PLUS 1 and Addison play at Sailor Bar is tonight. The shows have been getting bigger; they've even been asked to open for an Australian indie band that's playing at a bigger downtown music venue the next month.

'No one's gonna expect you to be there. I'll just do a DJ set,' PLUS 1 says.

They're outside the gym, sharing a vape. PLUS 1 has the occasional vape; Addison hardly ever. But today she wants one.

'Are you going in to the call centre?' PLUS 1 asks.

'Yeah. I think so.'

PLUS 1 knows why Addison really wants to head back to Gen Helpline. She hasn't been able to get the call from the young woman with the frightened voice out of her mind.

'Like your mum said. It was a fake-out. They're not gonna call again.'

'But what if they do? And I'm not there?'

Addison takes another drag on the vape.

'I don't know. Being there, just in case,' she exhales. 'It makes me feel like I'm doing something, you know?'

Dax comes out through the front door. He's got the money they just gave him for the session.

'The boss heard about your dad. Today's on the house.'

Addison gives Dax a thank-you hug.

'That cop with the artificial leg,' Dax says, when she lets go. 'He's your mate, eh?' His voice has shifted. It sounds awkward.

'Stan Riordan?'

'There's more than one cop with one of those things?'

Addison laughs. 'Yeah, he's our friend.'

'He's been training here,' Dax says. 'He's got a fitness test coming up, right? Trying to get back into the cops.'

Addison and PLUS 1 know all about the PCT test: Stan describes it in slightly obsessive detail every time they see him. It's a fifty-metre sprint, scaling a rope wall, another sprint, crawling flat to the ground under a ten-metre obstacle, yet another sprint, jumping through a hole in a free-standing wall that simulates a window six feet off the ground, then a final fifty-metre sprint.

'Yeah, he's pretty fixated,' Addison says.

'No shit,' Dax replies. 'It's all he can talk about.'

Addison can see Dax is a little edgy. There's something on his mind. 'What's up?'

'My mate is his trainer. Stan asked her if there might be any supplements he could get hold of that could help him.'

'Like protein supplements?' PLUS 1 asks.

'My mate didn't think that's what he meant. She thought he was asking if he could get 'roids.'

'Steroids?' Addison frowns.

'He never said it straight out. But that's definitely what she thought.' Dax looks back towards the owner, behind the counter of the gym. 'This place is clean. It's a family business. We didn't tell the boss. He'd ban the guy.'

He starts to head back in, glancing back at Addison as he swings the door open.

'Just thought you should know.'

The call comes in at almost the exact same time as the last one.

Just after 9:30pm.

Addison had checked in for her shift at four. There's one other volunteer on duty, and there'd only been a few calls, with nothing requiring a referral to Suicide Crisis or an emergency medical call-out or anything like that. At the call centre, they've found that most calls come in later at night. Someone unable to sleep. Staring at the mirror, staring at the bottle they've drunk, staring at a future without the person they thought they were going to be with for the rest of their lives.

As she waited at her station, Addison thought about what Dax had said about Stan. It had thrown her a little. Stan is almost definitely the straightest human being under the age of thirty she's ever met. The idea of him trying to buy black-market anabolic steroids makes zero sense. You might as well have told her he was planning to blow up the downtown train station. It just didn't fit with the by-the-rules guy with the side-part and the clean-shaven jawline. Sure, Addison has seen how motivated Stan is to get back into the cops. The obsession with the obstacle course, with getting his badge back.

But still.

The trainer must have made some mistake. It wasn't possible.

The red light in front of Addison flashes.

'Kia ora, Gen Helpline.'

'Is that you?'

Addison instantly recognizes the voice, the staticky buzz on the line. It's the young woman.

When she'd first started her shift that evening, Addison had chosen the seat at the end of the second row of call stations, as far away as possible from the other volunteer. She'd done a bit of prep, in case the young woman called back, discreetly unscrewing one of the earpieces of her headset and positioning it close to her phone's mic. Now she glances towards the other volunteer. They're deep in a conversation with a client. Taking a deep breath, Addison hits record on the voice memo app on her phone, very aware she is breaking the most fundamental rule of the Helpline: calls are anonymous and unrecorded.

'It's me,' she says. 'We talked the other day, right?'

'I said this was gonna happen,' the young woman on the other end of the line says, with the same angry edge. 'He's been set up. The cops have it in for him.'

The selfie of Toa Davis and his name and details are on every news feed, identifying him as a person of interest in the shooting. When she speaks again, the young woman's voice is shaky.

'I'm scared. I'm really scared.'

There's silence for a moment. From the other end of the call, Addison hears the same sound in the background as she did the last time, like the distant ringing of a car alarm. As the sound continues, she thinks about what the young woman just said.

'Is he making you say all this?' she asks quietly.

'What?'

In the background, the high-pitched ringing sound stops, as abruptly as it began. The silence is swallowed by the same continuous, vague buzzing as before.

'You said you're scared. Is that why?' Addison says quietly. 'Is he forcing you to make this call? Will he hurt you if you don't?'

'Fucksake.' A snort of what sounds like laughter from the other end of the phone, but Addison can't tell if it's contempt, or a terrified young woman trying to cover her fears. 'All the stuff you sing about. Brown people getting eaten up by the system. That's just talk. You believe their crap as much as anyone. You're on their side.'

'That's my father in that hospital bed. I'm not on anyone's side except my dad's.'

Addison takes a deep breath. Knowing she has to try to keep the woman talking, to get some kind of useful information from her.

'Tell me where you are,' Addison says. 'I want to help.'

The line goes dead.

'That's the sound of cars, right?'

It's past midnight. After Addison finished her shift, she drove straight to Sailor Bar and picked up PLUS 1 and their turntables before heading home. PLUS 1 does the recording and sound engineering for all their music, and they recently invested some of the money from the Sailor Bar gigs to buy audio sweetening equipment, with a whole bunch of filtering plug-ins.

PLUS 1 downloaded the recording from Addison's phone to their laptop. The message is two minutes long. There are a few pauses in the conversation, and PLUS

1 takes one of these, a ten-second gap towards the end of the call, and loops it. Both listen to the distinctive sound of passing vehicles.

'There's only a few cars,' PLUS 1 says as the section loops again. 'They speed up and slow down or stop. Wherever she is, it must be next to a road, not a motorway. If it was a motorway, it'd be constant. And the cars would be going faster.'

Addison's not sure what she's trying to achieve with the illegal recording. But she has an instinct that finding some clues to where the call is coming from might just help.

'The sound in the middle,' she says. 'Just after she says she's scared. The ringing noise.'

PLUS 1 goes back to that section, looking at the LED readouts of the soundwaves.

'It's a different pitch to both your voices. That's gonna make it easier to isolate.'

PLUS 1 makes a copy of that section of the recording. They dial up the playback of the high-pitched sounds, using another filter to isolate out the young woman's voice, then Addison's.

'Here we go,' PLUS 1 says.

They push play. Removed from all the surrounding sounds, the background noise becomes clearer.

'What do you think?' Addison asks. 'A car alarm? Or a home security system going off?'

'There's something else underneath.'

PLUS 1 pulls up the lower, more bassy sound that starts a little bit after the ringing begins and ends before the ringing stops. A rumbling, something large and heavy. Playing it back, with the ringing minimized, the sound is unmistakeable.

'A train,' Addison realizes.

'Which means, the ringing is warning bells.'

'She's near a rail crossing.'

It takes them another couple of hours to work their way through the Auckland Rail timetable, looking at all the suburban routes, figuring out where trains would be passing at the exact time of the recording, between 9:37pm and 9:39pm. Auckland isn't overly blessed in terms of its public transport system, and that evening one of the three main rail corridors was being repaired. That left two lines, and at that time of night, after rush-hour, there were only a couple of services running.

They download a map of the greater Auckland metro area. Addison circles the three areas that a train was passing through at the time the young woman called.

'I'm sure,' she says. 'She's in one of those three places. Which means the guy's probably there too.'

PLUS 1 looks at the determination in Addison's face. After the initial adrenaline buzz of figuring out the bits and pieces of the puzzle, the reality is sinking in.

'You know this is completely wrong, eh? You're breaking privacy laws. You signed that contract when you joined the Helpline, that any conversation is one hundred per cent confidential. They could take you to court.'

Addison looks again at the three areas on the map, circled in green. The places the gunman might be hiding.

'I don't give a shit. It's my dad.'

11

RED LUCKY STAR

It's the end of another busy lunchtime at Moon Lake Bistro and Lounge. A man makes his way through the tables in the main room, approaching the gold braided rope across the entry to the private lounge.

He's casually dressed, but the kind of casual that says, *I have money*. He takes a menu, lifts the rope, relatches it behind him and takes a seat alone in the private room. A waiter hurries from the main dining area. Recognizing the man as Asian but not Chinese, the waiter speaks to him in English.

'I'm sorry, this is a private room.'

'Does anyone here speak Korean?' the man asks in heavily accented English, his eyes not leaving the menu.

'This is a private room,' the waiter repeats. Terse this time.

The man still doesn't look up. He flicks to the pages that have pictures of the various dishes.

'Sir,' the waiter says slowly. 'You need to go back out to the main dining area.'

The man makes no indication that he understands what's being said. He reaches into the leather satchel at his side. He pulls out a bright red carton of Red Lucky Star cigarettes, a favourite brand for many Asian immigrants, sought out with the same yearning as a signature dish from their favourite restaurant in their hometown. In the VIP-lounge smoking booths at the casino, Red Lucky Star is the preferred brand of most of the high-value Asian clients. It's more than a cigarette. It's currency.

'A gift for the owner,' the man says, in his slow, halting English.

The waiter takes the box of cigarettes, heads to the office.

Alone again in the private room, Sebastian Kang studies the pictures on the menu.

The evening before was the weekly group swim down at the inner-city beach. Hana sat on the low concrete platform above the beach, waiting as Sebastian came out of the water with the other hardcore swimmers who had made it this far into an increasingly bleak Auckland winter.

'Good swim?' Hana asked.

'Getting colder. Not sure how much longer I'll keep going.'

It was the first time they'd seen or spoken to each other since the difficult conversation on Hana's doorstep. Sebastian towelled off as the others in the group headed up the wooden stairs towards their cars.

'How's Jaye?'

'The doctors say he's improving faster than they expected. It's looking hopeful.'

'That's welcome news.' Sebastian sat down on the concrete platform, next to Hana.

'What we talked about the other morning,' he said. 'No two people get to the same place at the exact same time. I thought you were feeling the way I was feeling. I had no right to assume that.'

'Right now, I don't know what the hell I'm feeling. I do know I'm sorry if I hurt you. I didn't mean to do that.'

Sebastian nodded, *thank you*.

'There's something else, isn't there?'

There was.

Hana told Sebastian about the lack of progress the cops had made in finding Toa Davis. They knew he had a connection to Moon Lake, but Gold Brother's operation was a closed door.

'I have no right to ask this. I fully expect you'll tell me to go to hell.'

'Ask what?'

'Customs confiscated a container of Red Lucky Star cigarettes a couple of months ago.'

Sebastian whistled. From his time in the CIB, he knew well enough the value of this brand of Asian cigarette in the right marketplace.

'It's worth maybe $200k,' Hana continued. 'DI Williams and I think maybe that's a way in. Setting up a sale. Once someone's in the door, something might slip.'

'You said there was no one on the inside.'

'You speak Mandarin.'

It took Sebastian a moment to realize what she was saying.

'If they know I speak Mandarin, they're not going to say anything.'

Hana nodded, *exactly*. 'That's the point. You're a Korean businessman with a small fortune in black-market cigarettes. There's no reason for anyone to think you speak Mandarin. And you don't let them know.'

From where they were sitting, they could see Rat Island and the yachts moored beyond. Sebastian watched the boats drifting slowly in the water.

'Of course I'll help,' he said.

New Zealand Police are traditionally risk averse. There are stringent tests and preconditions to be met before someone is sworn in as a temporary officer. But Elisa Williams is facing a situation that is singular, and urgent. Most senior cops in her role wouldn't make a call this big. They wouldn't bend the rules.

But she made the call.

In Williams' office, Sebastian swore the same oath of allegiance as Hana had, becoming a temporary constable in the New Zealand police force. Williams assigned a junior detective constable to work with them both, and an unmarked car.

'It's all I can spare. If you find anything, if you get any sense they're harbouring the guy, you're now authorized to make an arrest. If anything goes wrong, call out and we'll come running.'

In the private lounge, Sebastian has been brought a pot of tea. It's been ten minutes since he handed over the carton of cigarettes to the waiter. As he pours himself a cup, Gold Brother comes in, sits down. Two burly waiters stand watching from the door, Hàoyŭ beside them.

Gold Brother has a pack of Red Lucky Star from the carton. He puts his phone on the table. It's open to a translation app, Mandarin into Korean.

'How many do you have?'

Sebastian reads the translation. He replies in fluent Korean, with the accent from the Daegu region, where he was sent by his parents most school holidays to spend as much time with his grandparents as possible. So he'd know his family, his culture, his mother tongue.

'I brought in a container a few weeks ago.' Sebastian waits for the translation into Mandarin. 'It was concealed in a consignment of wide screen TVs. Half the shipment is Red Lucky Star.'

Gold Brother reads the translation. He nods, impressed.

'Half a container. Maybe one hundred fifty thousand packs?'

Sebastian waits for the translation, although he immediately understands the Mandarin.

'More like two hundred thousand.'

Gold Brother looks out towards the main restaurant. At the front door, a group of customers are gathered, smoking. He doesn't need to be near them to know they're all smoking Red Lucky Star.

'You import electronics? That's your main business? This is on the side?'

Gold Brother pushes the phone towards Sebastian.

'I'm a businessman,' he replies in Korean. 'I do a lot of things. I'm sure it's the same with you.'

Gold Brother reads the translation. He kills the app. Types a number on the screen.

Sebastian looks at the number. He drinks the last of his tea.

'Don't insult me.'

Gold Brother doesn't need a translation to understand what was just said.

Sebastian rises from his chair, lifts the gold rope and walks away, out through the restaurant.

Gold Brother catches up with him outside the front door. 'Okay, okay,' he says.

He hands Sebastian the phone again. Sebastian types

in a different number. It's the number Gold Brother typed, plus fifty per cent. Gold Brother looks at the new figure.

'Come back tomorrow.'

As Sebastian leaves, Hàoyǔ joins Gold Brother on the pavement.

'Do you trust him?' Hàoyǔ asks quietly.

Gold Brother hands the packet of Red Lucky Star to one of the regular customers gathered smoking.

'I don't trust anyone,' Gold Brother says.

He and Hàoyǔ watch closely as Sebastian walks away down the street.

In the nearby street where Hana and the junior detective were waiting in the unmarked police car, Sebastian fills them in on the negotiation.

'You bargained?' the junior detective asks. Her name is Ruby; she's mid-twenties, a practical, strong-jawed young woman who worked in a metal joinery before she joined the cops. She's a little starstruck to have been assigned a job with these two experienced former detectives.

'He was ripping me off,' Sebastian says, as calm and collected as if he'd just gone to the corner store to buy a pint of milk. 'You have to have standards.'

As the unmarked car pulls away from the kerb, Hana grins, impressed, knowing that she and Elisa picked the right guy for this job.

12

I HAVEN'T BEEN SLEEPING

Stan is driving PLUS 1's car. An old 1995 Honda Civic with a bit of a rust problem, PLUS 1's big brother gave it to them when he was completely done repairing it. It's a stick drive, which is actually better practice for Stan as he gets his new leg used to the pedals, and every week or so Addison and PLUS 1 pick him up and they go driving for an hour or two.

'All you need is red and blue lights behind the grill, and it's exactly like my old one,' Stan says with a grin.

It's not. Stan's unmarked police car was a Holden Equinox with a two-litre turbocharged engine; it could accelerate from a dead stop to one hundred miles per hour in a smidge over eight seconds. Stan knows this because he tried it once, after he'd dropped Hana home and decided to head back to the station via a section of motorway he'd made sure had no speed-camera police patrols that night.

'My car has four wheels. That's where the similarities end,' PLUS 1 says from the back seat, pushing a few stray pieces of cushioning back into the splits which have formed in the faded vinyl upholstery. 'Unless you're talking about how your car was *after* it blew up.'

From the front, Addison shoots a look at PLUS 1.

'Sheesh, babe. That's a bit dark.'

Addison has always had a teasing relationship with Stan, and PLUS 1 has happily joined in. But it's only a bit over a year since Stan lost his lower leg and his career as a detective stopped dead.

'Too soon?' PLUS 1 asks tentatively, realizing what they just said. 'Sorry, Stan.'

'Nah, I'm tough. When shit like this happens, you learn to count your blessings. Anyway. This thing is maybe better than the old one,' Stan says, as the titanium shank of his artificial limb pushes down on the clutch pedal. 'I'll never get arthritis in this ankle or pull a calf muscle. And I instantly lost five kilograms in body weight.'

'Who's being dark now?' PLUS 1 grins.

Ahead of them, the hazard lights of a rail crossing start flashing and warning bells sound. Stan pulls to a stop as the barrier arm descends.

'We don't usually come out this side of town for driving practice,' he says.

PLUS 1 looks at Addison. 'Do you ask him, or do I?'

As the train passes, Stan looks between them.
'Ask me what?'

After they'd identified the three areas around Auckland that were near active railway crossing bells at the time of the call, Addison had a brainwave. Get Stan to help in the hunt.

'You and I go knocking on doors,' she said to PLUS 1. 'Two teenagers with tatts and nose-rings, someone's gonna think we're scoping out the area to nick something. But Stan can flash his ID card.'

'He's not a detective anymore.'

'It's still a New Zealand Police ID. No one knows he sits at a computer.'

'What if he tells us to piss off?'

'What if he doesn't?' Addison said, texting Stan that they were coming to pick him up for driving practice.

When they arrived at the house Stan rents with his sister, he was finishing a training session. The place has a big backyard with an old chestnut tree, and he'd made a bunch of makeshift conversions to replicate the police PCT course.

'Watch,' he said, taking a starting position at the top of the rear deck. 'Time me.'

PLUS 1 opened the timer on their phone. 'Go.'

Stan took off down the steps, hurtling across the backyard to where he'd fixed a climbing rope to the side of the garden shed; he shimmied up the rope to touch the roof, then down again, sprinting back across the yard and crawling on hands and knees through a series of old car tyres he'd got from the recycling centre, before running back across the yard to the chestnut tree, where he'd hung a pull-up bar from the lower branches, measuring the chains to hang six feet from the ground – the same height as the window in the obstacle course.

'How long?' he grunted out, grabbing the pull-up bar and hauling himself up.

'One minute fifty.'

Stan slid over the bar and fell to the ground in a tumble drop, rolling straight up to his feet. He went all out for the final sprint, back up the steps three at a time.

PLUS 1 clicked stop on the timer. 'Two minutes, ten seconds.'

'Best I've done is two minutes four,' Stan gasped, chest heaving. 'I'm so close.'

As Stan jumped through the shower, Addison and PLUS 1 timed each other on the course. PLUS 1 took just over fifty seconds longer than Stan had; Addison needed a couple of attempts before she managed to haul herself over the pull-up bar and she ended up a full minute slower.

Stan's time was impressive. If anyone was going to come back from what he'd been through, Addison thought, it was him. But she still hadn't worked out how to tell him about illegally recording the Helpline call, or the slightly unhinged mission she needed his help with.

The young woman's voice is coming out of the loudspeaker on Addison's phone.

'*All the stuff you sing about. Brown people getting eaten up by the system. That's just talk. You believe their crap as much as anyone. You're on their side.*'

Stan listens until the recording finishes. Then PLUS 1 plays him the filtered sound of the railway crossing bells.

'We figure, wherever the house is, it's in hearing distance of crossing bells.'

Addison shows Stan the map they made; the three areas where trains would have been passing during the two minutes of the phone call.

His fingers drum on the cracked lining of the steering wheel. His shoulders are stiff, his face tense.

'You've broken so many laws. You've got no authority to do any of this stuff. Nor have I. This is like those half-arsed podcasters who try to solve true crimes and end up fucking everything up.'

'PLUS 1 said you'd tell me to piss off.' Addison sighs. 'Mum thinks the caller's just a troll, messing with my head.'

'She's probably right,' Stan says.

The rail crossing warning bells start clanging again.

'Okay. Message received. Sorry we wasted your time.' There's a defeated look on Addison's face, sure that Stan's not going to help. She's run out of options.

They sit without speaking as the train approaches. Stan watches it pass, deep in thought. Finally he turns towards them.

'You're not half-arsed podcasters,' he says. 'There's nothing half-arsed about you. Taking that recording, filtering out the bells, working out the train timetables. That's bloody impressive.' He looks at Addison. 'Impressive. Also fucked-up and wrong.'

From the back seat, PLUS 1 can see that Stan's hands are gripping the steering wheel so hard his knuckles are white. 'Are you okay, bro?'

It takes a moment for Stan to answer.

'No. Not really,' he says at last, his voice tight. 'What happened to Jaye. I'm stuck pushing keys on a computer. Filing reports. Not being able to do a thing that's useful, that might actually help.'

The last carriage of the train passes, the lights stop flashing, the barrier arms rise. Stan lets go his iron grip on the steering wheel. He flexes his fingers, getting the blood back into them.

'How do we do this?' he asks.

Addison beams, surprised and delighted.

'I dunno. I'm not the detective.'

'You remember that now?'

'All I know is, if we knock on the right door and I hear her voice, I'll know it's her.'

'This is such a long shot.' Stan starts the car. 'But what the hell. Let's do it.'

By trial and error, they work out that about two hundred yards away from a crossing the sound of the bells is just audible, but probably too faint to show up so clearly through a phone call. They figure out a routine quickly. Stan knocks at the door, his police ID lanyard around his neck.

'We're conducting an online survey on satisfaction with police services. Would you like to have your email added to the database?'

It was PLUS 1's idea, an approach which almost guarantees a response of some variation on *'Thanks but no thanks,'* and no need for further conversation. But in the meantime, they have a chance to see who opens the door. It's surprising how long it takes them to knock at all of the houses within hearing distance of the first crossing bells. A two-hundred-yard radius in a built-up suburb means a dozen or so streets and cul-de-sacs.

Which also means a lot of doors to knock on.

They finish the perimeter around the first level crossing by mid-afternoon, and as they start on the second of the three areas, Stan calls in to the office to say he's come down sick and won't be in to work the next day.

'If we don't have any luck today, we can do the last zone of interest first thing in the morning.'

'Wow, zone of interest. You're really getting into this,' Addison says, smiling.

'It's been a while.'

There were a handful of houses where a young woman answered the door – someone who looked about the right age to be the person who'd called Addison – and at those houses, Stan ad-libbed a couple of follow-up questions, to get the person to talk a bit more. Each time Addison was certain it wasn't the caller. The woman had that distinctive way of speaking: a hesitancy at the start of each sentence, like she was working out what she wanted to say, then fast and certain once she'd begun. None of the young women who answered the door had that particular tic, and they didn't seem fearful and under stress, as the woman who'd called certainly was.

They finish the area around the second of the rail crossings as the streetlights are flickering to life.

'Takeaways? Then we'll drop you home,' Addison says.

At the kebab place, PLUS 1 goes in to make the order. Alone in the car with Stan, Addison glances his way. 'How are you doing?'

'Starving. Looking forward to demolishing a kebab.'

'I mean, is everything all right?' Addison chooses her words carefully. 'Are you sleeping okay?'

'Yeah. I'm fine.' He turns to her, a little surprised by the question. 'Why?'

'This morning. I saw your bathroom cupboard, Stan.'

Earlier that day, just before they were about to set off, Addison had to use the bathroom. Stan told her to use his ensuite. There was no soap, and when she opened his cupboard to find a new bar, it took her a moment to realize what she was looking at. It was like a dispensary. Sleep medications, a lot of them, and Addison could see they were maximum strength.

And something else.

Unlabelled bottles of a clear fluid. Hypodermic needles. Addison had tried to dismiss what Dax had said. But if Stan really was looking for black market steroids, it sure looked like he'd found them.

'You spied on me?' There's a dark look on Stan's face.

'You'd run out of soap. You know how I am with hygiene. I'm sorry. But I can't un-see it.'

Through the window, Addison can see PLUS 1 is still waiting for the order. They're free to talk uninterrupted for a minute or two.

'What's going on?'

Stan stares straight ahead out the window.

'If anyone finds out about this. Anyone in the police. I'm fucked.'

'I'm not the cops.'

'I can't believe you looked in my fucking cupboard.'

Addison puts a hand on Stan's. He flinches, shifts his hand away.

'Stan,' she says quietly. 'I'm your friend.'

He blinks a few times. When he speaks again, his voice is very quiet.

'It's been almost eighteen months. Since what happened.' He looks down at the titanium shank. 'After the operation. After they took me off the painkillers and the sedatives. That's when it started.'

'What?'

'Every time I'd start to fall asleep. I was back there. Back in the industrial yard.'

The explosion that cost Stan his leg had happened in a sprawling, high-fenced yard that stored empty shipping containers.

'I'd start to drop off, then the same thing. Playing it all back, moment by moment. That huge flash . . . It's hard to describe. It's not like looking at the sun. It's a hundred times brighter. The rush of hot air hitting me. Like when you've forgotten a roast chicken in the oven and you open the door and *whoosh*. This super-hot, dry blast of heat hitting me, but no noise from the gelignite, like the explosion moved so much faster than the sound. They said later that both my eardrums were ruptured, so maybe that was it . . .'

Stan pauses. Addison reaches out again.

This time, Stan doesn't move his hand away.

'Then I'm just lying on the concrete, looking up at the shipping containers stacked three containers high. Counting them. One, two, three. And the feeling in my leg. Actually, the lack of feeling. I knew straight away; it was gone. I just kept counting the containers. So I didn't have to think about anything else.'

There's a tremor in his voice that Addison's never heard

before. She glances back through the window of the takeaway shop; PLUS 1 is selecting sauces for the kebabs.

'After six months, I just had to accept that the flashbacks weren't going away. I got sleeping pills from the doctor. Then I asked for stronger ones. Finally, she let me have the heaviest safe dose.'

'The steroids, though . . . I mean, I know *why*. You want to pass the physical so bad. But what that shit does to you, bro.'

'It's okay. Really, it's okay. With the sleeping pills, I get a couple of hours sleep, on a good night. The fitness, the obstacle course, the boxing. It's all self-medication. The 'roids mean I can keep pushing myself. That's what I need to do, Addison.'

'I googled it – steroids interfere with sleep as well. You're making everything worse.'

'I'm giving myself a fighting chance of getting my badge back.'

'I don't know what to do with all this, Stan.'

'Nothing.'

He turns to meet her eyes.

'You don't do anything,' he says. 'Once I'm back in the CIB, I'm gonna be fine. I just have to do what I'm doing. Get through the other side. Get my life back.'

'Does your sister know?'

He shakes his head, *hell no*.

'I'm driving Melody nuts already. The obstacle course. Trying so hard to get back to a job she hated me doing anyway, even before the accident.'

'You need to talk to someone. A counsellor.'

'How's that gonna look? When I go for my badge? I'm climbing Mount Everest already. If I'm on record as being lala, needing a psychiatrist, there's no way they're going to let me back in.'

'This is your health.'

'It's not forever. It's just for now.'

The door of the kebab shop opens. PLUS 1 heads for the car, laden down with food and energy drinks. Stan lowers his voice.

'Please. This is between us. Promise me.'

Addison can feel the trembling of his hand in hers.

'I promise.'

She squeezes Stan's hand as PLUS 1 gets back into the car.

13

POWER PYLONS

'You got children?'

The translate app is on loudspeaker, the Korean translation from the Mandarin question read aloud by an electronic voice. It's painstaking, and the translations aren't always exact, but it means the conversation can happen while Sebastian drives.

'None yet.'

'That's unusual for you people, Mr Samsung.'

A half-hour earlier, Sebastian picked up the manager of Moon Lake Bistro and Lounge, Hàoyǔ, and one of his men. He's taking them to the container of Red Lucky Star cigarettes, to confirm the quantity and quality of the product. Sebastian gave Gold Brother and Hàoyǔ the assumed name he'd decided on: a very ordinary Korean family name, a little less common than the equivalent of Smith, maybe more like Johnston or Reilly. But Hàoyŭ decided on a more easily remembered nickname, informed by Sebastian's story of being an importer of household electronics.

'You Koreans, you like your two point five kids. No kids is surprising, Mr Samsung.'

'I haven't got around to having any. Yet.'

'Two point five children, and a pretty wife with round eyes. What is it with Koreans and plastic surgery?'

'I haven't had any of that either.'

'Bet your wife's had surgery.'

'No wife.'

'That's too bad.'

Sebastian's jaw tightens. He knows this guy's reputation. Hàoyŭ is thought to have ordered the killing of at least one of the victims found in shallow graves on the Desert Road, and he could well have been hands-on in the murder. It's kind of surreal, sitting next to this ruthless enforcer of a serious organized crime syndicate, having a conversation about families and plastic surgery through a translation app.

'You don't want kids? Me, I've got three.'

As Sebastian drives through an industrial area in the south of Auckland city, several suburbs away from Moon Lake Bistro and Lounge, Hàoyŭ flicks to his phone's gallery. He pulls up a photo of three smiling, good-looking young people, early twenties, their arms around their mother and father, and holds the phone out for Sebastian to see.

'They're grown now. All studying arts and literature. *Arts and literature.* Too many New Zealand friends with their free-thinking ideas. How will they ever make money? So, I have to keep working. No one's going to be looking after my wife and me if I retire.'

'They look like good people,' Sebastian says.

He looks up from the photo to the rear-view mirror. In the back seat, Hàoyǔ's guy has been texting ever since they left the restaurant. Through the rear window, the plainclothes car is nowhere to be seen, but that doesn't worry Sebastian. Hana and the young detective constable know where he's headed; there's no need to risk tailing too closely behind.

'You don't want kids?'

'It just hasn't worked out yet,' Sebastian says. Partly this explanation is to stay true to the character he's playing, given that clearly Hàoyǔ's expectation is that all Korean men want a family. But also, it's just true.

Sebastian *would* like kids. It just hasn't worked out yet.

'Might have left your run a bit late.'

'I'm only thirty-six.'

'You don't wanna be an old guy with wrinkles changing diapers, Mr Samsung.'

The guy in the back seat laughs with Hàoyǔ. Sebastian waits for the translation app to process the words he already understands. Then he laughs too.

Leaving the main road, Sebastian turns his car down a long concrete driveway, past a series of factories. The last factory is empty and available for lease. At the rear of the building is a deserted parking area where the shipping container holding the seized consignment of illegal cigarettes was moved by the customs police earlier that morning. As Sebastian pulls up, Hàoyǔ turns to the guy in the back seat.

'Anyone heard anything about the little prick?' he asks in Mandarin.

Sebastian glances in the mirror. The guy in the back seat shakes his head.

'Nothing.'

Sebastian wishes he could look at the guy's messages. He's sure they're talking about Toa Davis, and that Toa is the reason for the incessant texting. Maybe there are communications on the phone from the gunman himself.

Hàoyǔ snorts in irritation, turning back to Sebastian abruptly. 'Come on, show us what you've got,' he says. Sebastian knows exactly what he has asked, but Hàoyǔ hasn't used the translator app this time. He replies in halting English.

'Don't understand.'

Tiring of the app conversation, Hàoyǔ nods towards the shipping container.

Getting out of the car, Sebastian reaches for the keys in his pocket, provided by the customs police. There are three heavy-duty padlocks on the door of the container. As he unlocks them, he hears Hàoyǔ speaking to the young guy behind him.

'Anyone sees three padlocks, they're gonna know there's something inside worth stealing. Fucking amateur.'

Sebastian opens the door, still as if he hasn't understood a word. Inside the container, he moves aside several big boxes holding giant flat-screen televisions. Behind them, there's a mountain of cigarette cartons. Red Lucky Star. Hàoyǔ nods at the young guy, who steps forward and digs through the cartons, selecting a few at random and opening them to make sure they're not empty boxes stuffed with newspaper or polystyrene chips. He nods confirmation to Hàoyǔ. Everything is as promised.

'We're in business, Mr Samsung.'

Sebastian relocks the container. As he gets back in the car, to his surprise, Hàoyǔ has opened his glove box. That morning, before he went to Moon Lake Bistro and Lounge, Sebastian had carefully removed anything from the car that related to his true identity, like the flyer he had for his parents' church bingo night, or the repair slip for recent work on the vehicle that had his name on it. Now he's glad he was thorough. He speaks into the translator app.

'Something you're looking for?'

'I'm a naturally curious individual.'

Hàoyǔ closes the glove box. His eyes rise to the stickers on the bottom corner of the windscreen. The Warrant of Fitness certificate; the vehicle license label.

Sebastian suddenly wants to groan.

Hàoyǔ is staring at the local resident on-street parking permit. Karangahape Road.

'You live on K Road? Not ideal for a family. But I imagine for a young, good-looking bachelor like yourself, must be quite the place.'

'I guess so.'

Sebastian starts the engine, pulls away, hoping that's the end of the conversation.

It isn't.

'Tell you what. Let's make a stop at your apartment.'

'What for?'

'We can iron out the details. Shake hands on the deal, the civilized way. I like to get to know who I'm doing business with.'

As he waits for the translation app to interpret, Sebastian's heart is racing. The words are cheerful enough, but it's clear this isn't a polite suggestion. Hàoyǔ's not about to take no for an answer.

Sebastian turns out from the driveway, heading back through the industrial area, passing a car parked a hundred metres down the road, facing the opposite way. The two women in the front seats are having an animated conversation, taking no notice of the passing car, but for the briefest moment, in the passenger seat, Hana's gaze flicks towards Sebastian's.

Their eyes meet. She sees the worried look on his face.

But there's no way for Sebastian to tell her how things have suddenly gone so badly wrong.

'I don't get it.' Addison frowns. 'Mum and Dad and you. You're all so smart. You could all do anything you wanted. You could be doctors or lawyers or anything.'

'You could be an accountant, Stan,' PLUS 1 says. 'You've got the wardrobe for it.'

As they walk towards the next house, Stan gives PLUS 1 the middle finger. PLUS 1 cheerily returns it, both hands. They're in the third and final zone of interest, in Stan's cop-speak, and they've covered about half the streets they mapped out. Still no luck. Before they came out this morning, Addison and PLUS 1 visited the hospital. They sat with Jaye for an hour, while Marissa dropped the girls at school. Addison held her dad's hand the whole time.

'Isn't there something easier?' Addison continues. 'Something where you don't end up in a hospital bed? Or losing part of your body?'

Stan pauses beside the letterbox of the next house.

'I know why you're asking this stuff. Your dad getting shot. I mean, it's shit. Of course it's shit. For you more than anyone. And my accident wasn't the best day of my life. But if you're saying that should put me off doing the job . . . ?'

Stan looks for the right words to explain.

'It's the opposite. It makes me know that being a cop is – I don't know – it's a job that needs doing. And it needs doing by the right people. If we get to where the only ones lining up to put on a uniform are overgrown boys who like driving cars really fast and zapping people with tasers, we're fucked.'

'You're an overgrown boy who likes driving cars really fast,' Addison says. Stan had told her about the zero to one hundred thing on the motorway late at night.

Stan ignores the joke. 'You're missing my point. If it's inside you, if you're born for this job, you don't have a choice.'

He raises his hands, palms upwards, fingers extended. As in, empty hands. 'It's maybe not the explanation you're looking for,' he says. 'But it's all I've got.'

Stan heads up the concrete path towards the next house.

Sebastian takes the off-ramp from the motorway, the exit that heads into the city centre and then on to K Road. He keeps driving. He has no choice. Hàoyŭ now knows the part of town he lives in, down to the exact zone of resident parking he's got a permit for. Telling these guys he can't take them to his apartment will set alarm bells ringing. Hàoyŭ will know something's very wrong.

But Sebastian *can't* take them to his apartment.

His flat is also his office. He can't remember if there's a power bill sitting on his table or if his gym membership card is lying by his bed. All it would take would be Hàoyǔ opening a drawer of his filing cabinet, the way he happily dug through Sebastian's glove compartment, looking inside at one of his client's files, and Sebastian would be fucked. He'll have pissed this guy off, seriously.

Hàoyǔ isn't a guy you want to piss off.

He looks up to the rear-view mirror. After he drove away from the container earlier, he saw the unmarked car following him onto the motorway. But Hana and the young detective Ruby would have been expecting him to head back towards Moon Lake. The last place they'd think he'd be going is his apartment. And now, he can't see any sign of them.

Did they miss his car as he took the exit?

'I tell my children. Don't end up on K Road. It's full of drug addicts and perverts. No offence,' Hàoyǔ says.

Sebastian waits for the translation. 'No offence taken,' he replies in Korean.

Even as he's trying to work out what the hell to do next, he's also listening hard to the conversations in the back seat. The young guy has been texting non-stop throughout the trip and, on the return leg, he's started to make some increasingly terse calls. Sebastian has heard only one half of each of them, of course, so they don't make complete sense. But it's intriguing, and he's certain now, the conversations are about Toa Davis. What he's heard – he's sure – will be useful to Hana and DI Williams.

Ahead, on the right-hand side of K Road, is the taco place where Hana and Sebastian eat. His apartment is a couple of hundred yards beyond, as is the side street for the resident's parking zone he has a permit for. He slows, indicating to turn into the side street. Waiting for oncoming traffic to pass, he frowns. It all happened so fast. He thought he'd be able to figure out a plan between the industrial area and K Road.

But he doesn't have a plan.

The cars pass. Sebastian starts to turn, with no idea what he's going to do after he parks.

Then, *whomp*.

The car behind rear-ends him, hard, with enough force that all the airbags in the car explode at once. The phone conversation in the backseat abruptly ends; the car is shunted sideways.

'What the fuck?' Hàoyŭ says in furious Mandarin.

Ears ringing from the explosive charges of the airbags, Sebastian manages to pull himself out of the car. Behind it, the driver of the car that rear-ended his is stalking towards him.

It's Ruby. The junior detective.

'Are you a fucking idiot?' she barks at Sebastian. 'You didn't indicate or anything.'

Sebastian's never been happier to be involved in a car crash, or to have a young wild-eyed woman furiously screaming at him in the middle of K Road.

'Look at my car. Who's gonna pay for this?' Ruby yells, her voice and anger escalating. 'I think my mum's got whiplash.'

In the front seat of the unmarked police car, Hana

has her head down, rubbing her neck, glad to let the young detective carry on with the quite exceptional job she's doing.

A few minutes earlier, after they'd followed Sebastian's car off the exit, Hana began to get worried. As they tailed him along K Road, getting ever closer to his apartment, she started to figure out what was happening.

'Shit. They're making him take them to his place.'

Behind the steering wheel, Ruby thought this through. Ahead of her, Sebastian indicated to turn. Ruby gripped the wheel, aimed square at his bumper bar and hit the accelerator hard.

There's quite a crowd gathering, enjoying the spectacle of the enraged young woman yelling at the poor guy whose car she just ran into. 'I'm calling the fucking cops,' Ruby screams, as Hàoyǔ and the young guy drag themselves out from behind the airbags. She waves her cell phone at them.

'You fuckwits aren't going anywhere. The cops are coming, and you're involved.'

From the plainclothes car, Hana watches as Hàoyǔ and the young guy realize this is one hundred per cent the wrong place to be. They drift off in the opposite direction down K Road, any plan to visit Sebastian's apartment forgotten.

The young detective keeps screaming at Sebastian until, out of the corner of her eye, she sees the pair get into a nearby taxi. As the car pulls away, Ruby finally stops shouting.

'Shit, you're good,' Sebastian says quietly.
'Uh-huh,' the young detective agrees, smiling.

In the distance, the sound of bells clanging.

The railway crossing is about a hundred and fifty yards from the long, winding cul-de-sac that Addison, PLUS 1 and Stan are working their way down. Towering metal pylons stand at either end of the street, part of a long pathway of high-capacity power cables carrying millions of volts into energy-thirsty Auckland from the many hydroelectric dams scattered across the country. To keep the heavy-duty cables on as straight a line as possible, the huge pylons, up to fifty metres high, march straight through the outlying suburbs. The structures were inevitably located in the lower socio-economic areas, where homeowners were less likely to be able to afford lawyers to challenge the arrival of the metal monstrosities. With the constant static electricity in the air, and a skyline now dominated by steel towers and high-voltage wires, the values of properties along the pathway plummeted. You only live beneath a million volts of electricity passing overhead night and day if you can't afford anywhere else.

As they walk up the driveway towards the door of the next house, Stan makes sure his police ID is sitting right, so it's immediately seen by whoever opens the door. This house is one of the unlucky ones. Four massive metal pylon legs occupy the whole of the back yard, overshadowing the building like a rusty Mount Etna.

Stan knocks at the door. Addison's eyes rise to the huge cables hanging over the house. Something sounds familiar . . .

Stan knocks again. With a jolt, Addison realizes what she's hearing.

'Listen,' she says to PLUS 1.

In the air, the buzzing of enough electricity to power a city, passing directly overhead.

'On the phone call,' Addison says. 'The buzzing sound.'

PLUS 1 blinks.

It's the same sound.

The door opens.

Standing in front of them is a woman. Late teens, Māori. She looks at the ID around Stan's neck. Her eyes turn to the other two on the pathway behind him. She instantly recognizes Addison.

'Oh, fuck.'

The door slams in Stan's face.

'Hey!' he yells, knocking again, harder now. 'Open the door!' But even as he's hammering on the door, PLUS 1 hears movement at the back of the house. They hurry to where a guy can be seen frantically scaling one of the giant metal legs of the pylon. As he pulls himself up onto the top of the back fence, the young man looks back for a moment.

It's Toa Davis.

'It's him!' PLUS 1 shouts, as Toa leaps over the top of the fence and disappears from sight. 'He went over the fence!'

Instantly, Stan is sprinting down the side of the house, PLUS 1 and Addison on his heels. Stan leaps at the fence, grabbing the top railing: with the same upper-body strength that he's been obsessively building on the backyard obstacle course, he hauls himself up and over, tumbling down the other side and landing in a narrow pedestrian alley, losing his footing for a moment and going sprawling.

He looks up to see Davis sprinting away down the alley.

'Wait! Police!'

Stan knows even as he's saying it that if he hadn't crossed a line before, knocking on hundreds of doors with his police ID, now he's for sure breaking all kinds of regulations against imitating a police officer.

But fuck it.

This is the guy who shot Jaye.

'STOP! POLICE!'

Davis doesn't even pause; he sprints harder, disappearing around a bend. As Addison and PLUS 1 help each other over the fence, Stan takes off after the guy, emerging from the end of the alley onto a narrow road, the footpath starting again on the opposite side.

Stan's eyes hunt the length of the road. Both directions. No sign of movement.

Nothing.

Then, coming from the next section of alleyway, the sound of a dog barking, disturbed by something, or someone. Stan takes off across the road, sprinting past where the dog is going crazy behind a high wooden fence towards a hard right-hand turn ahead. He races around it to see, not fifty yards away, where the walkway hits a dead end, Toa Davis clambering up a pile of discarded planks of wood from where a gate has recently been repaired, scaling the fence that cuts off the path.

'Stop!' Stan screams, still running, adrenaline racing. He throws himself at Davis, just managing to grab one of his legs, hauling him back down. Davis lands heavily, the wind knocked out of him, but he's instantly on his feet, all wild eyes and swinging fists. He punches Stan hard, square in the face. Stan stumbles backwards. Seeing stars. But as Davis lunges for the fence again, he regathers himself.

'You piece of shit!' Stan screams, pulling the other guy back down again, standing over him where he's sprawled on the ground. Furious, relentless, he starts pounding Davis in the face, the abdomen.

'I know what you did!'

Stan has at least three inches of height on his opponent, and a lot more body weight, and now he's face to face with the guy who shot Jaye, the red mist has descended. He hauls Davis to his feet and lets loose with a hard, straight punch, sending him tumbling onto the pile of discarded building materials. Sprawled among the debris, Davis gasps for air as Stan towers over him.

'Jaye Hamilton is my friend,' Stan spits out.

On the pile of wood, the guy is bleeding, winded, done. Stan sucks air into his lungs. From back down the alleyway, he hears the sound of Addison and PLUS 1.

'Stan! Where are you?'

He turns, just long enough to call out in their direction. 'The end of the walkway.'

It's a split second. But that's all the desperate young man needs. Toa Davis grabs a heavy length of 4 x 2 wood from the pile of building debris and, even as Stan is turning back from yelling out to the others, he swings it with everything he has. It hits Stan full force in his solar plexus, knocking the wind from him; his legs give way and he falls into a hunched heap on the walkway.

Stan doesn't know what's hit him, groaning and puking and trying to gasp air all at the same time.

'Stan!'

Addison and PLUS 1 rush round the corner to see him on his knees on the concrete footpath, clasping his gut. Unable to speak. Unable to think from the sheer pain.

There's no one else there.

As Addison hurries to Stan's side, PLUS 1 scales the pile of building materials, looks over the fence. Toa Davis is already racing past a rusted-out vehicle in the next property's yard, slamming through the wooden gate and knocking it off its hinges, then out onto the street and away.

As PLUS 1 watches, Davis sprints to the end of the road, turns the corner and disappears into the distance.

14

IF ANYONE SHOULD KNOW

A heavy winter rain shower drums a rhythm on the iron roof as Hana looks around the kitchen. There's a frying pan on the stove, scrambled eggs in the pan – a meal for two. The food is blackened around the edges, Hana notices; Toa and the young woman must have been cooking when they were interrupted by the arrival of Addison, PLUS 1 and Stan, the scrambled eggs burning in the chaos that followed.

DI Williams is talking with the crime-scene team, who are working their way methodically through the house, looking for the weapon Toa Davis used in the hold-up, or any other evidence linking him to the shooting. The young Māori woman who answered the door to Stan has been taken to Central Police Station. Her name is Gracie Huia. No prior criminal record, nothing known about her that could have linked her to Toa. Hana and Williams assume she's a girlfriend who has never previously been on anyone's radar. What neither cop knows yet is whether or not Gracie is enmeshed in Toa's criminal activities.

Specifically, if the young woman was involved in the hold-up and shooting.

As the house is worked over, Hana takes the opportunity to look around, building a picture for herself of the life these two were living. The house isn't anything fancy, and that's an understatement. But it's clean, tidy. Hana notes the food in the kitchen. The scrambled eggs, the vegetables in the fridge. Healthy. A few beers, sure, but only a couple, and none of the fried chicken takeaway containers she'd expect from two teenage kids playing house.

She looks up as Williams comes into the kitchen. 'No sign of the weapon.'

'He's had lots of time to dump it,' Hana points out.

'But he could still have it. We should assume the worst.'

The forensics team have finished in the bedroom. Hana goes in. It's as cramped as the rest of the house. One window has been flung open where Toa jumped out and ran. There's a cheap three-bar heater. A duvet, new, but an inexpensive brand from a discount warehouse store. The house has the feel of two young people on their own without a lot of spare cash, struggling to get through a cold Auckland winter.

The mattress sits on the bare floor, and something above it catches Hana's eye. There's a sheet of paper pinned to the wall. On the paper are two drawings, made in pencil, that look like two different depictions of a little girl.

Hana moves closer to get a better look.

One of the drawings is a stick figure, arms and legs described with single pencil lines. A round face with a big smile. A few pencil strokes for a tuft of hair on top of the head. It's the kind of sketch you'd expect from someone who says, 'I can't really draw.'

Next to the stick figure, the other drawing is clearly the work of a much more confident artist. This little girl wears a dress patterned with flowers; her hair is in pigtails. Her eyes are carefully shaded, the dark pupils staring out from the page with a serious look.

Written underneath the two drawings, a name.

Arihia.

Outside, the rain is falling more heavily.

'We should get back to the station,' Williams says from the doorway, above the sound of heavy raindrops hitting the metal roof.

Hana takes another look at the pencil drawings pinned to the wall.

Then she follows Williams out through the rain to the car.

'We know what Toa does. We know exactly how he makes a living. He works for Moon Lake, couriering narcotics for the syndicate. We have his criminal record.

But I'm not going to waste your time with any of that. That's not why you're here, Gracie.'

In the interview room in Central Police Station, DI Williams sits on one side of the small table, Gracie Huia on the other. Hana watches from a nearby room, through a feed from the video camera recording the interview. The young Māori woman sits with her hands on the table, one on top of the other, with a look on her face like she's not listening, or, if she is, like whatever's being said by the cop on the other side of the table is the least interesting thing she's ever heard. But Hana knows the reality is very probably the exact opposite. Hana is willing to bet that the young woman's stomach is churning. She probably wants to go to the bathroom, kneel on the floor and throw up.

'The drugs, the stolen cars. I don't care about any of that. I want the same thing you do. I want Toa to be safe.'

Williams' voice is soft. She lets what she's said hang there for a moment. Through the video feed, Hana sees a little telltale movement of Gracie's head. Waiting for what's coming next.

'I'm worried this is going to end very badly for Toa,' Williams continues slowly, letting every word sink in. 'He's out on the streets, on the run. With a gun. When we find him – and we're going to find him – it could all go very wrong.'

She reaches across the table. Gently touches the young woman's carefully crossed hands.

'I don't want that to happen, Gracie. And I know you don't either.'

Hana watches as Gracie looks at Williams' hand on hers.

'Please don't touch me.'

Williams nods, *okay then*, and withdraws her hand.

Hana knows why Williams broke the unspoken rule about contact between an interviewing officer and someone detained for questioning. Williams is a brown woman, probably the age of some of the older women in Gracie Huia's whānau. Human contact, the touch of a hand – it might just be a way of breaking through the staunch *go-fuck-yourself* silence. It seems to have worked.

'You don't know anything about Toa. You've made up your mind about him. But you've got it all wrong.'

'Okay. Tell me what we've got wrong,' Williams says.

Gracie's head rises, the first time she has met Williams' eyes since the interview began. Through the camera feed, Hana can see the young woman's jaw is set. She's come to a decision. She knows her boyfriend is in a lot of trouble. Staying silent now isn't going to help him.

'He does jobs, yeah. I'm not gonna bullshit about that. He delivers packages for the Asian guys. Picks up stuff from fishing boats, drops them off where he's told. But fuck, what else is he meant to do? He got busted for nicking a car when he was fifteen. Just a dumb kid caught up in dumb kid shit. But because the others walked away and Toa got the blame, now he's screwed. Try turning up to a job interview when you're brown and young and you've got a record. He does what he has to.'

Gracie's hands unfold, then start to unconsciously ball into fists.

'What you said on TV. About the car and the gun. You got all that completely wrong.'

'His fingerprints were in the car. We found his phone, dumped nearby,' Williams says, her voice measured.

'The car was his. I mean, it was a car he stole. He was using it for his work. To do deliveries. But a few days after Toa took the car, someone nicked it off of *him*.'

'Who stole the car from Toa?'

'How the fuck would I know?' Gracie says, her voice rising. 'He came home, middle of the day, maybe a week ago. He'd just picked up a delivery, he had to go drop it off at the restaurant. But he was worried I was hungry. He got me some food, we ate together. Toa wasn't inside the house more than fifteen minutes. When he went out again, the car was gone. The car. His phone. The package he'd just picked up.'

Gracie consciously straightens her fingers, laying her palms down flat on the surface of the table.

'He knew he was screwed. The stuff he was meant to deliver was gone. How the hell was he gonna pay those Moon Lake fellas back? They're scary, man. Then it gets worse. He sees the car on TV. And you, saying the guy whose car it was shot a cop.'

The young woman considers her next words. When she speaks again, her voice is flat.

'That's why I called the girl, Addison, at the Helpline. I didn't know what else to do. I didn't think she'd fucking turn up at our door . . .'

Gracie trails away. In the silence, the door opens. Hana comes in. She looks at DI Williams.

'Is it okay if I ask a couple of questions?'

Williams nods. Hana sits down opposite Gracie.

'How far along are you?'

Gracie looks up with a jolt.

'Sorry?'

'I saw the drawings above your bed. The little girl. Was it you and Toa, taking turns, trying to imagine what she might look like when she arrives?'

Hana can see the rush of emotion in Gracie's face. Her hand goes to her abdomen, the slight beginnings of a curve there. Hana has guessed right.

'You can really draw,' Hana says. 'I loved the flowers you did on the little girl's dress.'

Despite everything, there's a hint of smile at the corners of Gracie's mouth.

'The stick figure is mine. Can't draw to save myself. But Toa, he's amazing. Put anything in his hand – a pencil, a crayon, a burned piece of wood – he'll make something beautiful.'

Williams watches, impressed, and happy to let Hana keep going.

'You two, you're looking after each other,' Hana

continues. 'Good food, keeping the place warm. Getting ready for the baby. You're taking this seriously.'

'Of course we are,' Gracie says, her hand still on her abdomen. 'It's a kid. She's coming. She can't look after herself.'

'You'll be a good mum.'

'Toa's gonna be a good dad,' Gracie says without hesitation.

'I'm sure you're right.'

When Hana speaks again, the trajectory shifts a little, but she keeps the same gentle, reassuring tone. 'Your instinct is to protect Toa. But you're not protecting him if you don't tell us the truth.'

'I have told you the truth.'

'Have you, Gracie? Here's what we think. Toa wants to be a good dad, maybe more than anything in the world. Maybe he was scared he wouldn't have enough money to look after you and your baby. So he went and found a gun. Went to that liquor store. Things got out of control.'

On the other side of the table, Gracie's hands are forming fists again.

'We want the same thing you want, Gracie. We want Toa to be safe. Most of all, we don't want him using the gun again.'

For a moment, there's only the slight electronic sound of the video recording device. Finally, Gracie speaks, her eyes still on the table.

'Toa sleeps every night with his head against our baby in my tummy. He wants this kid more than anything on earth. He wouldn't risk everything – me – our baby – for a couple of hundred bucks from a booze store. Toa does what he has to do to get money for rent and food. He's never hurt anyone. Never.'

Gracie lifts her gaze. She looks from Hana to Williams. If she'd been scared earlier in this conversation, and she had been, that fear is gone now. Replaced by something else.

Anger.

'You two. You make me sick.'

Gracie's eyes well. It's involuntary; she absolutely doesn't want to show Williams and Hana what she's feeling. Still, an angry tear falls on the table.

'If anyone should know how hard it is for brown people at the bottom of the pile, it's two fucking brown women. You should be ashamed.'

The young Māori woman uses her cuff to wipe her eyes. She regathers herself.

'He doesn't have a gun,' Gracie says finally. 'He's never had a gun. Toa didn't shoot that guy.'

In the police car park, two uniformed cops put Gracie into a police vehicle.

Hana waits with DI Williams as the car heads away,

taking Gracie back to the house with the drawings of her unborn baby on the wall. As she passes, Gracie stares straight ahead. Not even glancing towards them.

'What do you think?' Williams asks quietly.

'I think she's scared. Scared enough to lie.'

Williams and Hana watch as the police car heads down the ramp towards the road.

'But maybe she's scared enough to be telling the truth,' Hana continues, as the car turns into the street and drives away.

Later that night, back in her house, Gracie is making food. She's thrown away the burned scrambled eggs that have been sitting for the last few hours in the frying pan. There were a couple of eggs left in the tray – enough for a semi-decent meal. She's got zero appetite. But she has to eat. For their baby.

As she cooks the eggs, Gracie looks out of the window.

There are two unfamiliar cars parked on the street. Two people in each of them; she can see their shapes under the street lights. Gracie knows they're cops, and they'll be there 24/7.

If Toa tries to come back, he's going to be arrested.

She looks out into the night, past the police cars. It's going to be a cold one. They struggle to pay for the electricity at the best of times, and now, with no money coming in at all, it's going to be impossible. But she'll cross that bridge when she has to. She can't afford the electricity, but she can't afford to get sick. She's going to have the heater on tonight. Two bars, maybe even three.

As she eats, Gracie looks out into the darkness.

Wherever he is right now, she hopes Toa is keeping warm.

15

TEXTBOOK

After the girl with the wavy hair and the braces on her teeth.

After the magpie he healed, which came to love him.

After stepping over the old woman's body where it lay fallen on the floor, so that he could make a sandwich with luncheon sausage and the new mustard.

After he knew for so long he was different.

After he tried so hard to be the same.

There came a point when he understood that he didn't need to try to be like everyone else. Every snowflake that falls from the heavens is different, he'd read when he was younger. It had seemed unlikely to him, at the time. What are the odds that no two snowflakes had ever been exactly identical in the entire history of the world? But the further he moved down the specific and curious path that was his life, the more he knew that he wasn't like everyone else.

That he wasn't like *anyone* else.

Whatever the genesis of his identity; whatever the intersections between the double-helix configuration of his DNA at the moment of his conception, his isolated childhood and the things he experienced in the garden shed; however those forces had collided and come to form him, he was who he was.

He couldn't fight it.

But he could try to understand.

Finding the book in the library was the thing that finally made everything clear.

It was the *Textbook of Abnormal Psychology*. When he found it on the shelves, he was immediately drawn to it. In its pages he found descriptions of all the ways that miswiring can happen. The divergences, the aberrations, the varied misdirections of human psychology and behaviour. He read and he read and he read, and when he finally paused and glanced at his watch, he realized that several hours had passed. He hadn't moved a step. He hadn't looked up from the pages once.

He put the textbook in his bag, walked out the front door and took it home, stealing it so that he would never have to return it. He knew he would read this book from cover to cover, and that he would return to it again and again. Its pages gave him a context he had never had before. Ways for him to define himself. To understand why he'd had more feeling for the sandwich made of luncheon sausage and mustard than for the old woman lying dead on the floor. Why he'd felt nothing inside, nor in his pants, when the girl with the wavy hair and braces had squeezed him and pressed her mouth against his. But why he'd felt such a stirring, such a giddying wave of hormones and adrenaline, such a rush of blood to his loins, when he'd snapped the magpie's neck.

With the textbook, at last, he understood himself.

He understood his needs.

And he understood, now that he had context and insight, that he wouldn't seek a cure. There was nothing in the pages of the textbook that was even remotely 'abnormal' to him.

It was just who he was.

And henceforth, he would be true to himself.

Weird shit happens in Australia.

It felt like the right place for the first one.

It was a year after he'd stolen the textbook from the library. He'd begun to teach himself the art and craft of breaking and entering, and, as with all things he turned his hand to, he was a fast learner. With the earnings from a few well-executed burglaries, he bought a passport and a return ticket to Sydney.

He wasn't there long. He knew exactly what he wanted to achieve. It wasn't sightseeing.

He had heard about South Head. The beachside suburb

with the sheer cliffs where the depressed and the unstable went to step into thin air. It was a good place for a life to end, apparently. Few people survived the fall, and, if they did, they would almost certainly be knocked senseless and drown.

He took a bus from the airport to the beach. This was deliberate and canny; he was already working out the angles, honing a capacity for careful forward-planning that would come to serve him well. A taxi driver might remember the face of a passenger he dropped off. A bus driver with thirty other customers on board, not so likely.

He found a bench at the top of the cliffs and sat watching the spectacular sunset, waiting for darkness. After night fell, he scouted a place along the clifftop where the street lights were spaced sufficiently far apart that there was a decent stretch of shadow to move in. In no hurry, he scanned the faces of passersby, wanting to make the right choice. Savouring the possibilities.

As it got later, there were fewer and fewer people.

That was going to be a good thing.

Towards midnight, he saw the guy running up the hill.

He was brown, Fijian perhaps, with a burly rugby league player's frame and wearing a South Sydney Rabbitohs jersey. He watched the guy as he passed under a street light. He was a few years older than him. Definitely Fijian, he decided as the man drew closer and he could see the tightly curled frizz of his hair. Watching the runner's laboured gait, he decided that if the guy was still playing footie, he was probably near the end of his career. Rugby league really screws with your joints. Somehow that made everything just that much more right. Like the stars were aligning.

Excuse me. Got a ciggie? he said.

The league player pulled up, puffing, a bemused look on his face.

Bro. I'm running. Why the fuck would I have a ciggie?

My bad.

The league player shook his head, started running again. As soon as the other man's back was turned, he took the large rock he had found earlier at the edge of the cliff, he ran the few steps it took to catch up, he brought the rock down hard on the back of the guy's head. He hit the sweet spot. The Fijian fell, and didn't so much as stir as he dragged him the twenty yards from the pathway to the edge of the cliff. He rolled the unresisting body off the rocky outcrop and watched, counting under his breath, as the heavy shape tumbled silently downwards through the darkness: *one apricot, two apricot.*

Just after *four apricot*, the man hit the rocks far below, the body bouncing into the incoming waves, the Rabbitohs jersey disappearing in moments into the dark waters.

And that was that.

In the morning he took the first bus to the airport for the three-hour flight back to Auckland.

He'd been in Sydney less than twenty-four hours.

He was home in time to make his evening meal.

16

THE CHOICE

'What if he'd pulled a gun on you?'

'He didn't, Mum.'

'But what if he had?'

'We'd have run like hell.'

Hana is at Jaye's bedside with Addison, giving Marissa and the girls a break. Vita and Sammie can have a meal cooked by their mum, instead of an egg sandwich from the hospital café. They can do their homework in their own house, instead of perched on the side of Jaye's bed.

They can pretend, for an hour or two at least, that their world is normal.

It's the first time Hana has been alone with her daughter since Addison and Stan and PLUS 1 knocked on the front door of Toa and Gracie's house.

'It wasn't just you,' Hana says. 'You were putting others in danger. Stan. PLUS 1, for God's sake. It was just irresponsible.'

'I can't help my DNA.'

'What does that mean?'

Addison gestures towards where Jaye is lying on the bed, then at Hana.

'Look where I came from. I can figure stuff out, apparently, like you and Dad. No surprise, really. You should actually be chuffed.'

'Have you heard a word I've said?' Hana tries to stay calm and even. She's not very successful. 'I'm not chuffed, Addison. I'm terrified.'

That word and the sudden shakiness in Hana's voice takes Addison aback. In many regards she is wise beyond her years. In other ways, like understanding the devastating effects her actions can have on those who love her, she's not that different to most teenagers. Hana's reaction gives Addison a short, hard jolt.

'Shit. Shit, Mum. I'm sorry.'

Hana can't reply for a moment.

It's been a crap few days. Things are getting frayed at the edges for Hana. What happened to Jaye. Trying to help DI Williams in the hunt for the gunman. Having to ask for help from Sebastian, after things between them had got confusing and awkward. Finding out that her daughter had stumbled-upon-slash-brilliantly-figured-out where the gunman was. If Hana was being honest, she was blown away by Addison putting together those pieces. But any admiration she feels is overshadowed by the thought of her daughter being in danger. Hana can deal with most things, but she can't conceive of how she'd cope if Addison were hurt.

'It's okay, love.' Hana clears her throat, her eyes going to Jaye, the bandaging around his head. 'Just don't try too hard to be like your dad and me, eh? We made a choice. But I wouldn't wish this world, this career, on you. Or anyone.'

As a vibrating buzz issues from Hana's hip pocket, she pulls out her phone, checking the caller ID.

'Hey, Dad,' she says, answering the call.

'Kia ora, e kō.'*

'You don't normally call this late.'

Eru is a five o'clock riser, like her; the habit of a lifetime. Meaning he's usually in bed and snoring not long after the sun goes down.

'Everything okay?'

'We're coming up. To see Jaye. And you and Addison.'

'Great,' Hana says, not missing his use of the word *we*. 'You and Daisy? When?'

'Look outside.'

Hana goes to the window next to Jaye's bed. Addison joins her mother. Looking down at the car park below, she squeals, 'Grandpa!'

Eru's distinctive red-and-white ute sits under one of the parking lot lights, he and Daisy standing alongside

---

* Kia ora, e kō – hello, my girl.

it, smiling up at the hospital wards. Addison grabs the phone from Hana's hand.

'I'm coming down to get you guys.'

As Addison hurries away, Hana watches Daisy from the hospital window as she gently straightens Eru's hat and kisses his cheek, her blonde curls all but glowing under the car park lights.

'Auē.* My boy. My boy.'

Eru is holding Jaye's hand, the hand that is free of the IV drip and the pulse monitor. He and Daisy had wanted to come up days earlier, as soon as they knew about the shooting, but at first visitor numbers were kept very limited and Hana had told them she thought Marissa needed a little time before the wider family came. Now that he's here, the reality of what's happened to Jaye is hitting Eru hard.

'You are not my blood,' he says in te reo, his voice heavy with love and pain. 'But you are still my son.'

Addison and Hana watch, both crying.

'Old man,' Daisy says, taking a tissue from a box on the bedside table, wiping Eru's eyes.

It's a couple of minutes before anyone feels ready to speak again.

'Have they found him?' Eru asks at last, still holding

---

* Auē – expression of distress and dismay.

Jaye's hand. 'The one who did it? It makes me weep. A young Māori boy. Why did it have to be a Māori boy?'

'It might not have been him, Dad.'

The words are out of Hana's mouth before she even realizes, surprising herself as much as anyone else. Addison stares at her mother. 'What do you mean?'

Hana takes a moment before she replies.

'It's possible Toa Davis didn't do it.'

The idea has been eating at her since the interrogation room earlier. Objectively, all the evidence points to Toa. The car. The cell phone. But she can't help asking herself a few questions. They still haven't found the gun, but if Toa has it, he didn't confront Addison and the others with it when they turned up at the door. Stan beat the boy, badly, and if there was ever a moment to take the weapon out to threaten someone, it would have been then. But he didn't.

Maybe Toa had already dumped the weapon somewhere else, thrown it into the harbour at high tide, or tossed it into another garbage bin ready to be emptied? But then why take it from the scene at all, especially as he'd already left other incriminating evidence behind? Even assuming he'd panicked, something about it didn't quite seem to add up.

And the other thing. Hana backs her ability to read someone in an investigation room.

Gracie said that Toa wouldn't hurt anyone; that he didn't have a gun, nor would he ever have one; that Hana and Williams were brown people being racist for being so ready to jump to conclusions. And it wasn't just what she said, it was the way she said it.

If Gracie was lying, she was a hell of a liar.

'Nothing's changed,' Hana says. 'We're still working on the assumption it was him. I'm just saying, it's possible there's another explanation.'

'What other explanation?' Eru asks.

'I have no idea,' Hana says. 'I can't say anything else. I shouldn't have even said that, and you can't repeat it.' The others can see her discomfort. They know it's not the right time or place to push her.

In the silence that follows, Daisy goes to Eru's side. Puts her arm through his.

'There's another reason Eru and I have come to see you.'

Eru takes his bushman's hat from where he'd put it beside Jaye on the bed. He clears his throat, unconsciously turning the hat in his hands.

'For a few months now, e kō, you've been a bit funny with me. Like you've got some something you want to talk about. And then when you found out about me and Daisy . . . your reaction. It just feels like there's something going on. Maybe something you're worried about.'

Daisy squeezes his hand, encouraging him to keep going.

'It took us a while to work out how you found out,' Eru says to Hana.

'Found out what?' Addison asks.

'It was the computer, wasn't it?' Eru continues. 'You saw my searches. Forgetfulness. Memory loss.'

Now Hana knows what Eru wants to talk about. The thing she has been fearing so much. The possibility he has dementia.

'I'm sorry, Dad. I wasn't meaning to pry.'

'No. It's me who should apologize,' he says, his eyes moist. 'I'm so sorry you had to find out that way. I just wasn't ready to tell you.'

Addison's eyes flick between Eru and Hana, with no idea what they're talking about.

'Mum, Grandpa. This is scaring me.'

'Haere mai,'* Eru says, holding out a hand, and Addison hurries across the room to be wrapped in her grandfather's embrace. 'Don't be scared. Don't be scared, moko.'†

'Your grandfather has an illness,' Daisy says gently.

'What? Grandpa . . . ? What's wrong?'

'It sounds bad, but really, it's nothing to be afraid of,' Daisy continues. 'He has dementia.'

'Grandpa,' Addison says, her throat tight.

Daisy's voice is soft. 'There are two kinds of dementia. Your grandfather has the good kind. Well. The less cruel kind.'

'It's not frontotemporal?' Hana asks quickly.

Eru shakes his head, *no*.

Hana feels a flood of relief. She's done a lot of reading; online forums, dementia websites. With frontotemporal dementia your inhibitions can disappear; you can become

---

* Haere mai – come closer.
† Moko (mokopuna) – grandchild.

aggressive, difficult, sexually inappropriate; you can lose the ability to feel empathy. It's the worst-case scenario.

'Eru has vascular dementia,' Daisy says. 'It's very early stage. It's true, there's no cure. It will progress. But it could be a very long time before it's really noticeable. And the kind of dementia he has, even if it gets bad, he's going to stay the nice guy you know.'

Addison is really crying now. Hana goes to her daughter and Eru, putting her arms around both of them. She has been fearing this conversation. But it's almost a comfort, having a reality to confront.

'How did you realize?' Hana asks.

'Little stuff. On the marae, I lost track of the words of a karakia* I've been saying since I was sixteen. That time when you were at my place, I forgot your mother's birthday. Things like that. Small, mostly. Inconsequential. For now.'

Eru's arms tighten around Addison. He leans his head against Hana's.

'It can take decades to go from where I am, to when things are not so great. I might have ten good years. But I might have twenty. I might have more.'

'I know it's been a shock, Hana,' Daisy says from where she is standing by the window, giving the whānau their space to be together. 'Me turning up. I'm not your mother. I don't want to replace her.'

'I know that,' Hana says.

---

* Karakia – prayer/prayers.

'But I know there's something else worrying you. The idea of Eru starting a new relationship. With this hanging over him.'

Hana nods. It's the truth. Daisy takes a step forward, her hand finding Hana's. It's the first time they've actually touched, Hana realizes.

Daisy's eyes are bright. 'When Eru started to suspect what was happening to him, he tried to break things off between us. He just said he didn't think we were a good fit. I knew it was a lie, I didn't let him get away with it. I finally got it out of him, why he was saying these foolish things. He was trying to save me from the disease. From what was coming.'

Addison holds tighter onto Eru.

'I told him,' Daisy continues. 'I said, you want me to stop loving you because God is an arsehole and cursed you with this thing? Fuck that.' She looks towards Addison. 'Sorry, love. I'm swearing like a sailor. I don't normally use that kind of language.'

She laughs, the familiar tinkling sound lightening the room for a moment.

'I want you to know something. Really know it,' Daisy goes on, serious now. 'I am with Eru because I love him. I've gone with him to the specialists, I've found out everything I can about the disease, I know exactly what could happen. And I don't care. I'm going into this with my eyes wide open. I want to be with him, every step of the way. I hope you can come to understand.'

'I understand,' Hana says, and she means it. 'Of course

I understand. And I can't say how grateful I am that my dad has you.'

Silence falls in the hospital room. Eru is holding Jaye's hand again, his other arm around Addison, his head against Hana's where she is standing by him.

Finally, he speaks.

'When you find out something like this,' he says, 'you have a choice. You can choose to keep living. Or you can choose to start dying.'

Eru looks at his daughter and granddaughter. His eyes shining.

'I've made my choice. I'm going to keep living.'

It's a busy evening at Moon Lake Bistro and Lounge. There's a gathering in the private room. It's the big night, the fiftieth birthday of Hàoyǔ's wife. The largest of the half dozen marble-topped dining tables is laden with presents, everyone making a point of displaying their generosity. All the women are dressed up. While the other men wear suits, as befits the occasion, Gold Brother is in his usual tracksuit and gold chain, sitting beside Hàoyǔ and his wife.

'I'm not the most emotional man,' Hàoyǔ says in Mandarin. Laughter, all around the table, everyone knowing that Hàoyǔ describing himself as unemotional is a little like a goldfish describing itself as being able to swim. 'But I am emotional tonight.'

Hàoyǔ turns to his wife.

'You have brought light into my life. You brought the light of our children's smiles into the world. Each day you give us all the gifts of light and of joy. And so, it is only right, my dear, that I give you back just a little of the light you have given me.'

He nods to a group of waiters who are standing at the ready. One dims the lamps of the private room, while another two carry something in, covered by a tablecloth. They place it carefully on the table at the head of the room, then lift away the covering.

Everyone there stares at the large object, which seems to be a glass plate sitting inside a heavy, ornately carved frame.

'Are you ready, dear?' Hàoyǔ asks.

His wife nods enthusiastically. Hàoyǔ approaches the framed piece of glass and flicks a switch. Instantly, a series of small lights set behind the glass illuminates. Gasps go up around the table. The surface has been hand-etched, by one of the finest glass artists in New Zealand. It's an image of Hàoyǔ's wife, taken from the formal photo of her on their wedding day. The soft back-lighting makes her smiling features glow, radiant and ethereal.

In the darkness of the room, it's as though her face is floating in the air.

All around the table, everyone claps. Glasses are raised, a toast to Hàoyǔ's wife.

The waiters bring more wine, the best available in

Gold Brother's premises, a significant gesture for the wife of his number two. Corks are popped; glasses are filled. As the celebration continues, someone slides into the empty seat next to Gold Brother.

'Sorry to intrude.'

He turns to see a new arrival.

'We haven't met,' Elisa Williams says, taking off the lanyard with her police ID and putting it on the table in front of him. 'This won't take long. I think you know why I'm here.'

Around the table, heads are turning. Several of Hàoyǔ's men appear at the entrance to the room as Hàoyǔ himself moves towards the unwelcome newcomer. Gold Brother gestures to him, *take it easy*. He turns back to Williams.

'How can I help you?'

'The young guy who works for you. Toa Davis.'

'Your people have already asked these questions. We know nothing about him. We don't know why our phone number was on his phone. He's not an employee.'

'I can't prove you're lying. But we both know you are,' Williams says. 'We're looking for him. You are too. For all we know, you may have found him already.'

Williams isn't bluffing or guessing. She knows exactly what she's talking about. After the incident on K Road when Ruby rear-ended his car, Sebastian debriefed her and Hana back at the station about what he'd overheard the guy in the back seat discussing on the phone.

'The young guy was calling around their contacts, their

associates,' Sebastian told them. 'He was phoning the people they distribute their drugs to. He told them that Toa had a package of Moon Lake's product. Everyone he called, he said the same thing. If they heard from Toa, if he turned up, if he tried to sell them the missing drugs, they were to call the restaurant and let them know straight away where he was. The guy promised them Moon Lake would make it worth their while.'

Sebastian's quasi-undercover work had almost ended very badly, and Williams and Hana agreed that the risks of him continuing with the pretence of selling the black-market cigarettes were too great. It had been worth the effort, however. Because of Sebastian's work, the cops now knew for certain that Moon Lake were actively looking for Toa, to reclaim their missing drugs.

'Have a look outside,' Williams says to Gold Brother.

His eyes turn to the front windows. A large white transit van can be seen parked on the footpath out front of the restaurant, full of uniformed police officers.

'When I leave, a dozen of my officers are coming into your restaurant,' Williams says. The whole of the private room is silent, listening to the cop. 'They're not here to eat. They are going to interview everyone. All of your guests. Every staff member. They will be checking working visas, immigration statuses. They'll be looking for any illicit substances that might be stored on the property.'

'This is harassment,' Gold Brother says, his eyes cold.

Williams picks up her police ID, slipping the lanyard back around her neck.

'As long as I have even the slightest suspicion that you know something about Toa Davis that you're not sharing with us, that van is going to keep turning up, when it's least convenient.'

She looks around the table. Her eyes settle on Hàoyǔ's wife, the stack of presents in front of her. 'Sorry to interrupt your celebration.'

She walks out the front door, and heads to her car.

At the entrance to the private room, Gold Brother and Hàoyǔ watch as the uniformed police file into the restaurant. For the guests, their evening is finished. And Hàoyǔ's wife's birthday is ruined.

Gold Brother looks at Hàoyǔ. He doesn't need to give voice to what he's thinking. Hàoyǔ is already thinking it himself.

Toa Davis has become a very big problem.

Addison tried very hard to get Eru and Daisy to stay the night in Auckland, promising a special breakfast with fresh bread from the local bakery and PLUS 1's scrambled eggs cooked with kawakawa.*

'I like my own bed, dear,' Eru told her. And there was no talking him round.

---

* Kawakawa – small native New Zealand tree, the leaves of which are used as a peppery herb.

Down in the car park, they're all standing beside Eru's ute as he and Daisy prepare for the drive home.

'I'm sorry I wasn't ready to tell you earlier about the bloody disease,' Eru says. 'Both of you.'

'It's okay, Grandpa.'

'When I first started to suspect,' Hana says, 'I talked to Jaye. He said you're a warrior. That you needed to figure out how you were going to fight this thing and you'd tell us when you were ready.'

Eru looks up towards the room they've just left, where Jaye is lying. 'He understands both of us so well.' His eyes turn back to Hana.

'I know how you think, love. You're a control freak. Please don't take that the wrong way.'

'Sheesh, Dad.' Hana raises her eyebrows. 'First you tell me I'm uptight and unable to relax. Now I'm a control freak. I'm not sure how else to take either of those things.'

Eru smiles, kindly. He's not being mean, just truthful.

'Running exactly the same distance every day. What is it?'

'Ten point thirteen kilometres,' Addison pipes up, remembering when Hana showed her the online running log she fastidiously keeps, with the exact same distance repeated day after day after day.

'If it was a hundred metres more or less, you'd be gutted. You need to run the exact same distance every time. You have to step in and fix all the wrongs in the world. You want nothing bad to ever happen to your daughter, or to anyone you love. That's just who you are. And I love you for it. But you can't control everything. And you definitely can't control what's happening to me. I can't either. Same as I couldn't control your mother dying. The longer I live, the more I know we can't really control much of anything. And maybe that's okay. Maybe that's just called being human.'

Eru kisses Hana. In his arms, she looks towards Daisy.

'You're two of the strongest people I've ever met,' Hana says.

'No, we're not,' Daisy says, her laughter echoing in the car park. 'We're just a couple of old singers with more wrinkles than sense.'

She and Eru climb into the ute, and Addison and Hana watch as it drives out of the hospital car park and heads off towards Tātā Bay.

17

RED LIGHT CAMERA

For days, the photo of Toa Davis wearing the backwards baseball cap has been the first thing anyone sees when they open their news app.

The sole suspect in an attempted murder is still on the run, possibly still in possession of the gun he used. The biggest nightmare for the CIB, and for the police hierarchy, would be if another incident happened, a member of the public being injured or even killed in some kind of confrontation with a desperate gunman. A hotline has been set up for information and reports of possible sightings are coming in, each one necessitating an armed response. In the past twenty-four hours there have been seven police call-outs for full-scale tactical responses. Uniformed police with sidearms, Armed Offenders officers bristling with semi-automatic weapons. Every reported sighting has proven false, and the unfortunate reality is that every erroneous report, though made with the best intentions, was about someone who fits the physical profile of Toa Davis.

Seven armed call-outs across Auckland; seven young Māori men confronted by armed police officers. None of them is Toa.

There have been no physical injuries in any of the call-outs to date, and Williams is grateful for the discipline of her officers. But understandably, those visited by the cops have responded with a range of reactions, from bewilderment to outright anger. Getting your door kicked down and guns in your face just because you are young and Māori. Hana knows, for the young men on the wrong side of this, it must feel a lot like racial profiling.

Williams has kept Hana on, at her temporary desk on the eighth floor. 'An objective set of experienced eyes,' she told her. 'Do what you do. Review everything. Look for what I might not be seeing.'

Hana pulls up a file. It's the video recording from the interrogation room the day before. The interview with Gracie Huia.

'If anyone should know how hard it is for brown people at the bottom of the pile, it's two fucking brown women.'

It's not like Hana needs to watch the footage again. The moment is etched into her memory. The young woman, staring at Williams and Hana. Using her sleeve to wipe away the tears in her eyes.

Hana hits pause on the video.

Gracie is a young mum-to-be, struggling to set up some kind of decent world for her baby to come into. Words like 'institutionalized racism', politically charged phrases that so readily roll off Addison's tongue – that's probably not how Gracie would talk. But Hana is sure that Gracie knows what it feels like to be walking down the road with friends or cousins, no ill intent, and for a cop car to pull up. She would bet a hundred bucks that at some point Gracie has walked into a supermarket, or a clothes shop, and slowly become aware that the same staff member happens to be finding something to do at the end of every aisle she goes into. Knowing that staff member has been told to keep an eye on 'the girl in the hoodie'.

The day-to-day little indignities. The labels that get put on you, just because of the colour of your skin.

And now Gracie's boyfriend has a new label.

SUSPECT IN SHOOTING OF COP

The headline above the photo of Toa in his baseball cap.

Hana stares at Gracie's face on the laptop screen, the young woman's bitter words still ringing in her head.

'*You should be ashamed.*'

Every Māori cop knows the problems with the system they're working in. It's just straightforward, undeniable stats. If you're young and Māori, you're more likely to be questioned for any given crime than a non-Māori is. If you're questioned, you're more likely to be arrested. If you're arrested, you're more likely to be convicted. If you're convicted, you're going to get a longer sentence than a non-Māori. There's nothing in the law books that makes this official policy – of course there isn't. There's nothing you learn at police college, nothing written down in the police code of conduct, nothing on any guideline or piece of paper or legislation that formalizes any of this.

But like every Māori cop, Hana knows this stuff is real. She knows fifty-three per cent of the prison population is Māori. Māori are only seventeen per cent of the New Zealand population. Māori are one of the most incarcerated Indigenous races on the planet.

At some point in the career of every brown cop, there has to be a reckoning. The justice system is far from perfect. In the treatment of Māori, it's deeply imperfect. You figure out your own balance sheet, you work out if you can look at yourself in the mirror. And you carry on.

Or, like Hana, you walk away.

It had made her want to scream, seeing the selfie on the gunman's phone. The exact same thing that broke her dad's heart. Why the fuck did it have to be a Māori kid?

But facts are facts. The phone dumped in the rubbish skip belonged to Toa. The car was the one he stole, to do his job as a donkey for Moon Lake, and it was full of his fingerprints and DNA.

One plus one equals two.

Hana exits out of the video clip.

Earlier that morning, Hana had dropped in to the third floor, where Stan works.

One of Stan's duties is the collating of data, including the video interviews relating to this investigation. Hana had brought the laptop she'd been issued, asked him to download all the relevant footage for her. But also, she'd just wanted the chance to see him. As the files were transferring, she pulled up a chair beside him.

'Are you okay?'

Hana knew that Stan had been reprimanded for what he'd done, using his police ID when he'd been working his way around those houses with Addison and PLUS 1.

'I mean, they had to give me a telling-off,' Stan told her. 'But how mad could they be? We got it right. Your daughter got it right. We found the guy. I got away without an official warning. But still. I don't know if it's going to make getting my badge back that much harder . . .'

Hana looked at Stan. The young cop she'd known before he'd been injured had never been the most easy-going guy. A bit socially awkward, always wanting to prove himself. It had helped that he was smart as hell, top of his class at police college. But since the explosion that took his leg, Hana has seen changes in Stan, and they worry her.

'After the accident,' she said quietly. 'You spoke to someone, right?'

Stan tensed up. 'What do you mean?'

'Counselling. The mandatory sessions with the police psychologist.'

'Yeah. Of course. That's what mandatory means.'

'Did you talk to them? Like, really talk to them?'

He didn't respond. Which answered Hana's question.

'You went through a lot, Stan. Really, a lot. That stuff can hang around. Some things are good to actually talk about.'

Stan's eyes stayed glued to the screen, his fingers tapping a fixed rhythm on the edge of the desk. 'That's not me. I self-medicate. You know. Running. Working out. It's the same result.' Hana could see he'd rather the conversation was over. But she wasn't finished.

'You lost a limb. You nearly died. PTSD isn't some made-up thing. It's real.'

Suddenly he turned to her sharply. 'Did Addison say something?'

She tried to hide her surprise. 'About what?'

He held her gaze for a beat. 'Nothing. It's nothing. Just . . . personal stuff. Forget about it.'

'Addison didn't say anything.'

It was the truth, Stan could see. He nodded, relaxing slightly, grateful that Addison had kept his confidence.

'But should she have?'

There was an awkward silence.

Hana waited it out. The files continued to buffer on the computer screen. Stan's fingers tapped the edge of the desk. Finally he spoke, his voice low.

'There's never been a detective in the New Zealand cops with an artificial limb. I'm going to do it. I'm going to make it so they can't say no. But if I do talk to the police counsellor, how do I know it's really confidential? If I'm on record saying I'm struggling, no way are they letting me back in.'

'I don't think that's true.'

Stan shook his head. 'They'll look for anything that feels like weakness. I've already got enough going against me.'

He looked around the room, very aware of the other workers nearby. He shuffled his chair closer to Hana.

'You don't want to be up there on the eighth floor, boss. You made a decision. You walked away from being a detective. I didn't make that decision. A fucking car blew up, it took my leg, and took the only job I ever wanted with it.'

The words were raw with emotion. Hana could see he was about to continue, but there was a ding as the file transfer finished. Stan unplugged the cable. Handed the laptop back to Hana. Turned back to his own screen.

'I don't have PTSD, boss. I'm fine. Don't worry about me.'

The red light camera.

Hana has worked her way through a number of the files. The footage from inside the liquor store. The CCTV footage of the stolen car from the street outside. After the car was found in the car park, the cops could retrospectively plot, with some certainty, the route it took, and pull footage from the relevant CCTV cameras. Professional video editors were brought in to help stitch together the various pieces of footage into one real-time sequence, from the moments after the shooting until the car was abandoned fifteen kilometres away.

The vehicle stayed away from the motorway, where Toa would have known he'd be more likely to be pulled over by the marked and unmarked patrols that drove the city's motorway network. There were quite a few sections of the journey where there was no CCTV coverage, so there are jumps in the video timeline, the car disappearing from one piece of footage, then being picked up again a mile or so later.

The edited sequence plays for twenty-two minutes. It's pretty much a straight line from the liquor store to the shopping centre.

There are a few things that stand out to Hana. After the shooting, the gunman hurries to the car and gets in. But there's no squeal of tyres, no hard acceleration away from the store. Even in the moments immediately after discharging a weapon into another human being, the driver is measured, careful.

Of course, Toa wouldn't have wanted to draw the attention of a passing cop. But all the same. It would have taken nerves of ice not to get the hell out of there as fast as possible.

Throughout the rest of the journey the car drives carefully, safely, well within the speed limits. None of the slight veers across the road that you might expect if Toa, fearful and with adrenaline surging, looked back over his shoulder to make sure he wasn't being followed. Every time the car makes a turn, the indicator light starts flashing well in advance.

If this was a video recording of someone sitting their practical exam for a full driver's licence, Hana thinks, *they'd pass with flying colours.*

None of this is surprising. Toa Davis is an experienced driver who's been behind the wheel since well before he was legally allowed to be. For the last couple of years, he's made a living out of couriering illegal substances around the city, a job where your income and your liberty depend on not drawing attention to you or your vehicle. On that level, the painstakingly careful getaway makes sense.

Except for the red light camera.

Hana finds herself watching the final section of the edited CCTV sequence again, focusing on the last thirty seconds. For the preceding twenty minutes, the car is driven so carefully it's almost boring. Then, at the traffic lights opposite the mall car park, it speeds straight through the red light.

Perhaps for Toa, after controlling his nerves for so long – after working so hard to keep the racing pulse and the near panic at bay – it all became too much. Perhaps he just wanted to get the hell out of the car, so he hit the accelerator instead of the brakes, turned into a random car park, threw away his phone and ran.

Perhaps.

Hana looks again at the last ten seconds of the red

light video. It's dark and shadowy. IT have done all they can to clarify the footage, getting rid of as much electronic buzz as possible, but it's still noisy. She slows down the frame rate. The balaclava-wearing gunman gets out of the car. He slams the door shut. He throws the bag with the orange circle into the skip. And he walks across the car park and into the night.

Hana rewinds the footage again, back to the moments just after the car pulls into the parking lot.

This time she slows it down even more. Frame by frame. The door opens. Toa gets out. He looks around. For a moment, he looks straight back in the direction he came from. Hana has thought a number of times that if he wasn't wearing the balaclava and they could digitally enhance the image enough to positively identify him, this would be the footage they'd play in the trial.

She pauses the video. There's a sketch pad and an art pencil beside her keyboard, a long-standing habit from when she was a cop. At every crime scene she'd sketch the environment, and the body if it was a homicide. Stan used to joke that she trusted her eyes more than forensic photos, but it wasn't actually a joke. It was completely true.

Hana sketches the stilled image in front of her. The face covered in the balaclava. She carefully shades the eyes she can see in the enhanced footage, staring back towards the intersection.

She looks again at the eyes as she has drawn them. Exactly as they are on the screen.

The eyes staring out from the balaclava are looking at the red light camera.

The gunman is looking *directly* at the camera.

Hana blinks.

Suddenly, she understands exactly what she is seeing.

'I didn't see this until maybe the twentieth time I watched.'

Hana is playing the footage for DI Williams, slowed down to five per cent speed.

'He looks around, making sure no one's in the car park.'

She forwards the footage frame by frame.

'Then he looks back. But look where he's looking.'

As Toa's head tilts upwards, Hana zooms in on the masked face.

'Straight at the red light camera. Not in the general direction. His eyes go straight to it.'

'So . . . are you saying . . . he knew where the camera was?'

'Exactly,' Hana says. 'He knew, because he'd been to the car park before. He planned this. He knew precisely where the red light camera was, and where to park to make sure it would see him after he ran the red light.'

Hana indicates the map of the route the car took from the liquor store to the car park.

'It's almost a straight line. He'd worked out the route in advance. Then he deliberately drove through the red light, to set off the camera.'

'Why would Toa Davis want the car found?'

Hana meets her eyes. 'What if Gracie is telling the truth? What if it wasn't him? What if the car *was* stolen from Toa. Used in the hold-up, knowing it would be linked to the shooting. Then it was dumped where the driver knew it would be found, along with Toa's phone and his fingerprints. Everything pointing straight to a young offender who would fit the bill when we went looking.'

Hana looks again at her sketch. The gunman's eyes, staring straight at the CCTV camera. Almost as if they are looking out from the page, at her.

'Jaye wasn't a random victim,' Hana says. 'The hold-up was staged, orchestrated. And the getaway afterwards was even more carefully planned, to point us straight towards Toa Davis.'

'You think this was a hit? An attempted execution?'

Hana nods. Williams can see there's now not the slightest doubt in her mind.

'Whoever did this,' Hana says. 'They wanted Jaye dead.'

18

THIS DOESN'T HAPPEN HERE

In the staff cafeteria, Williams takes her time, still stirring the milk into her coffee long after it's as mixed as it's ever going to be. She takes out the spoon. Lays it down carefully on a paper napkin.

'This is New Zealand,' she says, finally. 'This doesn't happen here.'

Hana knows what she's saying. If Jaye's shooting was an attempted assassination, it would be unheard of. In a country whose entire population is a little over half that of Manhattan Island, there isn't the kind of infrastructure in the organized crime world to readily find someone who will murder for money. Let alone someone willing to kill a cop.

'I'm not saying it's not possible. I'm just not sure who would be capable of it,' Williams continues. 'Or why.'

'Maybe it was a warning. An investigation Jaye was spearheading was getting too close for comfort for someone. Or maybe it was always meant to be more than a warning. Close down whatever inconvenient leads Jaye was pursuing by killing him.'

'I'll pull together the teams who are running active enquiries under Jaye's supervision, look at what cases are underway that might fit the picture.'

'It could also be payback,' Hana says. 'Someone Jaye put in prison. But that's going to be a long list. He's been a senior detective for nearly two decades.'

'We'll start with offenders he put away who've recently been released. Focus on those with the most violent records, or anyone who actually threatened him.'

Williams sips her coffee. It's thin and tasteless, the only kind served in the cafeteria. But today she doesn't notice as she works through the implications of this new angle. 'When we met,' she says quietly, 'I told you I left the SAS because I was done watching other countries tear themselves apart. I wanted to be back here in my own country, doing something to make the place better. That's the truth. But it's not the only reason.'

The room is almost empty. The only other people are at a far table, just as deep in conversation. All the same, Williams draws her chair closer to Hana, to say what she has to say next with as much privacy as possible.

'There was a situation I became aware of. The New Zealanders had made friends with some of the locals in an Afghani village we were based near for a few months. There was one woman, she was maybe mid-fifties. In Afghanistan, that's elderly. She asked me to her house one day – her daughter was there to translate. The women told me that a man from a neighbouring village had been detained by an officer from the Australian army forces. The young guy had tried to steal a box of supplies from the Australian mess tent, for his family. I mean, yeah, it was stupid as hell. And it's understandable the Aussie sergeant was pissed off. But no way did that even begin to excuse what happened.'

Williams takes another sip of her coffee. Not so much to taste it, but to give herself a moment. Hana waits, not sure where this conversation is headed.

'Do you know about blooding?' Williams continues eventually, meeting Hana's eyes.

Hana has heard of the practice. Junior soldiers on their first missions would be ordered by their superior officers to execute prisoners, so they'd get their first kills out of the way, the idea being that the next time they would be less likely to hesitate when they needed to use lethal force.

'The Australian sergeant had a junior soldier take the young guy to the edge of a rock face. He made the soldier shoot the thief in the head. Throw him off the cliff, then testify that the Afghani was running away with ammunition, weapons. They planted a sidearm on his body. It was ruled as a justifiable killing, to prevent a weapon getting into enemy hands.'

Williams puts down her coffee. Even now, years later,

talking about the incident is like the taste of vinegar in her mouth.

'What did you do, when the women told you their version?' Hana asks.

'I sat there, at their table. They'd made me tea and bread, food I knew they couldn't afford to give away. They treated me as an honoured guest. The young guy was a relative of theirs. Because I'd got friendly with them, they saw me as their only hope, to maybe have something done about what had happened.'

'The Aussies and the New Zealanders – were your camps near each other?'

'About ten kilometres apart. We'd have social nights with the Aussies. I'd met the Australian sergeant. I had a drink with him. He showed me photos of his kids. He was so proud of them. I genuinely liked the guy. I couldn't believe he'd do such a thing. He was hugely respected; he'd been decorated multiple times. No one had a bad word to say about him.'

Williams pauses, a little emotional at the memory.

'The old woman who made me tea and gave me food – she was the same age as my mum and aunties. I just imagined my mother in her situation. The courage it would take to speak up. The hope in her heart that maybe something could be done.'

Hana nods, understanding the awfulness of the situation Williams found herself in. But still not sure where this is going, or what it has to do with Jaye.

'I decided I had to look into it,' Williams continues. 'I

talked to other locals from the dead man's village. The incident had been seen by a number of the villagers. They were all too terrified to say anything, until they realized I was on their side. I took the information to our senior officers. To be honest, they would've preferred me to shut up and forget about it. But I made enough of a stink that they couldn't ignore it. Our senior officers passed on the information to the Australians, on an official level. They investigated. The Australian officer was court-martialled, sent home in disgrace. He did several years' prison time. It was the end of his career. His marriage. His family. And really . . . well, it was the end of my career in the army too. I didn't have the stomach for it anymore. War brings out the very best in people. It also brings out the very worst.'

Williams gestures around the building, the police HQ. 'This job can do the same,' she says, her eyes on Hana, letting the implication hang between them.

Hana's lips tighten. 'Let me get this straight. This story, about a soldier who crossed the line. You're saying Jaye might have done the same? He could be bent?'

'As uncomfortable as it is,' Williams says gently, 'we have to acknowledge the possibility.'

'The guy whose office you're sitting in doesn't have a corrupt bone in his body.'

'I know Jaye well enough to know it makes no sense. And you know him far better. But the Aussie dad who showed me the photo of his kids didn't fit the picture either.'

Williams chooses her next words carefully.

'Someone talks to a cop at the wrong moment, when they've had a shit week, when they're thinking seriously about getting the hell out of the job. A big offer goes on the table. Enough money to ensure your family's happiness and security for the rest of your life. This is the least corrupt country in the world. But it *can* happen.'

In the ensuing silence, Hana's eyes go to the cafeteria windows. Outside, the sun is setting. The skies are darkening over the tall buildings of central Auckland, black rain clouds threatening. It's going to be another cold, wet winter's night.

'Neither of us want to believe it,' Williams continues, gently. 'But we have to consider it. Jaye could have crossed the line. Gone down the rabbit hole with someone in the criminal world. The relationship went sour. The shooting was payback. Regardless of whether it was Toa Davis who pulled the trigger, we know there's someone in the equation with the kind of money to bribe a cop. And the kind of money to pay to get a cop killed.'

Hana immediately knows who she's talking about.

'Moon Lake.'

Williams nods. *Exactly*. 'Toa is in their orbit. He shifts product for them. He's disposable. Moon Lake are smart – smart enough to know that framing him would make sense to the police; a kid already on the wrong side of the law who takes the next step and holds up a liquor store.'

Williams puts her hands palms up on the table.

'I don't believe Jaye crossed the line. I don't believe it for a moment. But it's possible.'

Hana sighs. A sick feeling in her gut at even saying the words.

'It's possible,' she finally says.

Gracie falls asleep listening to the heavy rain on the rusted corrugated iron roof.

She's always liked the sound of rain at night. Rhythmic. Comforting. Kind of like a lullaby for grown-ups. The warm feelings the rain gives her make their way into her dream. She feels Toa slipping under the sheets, putting his arms around her. He's wet from the rain, but she doesn't mind as he holds her tight and puts his hand gently on her belly.

'You fellas miss me?' he says.

Gracie smiles in her sleep. She turns over. Her eyes open.

Someone is sitting in the shadows of the bedroom.

It's not Toa.

'What's the password for your phone?' Hàoyǔ asks quietly. He has Gracie's phone in his hand. The heavy he has brought with him translates just as quietly, both men crouched beneath the window. It's dark in the room; the curtains are drawn. But even so, they don't want the cops sitting in their unmarked car across the street to see any movement that might give them reason to break down the door.

'The password,' Hàoyǔ says again, impatient now. He's wet from where the two of them climbed silently over the back fence of the property, knowing that between the downpour and the darkness of the moonless night, this would be their best chance to get into the property unseen and question Toa's girlfriend.

He moves a little closer to the edge of the bed.

Gracie flinches. Her hand holds her abdomen protectively, as she'd just dreamed of Toa doing.

She tells the men the password.

Hàoyǔ's henchman takes the phone and opens it. Scrolls through her messages. He looks at Hàoyǔ, shaking his head. There's nothing from Toa there.

'I haven't heard from him,' Gracie says. 'I don't know where he is.'

The heavy translates for Hàoyǔ. In the darkness, Gracie watches, barely breathing, as the middle-aged man nods slowly. Once. Twice. Then Hàoyǔ reaches into his pocket. He pulls out a fistful of red $100 bills. Places them on the bedspread beside her.

'You're having a baby. Nappies and good baby formula are expensive. I know this.'

Another translation. Gracie looks at the pile of bills, illuminated in a shaft of light from a street light falling through a crack in the curtains. It's more money than she's ever seen in one place at one time.

'This is your chance, child,' Hàoyǔ says. 'Leave that

piece of shit behind. Find a man who will be a good, reliable father to the baby you are bringing into the world. The money is yours. Yours. I ask only one thing. The moment he contacts you, you tell us where he is.'

As the other man finishes translating the unfamiliar words, Gracie picks up the money. Weighs it in her hand.

'Go fuck yourself,' she says quietly.

She throws the pile of $100 bills in Hàoyǔ's face.

Instantly, the heavy's hand goes to the pocket of his jacket; Gracie sees cold metal glinting in the darkness. A knife. She braces herself, ready to scream as loud as she possibly can, loud enough to alert the cops maybe, though she knows by then it would be too late. But Hàoyǔ's hand moves to restrain his man.

'You made the wrong decision. Like you have your whole life, I suspect. Your baby deserves a better mother.' As the heavy translates, Hàoyǔ pockets the money.

The two men move silently back the way they came.

As the rain falls harder still, Gracie stumbles to the back of the house, watching the two silhouettes as they head across the rear yard, towards the fence. She locks the back door. Wedges a chair against the handle. Goes back and sits shivering on the side of the bed.

The sound of the rain has suddenly lost all ability to comfort. Gracie won't sleep again tonight.

19

YOU CAN'T HAVE EVERYTHING

There's a place Toa has heard about down at the far end of the wharves, where you can hand over a hundred bucks to the security guards, and they'll go off and have a meal at the cheap and cheerful Indian restaurant down the road. Gives you a couple of hours. Long enough to do what needs to be done.

Pāua fishermen bring their boats in to this part of the wharf. They send the guards off for their well-paid butter chicken meal breaks, and that's when the deals for their freshly gathered hauls are completed. Pāua are large, edible sea snails, known elsewhere as abalone. They're a protected species: recreational fishermen can only take five pāua per person, per day. It's a serious crime for any single person to have more than twenty pāua in their possession at any one time. Legally, pāua can only be harvested by freediving on the remote rocky coastlines just below the intertidal zone where they grow. You can't use scuba gear.

Those are the rules. On this shadowy part of the wharves, the rules get broken, a lot.

There's a thriving worldwide market for pāua, especially in Asia, the dark meat of the New Zealand abalone having a particularly big rep not only for the intensity of its flavour, but for its power as an aphrodisiac. In just a couple of days, a good pāua diver with oxygen tanks and knowledge of a thriving pāua bed can gather a small fortune. Easily as much as what a legit fisherman might make for a month or two of law-abiding catches.

You risk big fines. But the risk is worth it. The best divers call pāua 'black gold'.

Toa has been sleeping in a long-abandoned factory, holed up in what used to be the refrigerator room among old tarpaulins and cardboard boxes. Cold and getting colder. Last night, relentless rain made the factory floor a sea of puddles. Shivering alone in the dark, he thought about how nothing was going right. Just nicking food from the backs of takeaway shops was a risk, with his face on TV all the time. He felt like he was standing at the top of a very tall cliff, his toes right on the edge, about to tumble forward at any moment, into the darkness. How it looked to Toa, he had zero options on the one hand. No options on the other.

Then he remembered the stories about the pāua fishermen. The deals they made, down there at the dark end of the wharves. The huge amounts of money that passed from hand to hand.

He remembered about the black gold.

And Toa knew what he had to do.

There's a park with a big stand of tall trees, a few hundred metres from the narrow street where Toa and Gracie's house is.

After what had happened, after the people had come knocking at the door and Toa had fled out the back window, he had risked everything by coming back one night. He'd found his way through the relative safety of darkness, heading up to the stand of trees, where he could look down on the house in the distance with the metal pylon in the backyard.

He'd wanted to just look at where he knew Gracie was.

Even from that far away, Toa could see the cop cars on the street, watching the house. He knew he couldn't risk going back. The cops would be armed; of course they would – Toa was wanted for the shooting of a cop. If he tried to sneak in and see her and they came with guns, Gracie could get hurt.

Baby could get hurt.

He couldn't go and see her; he couldn't tell her what he was planning. But he'd let her know, as soon as he'd got everything fixed. He was going to make everything all right. Toa was going to get his little family back together again. Him and Gracie.

And, in a few months, baby Arihia.

Toa waits and watches, lying flat, his body pressed down against the cold steel of the shipping container he clambered up onto earlier, just after the sun went down. From here he can see the dark end of the wharves, without being seen himself. A half-hour ago, he watched as a fishing boat pulled in. A few minutes later, the two burly fishermen who had come in on the boat passed over a handful of fifty dollar bills to the security guards in their little white car. The car headed out of the main gates of the wharf, tandoori and garlic naan on the guards' minds. As they drove out onto the road, a van passed them, turning into the wharves, heading straight down to the newly arrived boat.

Toa watches as a series of iceboxes are unloaded from the boat, into the van. It's been a shitty week, the worst week of Toa's life. But at last, maybe now he's about to run into a bit of luck. The iceboxes of pāua nearly fill the van. It's a substantial haul. The two middlemen who are buying the pāua, before repacking them and shipping them off to clients across Asia, are delighted. They're going to make a killing. Everyone gets rich.

With all the iceboxes unloaded, one of the middlemen

hands over a bulging brown envelope before they drive away. These kinds of transactions are all in cash, of course. And whiskey. The fishermen end up with a couple of bottles of Johnnie Walker each, on top of the cash payment for the bumper haul of illegal pāua. A good day at the office in anyone's terms.

Toa keeps watching as the fishermen check the ropes securing their boat to the wharf are tied off properly. They climb back aboard, bringing out enamel cups, going to sit on the rear deck. They crack open the first bottle of Johnnie Walker. Toa watches as they start to drink. He has to be patient. Give it time. He turns over, looking up at the stars. He feels something in his back pocket, pressing against the steel roof of the container. He reaches back, finds a pencil there.

The pencil they used recently, when he and Gracie drew the pictures of their baby.

Toa was only two years old when his great-grandmother passed away. So young, he barely remembers her. But he has one strong memory, so vivid that he's completely sure it's real, not just something he's seen in a family photo or been told about.

'She was holding me,' he told Gracie. 'She looked old as the hills. Older. Skin like a ploughed field, if you were looking down at it from space. I remember her arms around me. Her smell, a bit like flowers, a bit like tobacco. She was old, but she held me so tight. I wasn't gonna come to any harm, in her arms. I remember looking up at her chin. Touching it. The blue carved lines.'

It was ten days ago. A few days before their world imploded. Gracie and Toa were lying in bed. All their clothes on, the red bars of the electric heater glowing in the darkness. Trying to keep warm together.

'She had a moko kauae?' Gracie asked, using the word in te reo for the small, finely rendered tattoos located on the chin, a form of tā moko* particularly reserved for women.

'It was so beautiful. When I got a bit older, I used to lie on the ground, looking all around the sky. You know, how it goes from really dark blue straight above you, on a really clear day, then through all these different shades until it's lightest down at the horizon?'

Gracie had to laugh. 'I can't believe you even see all this stuff. The sky's just blue.'

'I reckon her moko kauae would've been the colour of the sky right above your head when she was young and she first had it carved. Then over the years it faded till it was the shade of blue you get down near the horizon.'

Gracie took Toa's hand. She held it against the slight swell of her belly.

'She's going to be a girl,' Toa said quietly.

---

* Tā moko – traditional Māori tattooing.

'How do you know?'
'I just know. She's going to be a girl.'
Gracie smiled at Toa. Okay then.
'What was her name? Your great-grandmother?'
'Arihia.'
Gracie put her head against Toa's shoulder.
'She's going to be a girl,' she said. 'And we'll call her Arihia.'

It's well past midnight when Toa climbs carefully down from the shipping container.

In the time it had taken for the fishermen to finish the first bottle of whiskey, it had started to rain. There was nothing on top of the container to cover himself with, so Toa just had to grit his teeth and put up with it. He had to stay where he was, until he was ready to make his move. He couldn't come down to find cover from the rain and risk being spotted. It was all or nothing.

He has one chance. One chance only.

After twenty minutes or so the rain stopped, thank fuck. But the fishermen kept drinking, making their way through the second bottle. They had reason to celebrate. A bloody good payday. Finally, they finished the second bottle and went into the cabin. They must have been seriously boozed-up, Toa knew. That was a lot of spirits drunk straight from the little enamel cups. But he also knew he needed to take a wee bit more time. Be patient. Let them really conk out.

One chance. It's all he has left.

A full hour after the men went inside the cabin, Toa moves. He slips back down the side of the container, then makes his way through the shadows to the edge of the building closest to the fishing vessel. He hasn't seen the security guards for at least two hours. He figured they would maybe do the occasional drive around the wharf, if they were feeling particularly diligent. But there's been no sign of the little white car. Probably they're sitting in it over on the main area of the wharf. Sharing a joint. Or just snoozing.

Toa stands silent and still in the shadows. Listening hard. Above the gentle slapping of the water against the structural poles of the wharf, he can hear the sound of gulls crying. In his head he begs them to quiet themselves.

One chance. Just one chance to get his life back.

Toa slips off his shoes. He walks fast and silent, his socked feet making almost no noise against the wooden wharf. He climbs onto the rear running board of the boat, then onto the deck, sliding straight across to the cabin. The fishermen, two bottles of hard liquor in, have left the door unlocked. Through the crack he can hear whiskey-fuelled snoring. Encouraged, Toa eases the door a little further open, looks inside.

The two men are in their bunks, on either side of the cabin, dead to the world. Toa's eyes slide around the room and the wheelhouse beyond. Trying to pick out shapes in the darkness. A beam from one of the wharf's lighting towers falls through the front window of the vessel, and as the boat moves against its mooring ropes, the shaft of sodium-yellow light slides across the wheelhouse.

And Toa sees it. Tucked behind the wheel.

The brown envelope.

One chance.

He doesn't think; he doesn't hesitate. He just goes. Fast, silent, his feet falling carefully between the discarded whiskey bottles. Into the wheelhouse, grabbing the envelope of money, almost gasping as he feels the weight of the thing, *holy hell*, but he can't gasp. If he makes a noise and wakes the two men, he's completely fucked. He heads back past the sleeping fishermen, pausing for a split second to grab a cell phone that's lying on the floor by one of the bunks, then out onto the deck, jumping now, across the gap and onto the wharf, grabbing his shoes, not even stopping to pull them on. Running away as fast as he can, into the night.

One chance. Only one chance.

For the first time in what feels like a very long while, something has gone right for Toa Davis.

In the abandoned factory, in the long-unused refrigerator room, Toa sits on the pile of cardboard and tarpaulins and plastic on the floor. He's surrounded by $100 bills. He's counted them, counted them again, counted them again. Maths isn't his thing, so he had to make sure.

It's a bit over $27,000.

He looks at the money, still not quite able to grasp exactly what this pile of printed paper means. If he'd had $27,000 a few months back, when he and Gracie had just found out they were going to have their little girl, it would have changed everything. They could have left town. Gone somewhere nice, set themselves up. He'd have found a real job, who cares what; working on a farm or in a factory – it wouldn't have mattered. Anything would have been better than what he'd been doing. But they hadn't had the money then. Toa had had to keep doing what he was doing. And then what happened, happened. Now he's on every newsfeed. The guy who shot the cop in the head.

No use crying over spilt milk. Toa has the money now.

He'd been praying it would be enough to pay off Gold Brother for the missing drugs, get the nightmare of that debt off his back. But $27,000 pays back what he owes, plus interest. At least five grand of interest, Toa figures. It's more than he'd dreamed of.

It's a lifeline. A lifeline for him and Gracie and Arihia.

It's enough to buy him a spot on one of the boats that move through the night between Australia and New Zealand, bringing in the cocaine or ready-cooked meth-amphetamine. Five thousand bucks to Gold Brother will for sure get him a place on a boat as it heads back over to Sydney or Melbourne or Brisbane. He doesn't care where. As long as it's not here. In Australia, the wages are twice what they are in New Zealand, Toa has heard. He'll work, a real job; he'll set everything up for him and Gracie. It might take a few months before the cops stop watching her and she can get a passport organized and get on a plane without being noticed. Baby will probably be born by then. It breaks his heart that he won't be there for the birth the way they had it planned. But you take what the universe gives you.

And now the universe has given them $27,000.

A new start. A new life for Toa and Gracie and Arihia.

The little girl will grow up with an ugly Australian accent. But you can't have everything.

Toa waits until the sun comes up. He puts the money back in the brown envelope, tucks it under his jacket. Then he gets the phone he grabbed from the floor of the fishing boat, and he calls the restaurant. He asks for Gold Brother, using the fake name he's always used. He gets given the cell phone number and he dials.

The other phone is answered immediately.

'What the hell happened?' says Gold Brother. 'Where are you?'

Toa looks out at the sky. His eyes fall to just above the horizon, where the colour is the same faded blue as the carved lines on his great-grandmother's chin.

'I've got the money I owe you. And then some,' he says. 'I wanna make a deal.'

20

THE KEY

Two high school students in school uniform are sitting at a bus stop near where Hana's car is parked. They're on their separate phones but at the same time they're connected. They've got a pair of ear-pods, split between them – one in his ear, one in hers. Her left hand brushes against his right hand as they quietly sing along to the lyrics of whatever's playing.

In the passenger seat of Hana's car, Marissa stares through the windscreen, her eyes on the two teenagers. Her mind elsewhere. Outside, the pair begin to laugh and chat animatedly as the song comes to an end. Marissa shifts, the spell broken. She turns to Hana.

'Have you found something?' she asks.

Hana texted Marissa to meet her outside the hospital: she'd be parked two hundred yards from the visitors' entrance. For a while there'd been journalists camped out at the front door, getting in Marissa's face or trying to get comments from Hana every time they emerged, until it wasn't worth even stepping out for a breath of fresh air anymore. The journalists have gone now, but Hana doesn't want to risk what she has to say being overheard by anyone.

At the bus stop, the two teenagers scan the playlist on the girl's phone. There's a bit of debate, Marissa can see; two competing songs that just have to be next. They reach a compromise, and the young couple's heads nod in unison to the rhythm as the chosen song starts to play.

'I brought you coffee,' Hana says. She offers the takeaway cup. Marissa doesn't take it.

'What is it, Hana? What do you know?'

Hana sets the coffee down in the cup holder. Comes straight to the point.

'There's no easy way to say this. I think what happened was deliberate. I believe the person who shot Jaye went to that store to kill him.'

Marissa takes in a short, sharp breath.

Hana has the urge to reach out, take her hand, give this woman who has been through so much some kind of comfort in the face of still more awful news. But Marissa's fingers are wound tightly together. She wants to work through this on her own.

At the bus stop, the boy is doing a goofy dance. Kind of cool, but kind of not. The girl is trying her best not to laugh. Finally, she starts to giggle, punching him in the shoulder, both of them cracking up. Marissa watches. Two young people, nothing more to worry about than being in love for the first time. And not missing the next bus home.

Easy. Simple.

'I fucking hate this,' she finally says.

Hana hears the pain in her voice, the tiredness. But also something else that she can't quite put her finger on.

'The job Jaye chose. The job you chose. The things it does to anyone who wears a badge, to anyone who loves anyone who wears a badge. The endless brutality. It's not a job. It's inhuman. It's fucking legalized torture.'

Hana knows that Marissa needs to get this stuff out. And in truth, she doesn't disagree.

In the passenger seat, Marissa's hands continue to grip each other, the skin around the knuckles bloodless, like she is grappling with a choice she really doesn't want to make. At last her hands loosen. She takes her bag, unclasps the top.

She's made her decision.

'I found something, a couple of days ago. In the back of one of Jaye's drawers, when I was collecting some things to bring to his room.'

Marissa reaches into her bag, takes out a key. It's embossed with the name of a local storage unit company.

'I have no idea what it is. Why he has it, why he never told me he keeps a storage unit, why he keeps the key hidden away somewhere I'd never normally look.'

Marissa blinks. Finding the right words.

'I decided I wasn't going to use it. Not yet. There are questions I really don't want answered while Jaye is lying in that hospital room. Is he having an affair? What could he have to hide? I don't want to know. Right now, I have to be there for him, hold his hand, give him all the love I have. Will him to come back to me. While I'm being the homing beacon he needs, to find his way back, I'm not using this damn key.'

Marissa looks from the key in her hand to Hana. When she speaks again, her voice is very quiet. 'You're sure? You're sure it wasn't random? It wasn't just Jaye walking into the wrong place at the wrong time?'

'I can't know for certain. But it looks that way,' Hana says gently. She reaches out, takes Marissa's hand, and Marissa lets her.

At the bus stop, a bus pulls in. The two teenagers get on, and Marissa can see their shapes through the windows as they walk the length of the aisle, taking seats by the back window. Heads still moving to the music on their shared ear-pods. The boy puts his arm around the girl's shoulders. Marissa watches them kiss.

Simple. Easy.

The bus pulls away.

'Whatever's in that storage unit . . . Whatever he was keeping from me, from his colleagues . . . Maybe it's going to help you work out who did this. But I don't want to know.'

Hana feels the coldness of the storage unit key as Marissa presses it into her palm.

'When he's well, when he's healing, when I'm strong enough, then I'll ask. For now, I want to be able to be at his bedside, fighting for him to live. Not wishing he was dead.'

Marissa gets out of the car, hurries across the road. Hana watches until she disappears through the front entrance of the hospital, heading back up to the room where Jaye is lying.

Her eyes fall to the key in her hand.

21

DEVIL'S HORNS

Hana walks down the long rows of storage units, following the manager of the facility. Each unit they pass is identical: white walls, blue doors, about the dimensions of a large car garage in a decent-sized home. The manager is one of those people whose age you just can't guess. Could be twenty-five, could be forty-five, could be sixty-five. She is either incredibly well preserved, or gone prematurely to seed. When Hana showed her the key, she immediately knew who it belonged to, and what had happened to Jaye.

'I recognized him. All the news items on telly. The poor guy. He was always so sweet when he'd come in.'

'Did he come here a lot?' Hana asks, as they turn the corner from one line of identical units to another line of identical units. It reminds her of the old song. Little boxes on the hillside.

'Every so often. He's had the place a few years. He's such a good fella. He's one of those guys, he had a quick look at my name tag the first time he came in. Then after that, he remembered it, without even having to read it.'

'Sounds like Jaye.'

The manager stops outside a blue door with the number 661 stencilled on it.

'Is he going to be all right?' she asks.

'I hope so.'

The manager looks at Hana solemnly.

'What kind of animal would do that? When he's better, tell him hi from Dayna at the storage place. He'll remember.'

'I bet he will.'

As Dayna heads back to the office, Hana weighs the key in her hand. Staring at the door. Maybe there'll be nothing of use or interest inside. Or maybe she's about to discover something that forever changes her understanding of the man she shares a child with.

She takes the key. Slides it into the lock.

The roller door slides upwards, the chain and pulley mechanism a bit noisier than Hana expected, in need of a good oil. Even with the door open it's still shadowy inside. It takes a moment for Hana's eyes to adjust. There are piles of boxes, sealed up with masking tape. A couple of clothes racks in one corner; the mountain bike that Hana remembers Jaye talking about, the hobby he'd been threatening to take up to burn off the calories and the stress of the job. It's shop-new, Hana can see, barely ridden, and it certainly hasn't ever had a meaningful encounter with a muddy track. At the rear of the storage unit stands an old dressing table that Hana recognizes as one that five-year-old Vita had wanted to be painted Barbie colours. Jaye had dutifully complied, but a couple of years later Marissa's youngest decided she'd grown out of pink.

Hana has to smile. Jaye's mother was careful with her money, always had been; it was something she'd passed on to her only child. The senior cop just couldn't bring himself to throw away the bright-pink dressing table. Maybe he was saving it for when Marissa's daughters had kids, or when Addison did.

Breaking the masking tape seals, Hana starts working her way through the stacks of boxes. There's no apparent order to the contents. The first ones have Jaye's textbooks and notepads from police college, but in the next one down Hana finds the whites of a cricket uniform and a well-used bat, the pale wood marked with uncountable red distress lines from where the high school version of Jaye had faced tens of thousands of deliveries. Hana remembers him telling her he'd been the star batsman at his school, which didn't mean a lot, as it wasn't one of the posh schools that had money to throw into nurturing winning sports teams. He once took her to an indoor cricket facility, when they'd been dating for a few months. Hana had always been sporty, but the running and jumping and swimming kind of sporty; co-ordination of bat and ball wasn't her thing, and after reluctantly facing a couple of dozen deliveries from Jaye, over half of which bowled her out cleanly – one hitting her and leaving a bruise on her thigh that stayed for the best part of a month – she gave Jaye back his bat and said she needed a coffee. Jaye never suggested indoor cricket again.

Hana keeps going through the boxes. Treating the job methodically, thoroughly, as a cop. Not as someone prying, uninvited, into the things kept safe by someone she once shared her life with.

Opening the last of the boxes, she finds Christmas cards and letters from Jaye's grandparents, who were part of probably the last generation to habitually write letters. As she reseals it, she begins to think that maybe she's not going to find anything of use. And she's okay with that.

More than okay, actually.

The account of the Australian sergeant in Afghanistan wasn't a story DI Williams had needed to tell Hana. The moment she realized Jaye had been deliberately targeted, her mind went straight to the worst possible scenario. That Jaye might be corrupt, and that whatever bad choices he had made, it had all gone terribly wrong. If the instinct both she and Williams shared was completely misplaced, she would be very happy indeed.

Hana restacks the cardboard boxes as she found them. On the clothes rack, she spots Jaye's first police uniform, looking the worse for wear. Laundry was never his strong point. Next to it, there's a little onesie that Hana recognizes as Addison's first pyjama set. A leather jacket that she suspects was never fashionable even when Jaye bought it, and which looks worse now.

Finally, at the back of the storage unit, sitting beside the pink dressing table, a little rocking bassinette. It's the one they'd bought for Addison, but never really used, as their daughter somehow always ended up in bed with them.

Hana looks at the dressing table mirror. A photo collage lines the edge. Pictures of Marissa and her two girls; one of her first husband, the girls' dad, with a big smile on his face as they perch on his broad shoulders, one on each side. The cut-up photos progress through time, the girls getting older. At a certain point the photos of the dad stop, Hana assumes when he passed away, killed in action in the AOS raid he was leading. Then, at the bottom of the collage, photos of Jaye, as he became a part of the little family's life.

Hana understands now why Jaye couldn't take the bright-pink dressing table to the rubbish tip.

There are two sliding drawers. Hana opens the first. It's been cleared of all Marissa's daughters' belongings, but there's something tucked inside – a small, well-worn piece of paper. She picks it up.

It's a Destiny's Child ticket. The first date Hana and Jaye ever went on. It'd taken both of them months to work up the courage to actually make a move. Two cops at Police College, living hand in pocket with all the other cadets, under constant scrutiny from their peers and their tutors. They didn't want to be *that* couple, the one everyone gossiped about. But at the same time, neither of them could deny how they felt.

Then Jaye told her he had two tickets to the concert, coming up with a story that a mate had flaked on him. They danced through the whole thing, and it was fun, but they kept their distance, keeping up the pretence of just being two classmates who both happened to love the same music. Then the final encore started. 'Lose My Breath'. Hana thought, *Fuck it. One of us has to take the bull by the horns.*

Jaye was standing in front of her, and she leaned in, kissed the back of his neck. Not tentative, not a light brush, not something they could shrug off as an accident. Her lips pressed against the soft curls at the base of his hairline. They lingered there, for one beat, then another.

Jaye stopped dancing.

Hana stayed where she was, putting her hands around his waist, her lips pressed against him again.

The stage lights exploded with the final chorus.

In the middle of a maelstrom of sound and light and surging bodies, Jaye rested his head against Hana's.

As Beyoncé sang the last words, they kissed for the first time.

Hana puts the ticket back into the drawer. Slides it closed. She'll have to explain to Jaye later, when he's well, that she intruded into this private corner of his world. She hopes he'll understand.

She pulls the final drawer open, the bottom one. Nothing to be seen. But as she closes it, there's the smallest sound, like something displaced slightly by the movement. She eases the drawer open again. This time she kneels, looking more closely into the shadowy interior. There's a shape, right at the back. Hana reaches in, feeling something cold and metallic. She pulls it out, places the object on the surface of the dressing table.

It's a small gun-metal-grey safe, no bigger than a cash box, with a combination lock.

Between the montage of photos, Hana catches a glimpse of herself in the mirror, her brow furrowed, imagining what might be inside. Rolls of high-denomination cash, handed over in a darkened car park? Details of an anonymous Vanuatu bank account, with an impossibly large balance for someone on a cop's salary? A backdoor retirement fund intended to set up Jaye and Marissa and the girls and Addison for the rest of their days?

In her reflection, Hana's lips are tight and bloodless. She really doesn't want to open this safe.

But she has to.

She tries a few combinations. Jaye's birthday. The PIN

code they used to use for their cash cards. The number for the front door alarm at their first flat. The date Marissa and Jaye were married. None of them work.

Hana tries Addison's birthday.

The lock opens.

Nestled inside the safe is an old-school Nokia. Hana recognizes it as being similar to a model of phone she once had, from 2008 or so. There's a charger too; she'd spotted a power outlet in the storage unit when she was going through the boxes, and she plugs in the phone. It comes to life.

She opens the address book. There are a bunch of phone numbers that mean nothing to her, listed alongside a series of what seem to be comic book nicknames. Dog. Spanner. Harley. Boy. A couple of dozen others. The names mean nothing to Hana either. But an uneasy feeling is steadily growing.

She goes back to the menu, so much less intuitive than a modern smartphone. Finds the photo gallery.

The first image is of Jaye. It's from the same period as the photo Addison keeps beside her bed. He has the long greasy hair, the straggly unkempt beard. Hana realizes the phone is from when Jaye was undercover. Those two years of his life he's never talked about with her, or with anyone else outside the squad he worked with, as per the rules for undercover officers.

She keeps scrolling. There are no pictures of friends or family from his real world, from outside this undercover version of him. Which makes sense. If suspicion fell on Jaye and someone forced him to hand over his phone, he wouldn't have wanted links to his other reality. It also explains the names in the phonebook that Hana doesn't recognize – Jaye's associates from his time deep inside the world of organized crime.

Some photos were taken at night around fires burning in 44-gallon drums, or in rooms filled with bong smoke and empty bottles and drug paraphernalia. There are even selfies, from back in the days when the world was learning what the hell a selfie was. Jaye with various members of the gang he'd worked his way into. Lots of staunch faces. Fists in the air; raised middle fingers.

Hana remembers that soon after Jaye finished his time undercover, he cut his hair and shaved off his beard. But he was still re-entering. One time, he was holding Addison, getting a facecloth wet to wash her face. The water came out too hot, burning him, and he exploded. An angry outburst: *'Jesus motherfucker.'* Addison instantly started to cry, trying to wriggle out of his hands. It took Hana a good half-hour to calm her down, to persuade her that this really was her dad, even though he talked like a stranger she didn't know.

Hana clicks on another photo.

She stares at it. Unable to breathe for a moment.

She tries to pinch-zoom in on the other face in the photo, the person next to Jaye. To assure herself it really is who she thinks it is. But the Nokia was made a few years before touchscreens were invented and the screen can't zoom.

She steadies her hand. Looks closer. Finally takes a deep breath.

There's no mistaking it. Hana is sure now. She knows exactly who the person is with Jaye in the photo on the Nokia.

This changes everything.

22

KNOW THYSELF

He could have been an architect, say, or a forensic scientist, a business entrepreneur. Perhaps a celebrated journalist. If he'd been a lawyer, he would surely have joined a prestigious firm, and made his way up the ranks towards partnership. If he'd chosen the route of medicine, after graduating top of his cohort he would have charted a course towards becoming a specialist in ophthalmology.

When it comes to their eyes, people will pay anything.

You can name your price.

He read once that in ancient Delphi, the words 'Know Thyself' were inscribed in tall gold letters above the gateway to the Temple of Apollo. Sending the rugby league player plummeting from the cliffs of South Head was, for him, the moment of insight. The feelings he could barely contain as he counted *three apricot, four apricot* and the guy with the battered knees smashed into the rocks far below. The rush of visceral exhilaration told him all he needed to know about who he was. Who he would always be.

After that, he knew himself.

After that, he knew where he belonged.

A sunless place where he could move freely and unseen. A world where, like a flowering bloom that thrives by some kind of nature-defying reverse photosynthesis, he would blossom in the shadows.

The world of crime.

After Sydney, he worked hard to carefully curate his identity. An actor pulling on a costume to seamlessly inhabit the part. The look, the clothes, the tattoos. How to talk; how to be. Just as he'd closely watched the behaviours of his hormone-driven high school cohort to learn how to flirt with the girl with the braces, now he studied how he needed to be to survive and prosper in this new world he'd chosen.

And he learned the language. The dialect of aggression. The vocabulary of violence.

How to stare down all those who come up against you; how to intimidate; how to menace. The set of the eyes. The thrust of the hips and the chest. The tone of the voice. Every inch of the body saying loudly and unequivocally: *In this world of dog-eat-dog, I am the apex predator*. And when that doesn't work, then it's plan B. The only other plan that exists for the dwellers of this shadowland. You take whatever weapon is at hand, and you come at the other guy twice as hard and twice as fast as he is coming at you.

In this terrain he'd entered, blood gets spilled. He learned to make sure that the biggest pool of red was never his.

With the skill sets he was fast honing, he quickly caught the attention of a number of groups in the netherworld of crime and shadows. His reputation grew. He found his way into an organization hungry for his particular talents. He climbed the ranks.

But in truth, all this was no more than a way for him to hide in plain sight while he kept playing the game he liked to play. The only game that would ever rouse him; send the rush of blood to his loins. Play smart, and you'll keep playing for the rest of your life.

And he did keep playing.

The league player in Sydney was the first. There were others. Many others. The thrill never faded. The opposite. Each time he learned to savour the moment more.

But in the pursuit of pleasure, you had to be sparing and judicious, he knew this. Like with ice cream. You can have too much of a good thing. You can get greedy; you can get careless. You slip up. You get noticed.

Then along comes a chopper to chop off your head.

It was like the signs they had for campers in the national parks. *Leave only footprints behind.* Except, as opposed to those signs, he knew not to leave even footprints behind.

He was in the place he was born to be. He had found his home. It was all going so well.

Then Maffs turned up.

Maffs turned up and the role he'd seamlessly crafted for himself, the existence he'd curated as the apex predator moving among the shadows . . .

Maffs took a big rock and whacked the whole thing in the back of the head.

His world was shoved off a cliff.

Just like what he did to the guy at South Head.

Only this time, Maffs did it, to him.

Fucking Maffs.

23

DOMINOES

On the eighth floor of Central Police Station, DI Williams is deep in conversation with one of her detectives. It's been three days since Addison and Stan knocked on the door of the small house in earshot of the railway crossing bells, and there have still been no confirmed sightings of Toa Davis. The house he shared with Gracie has been staked out continuously; his family and known associates are being monitored.

Even though Williams shares Hana's belief that Toa may not be the gunman, that hasn't changed the urgent need to find him. If someone else shot Jaye, deliberately framing Toa, then he might have some idea of who that person could be. And as long as he remains at large, with no other suspects, there's the risk of a deadly standoff if he is spotted and feels he has nothing to lose.

'He can't just disappear off the face of the planet,' Williams says.

The detective doesn't respond, and really, there's nothing to answer; it's a plain statement of fact. The sole suspect in the shooting of a senior police officer has, impossibly, evaporated.

Williams takes a moment, rubbing her eyes. They feel like sandpaper. She hasn't slept more than an hour or two since the shooting, run ragged by juggling daily media conferences, growing pressure from senior management to find the shooter and endless necessary meetings with her senior staff and the multiple detective teams, uniformed officers and technicians. And that morning, something strange and potentially disturbing. A food delivery service dropped off a meal to her home address, a takeaway order she hadn't placed. It was slow roasted duck and savoury pancakes.

The speciality of the house at Moon Lake Bistro and Lounge.

There was no note attached, not even a hint of a threat, nothing that could feasibly lead to charges of intimidation against a police officer. But there didn't need to be. The message was clear. Walking into Gold Brother's restaurant had ruffled feathers, and someone at Moon Lake, likely Hàoyǔ, was letting Williams know her stunt hadn't been forgotten. Williams isn't alarmed, particularly; she's physically incapable of being intimidated – it's not in her genetic make-up – and she's come up against far worse and more overt threats in both her current and former jobs. For a moment she even considered sending the meal back with a complaint that the duck was overcooked, to let Hàoyŭ know she wasn't daunted. But she thought better of it.

More petty than staunch, she decided.

And actually, the duck was delicious.

'Boss.'

Williams looks up to see Hana approaching from the elevators. As she hurries through the maze of desks that has taken over the eighth floor while more and more officers join the enquiry into Jaye's shooting, Williams can see the look on the ex-cop's face.

'Hana?'

'I need to show you something.'

'Finding that photo. At first I thought what was on the phone might lead back to Moon Lake. But when I saw him – next to Jaye. All the dominoes started falling.'

Standing in her office, Williams looks down at the Nokia. In the photo Hana is showing her, Jaye holds the camera up, selfie-style, his hair long and scruffy; his undercover persona. His other arm is slung around a man wearing motorcycle leathers, the patches recognizable as belonging to a major national biker operation from the late 2000s. The guy has one hand out towards the camera, index and pinkie fingers raised.

Devil's horns.

In the storage unit, Hana instantly recognized the man. She knows him. She knows him better than she wants to.

It's Erwin Rendall.

The bully-boy gang leader she's had run-ins with in Tātā Bay. The guy who set up shop in a small town near her father's and has spent the time since then intimidating the locals. The standover guy who recruited Hana's nephew Tīmoti, the son of her cousin Eyes. Who trained him up in car theft and burglary.

Looking at the image of Rendall on the phone, Hana remembered the look on his face when she'd walked into his gang-pad, side by side with Eyes, and grabbed her nephew Tīmoti, dragging him away from the life of crime he had been seduced into with the promise of easy money and notoriety. As Hana and Eyes had taken Tīmoti away, Rendall had looked at her.

'Watch your back, Sheriff. 'Cos I sure will be.'

Then, Hana remembered something else.

After she'd first encountered Rendall in Tātā Bay and heard about the things he was doing, she'd asked Stan to run a check on his record to find out how serious the guy was. Stan had come back with an answer.

Erwin Rendall had spent nine years in Waikeria Prison, convicted and put away as the result of a complex long-term undercover operation in the late 2000s.

The photo suddenly made complete sense. Everything did.

Jaye was the man who'd put Erwin Rendall in prison for nine long years.

Rendall had been released a couple of years ago.

And now someone had pointed a gun at Jaye and put a bullet in his chest, and another in his head.

It couldn't be a coincidence.

'I think Rendall saw Jaye,' Hana tells Williams. 'I think their paths crossed when Jaye was in Tātā Bay.'

Six months before the shooting, an investigation into the discovery of a murdered body in the sand dunes led to Jaye spending many days in Hana's hometown. Erwin Rendall's gang-pad, a cheap former panel beating factory, is in a town not thirty miles away.

'I believe Rendall recognized the undercover cop who'd put him away. He decided it was time for payback. But he did what he always does. He found a way to set up someone else to take the fall. Rendall puts a bullet in Jaye's head. And Toa Davis gets the blame. We find the weapon that Rendall used, we've got him.'

'It smells right. It feels right. But it's not enough,' Williams says. 'Before I can get a warrant to bring him in and search his place for the gun, I need more.'

Hana knows it's true.

They need more.

'Can I have a look at your tā moko?' Hana asks Tīmoti.

A small group are gathered in the parking area outside a little tā moko studio in Mangere Bridge, a picturesque little suburb on the water, ten kilometres south of

Auckland central: the dividing line between the inner city and the sprawling suburbs of South Auckland. Tīmoti and his mum, Eyes, and dad, Matai, have been at the studio for the last two days, surrounded by the smell of calming kawakawa oil from a bubbling diffuser. They have begun every morning with karakia, before the tattoo gun begins its relentless buzzing and continues for the next six to eight hours, as Tīmoti has his first tā moko done.

Until six months ago, Tīmoti was a prospect with Erwin Rendall's gang. If anyone might be able to connect the dots between Rendall and Jaye's shooting, it could be him.

'Do you mind?' Hana asks, as Tīmoti leans against his dad's car. 'Might inspire me to get my own tā moko done.'

The conversation is going to be painful. It's a time in Tīmoti's life he's not proud of. Hana wants to at least try to make him feel a little at ease before the questions get difficult.

'It's only half-finished. Wait till it's done,' Tīmoti says. 'Besides. I'm not gonna take my T-shirt off out here in public. Don't wanna scare the locals, Auntie.'

Hana is glad to see the shy grin on her nephew's face. When Tīmoti was with Rendall and his gang, there was never a smile for Hana, no calling her 'Auntie'. Just dark looks and attitude. Away from Rendall's world, Tīmoti is finding his way back to being the amiable, smiley young man she remembers.

Tīmoti has been getting ready for the tā moko process for weeks, eating the right foods, cleansing. He's given up alcohol and marijuana since his mum and auntie walked into the middle of Erwin Rendall's gang-pad and dragged him away, then sent him to live with his dad in Auckland, far from the gang's reach. At first Tīmoti pushed back when Matai laid out the new boundaries. But now he's not missing the weed and the cheap alcohol as much. He's running with his dad, doing waka ama – traditional Māori outrigger-canoe racing. He's getting fit. Clear-eyed. And equally clear-eyed that this is where he wants to be. With the people who actually love him, as opposed to Rendall and the other gang members, who saw him as an asset; someone useful to nick cars and to sell weed. And to be the fall-guy if it all went wrong.

'I'm so sorry about what happened to your ex,' Eyes says to Hana. 'I really hope he pulls through okay. And that they find the guy soon.'

'Thank you,' Hana replies. She is touched by the words, which are full of concern and sincerity, despite the fact that Eyes and her son only met Jaye for the first time at Tīmoti's driving test. Hana's choice of a career in the police caused a rift between the cousins that is only now beginning to heal.

'You said you needed to ask Tīmoti some questions,' Eyes continues. 'What's up?'

Hana looks towards Williams and takes a step backwards, handing over to her.

'Last year, the human remains that were found in the sand dunes at Tātā Bay . . .' Williams says. 'I'm sure you remember.'

'The dead girl. Yeah, of course I remember.'

'Hana told me you were with a local gang at the time. Hanging out with them. Maybe working with them. Have I got that right?'

An unconscious flinch crosses Tīmoti's face.

'We're not here because of anything you did back then. We just need to ask a few questions,' Williams assures him.

Tīmoti looks at his mum and dad.

'It's okay, love,' Eyes says to him in te reo. 'You have nothing to be ashamed of. You left all that behind, son. You can answer the questions.'

'Yeah. I was with them,' Tīmoti says finally, his eyes on the concrete pavement.

'What did you do, while you were part of the gang?'

'I dunno. This and that.' It's barely audible, a mumble. Williams knows why Tīmoti is treading so carefully.

'I'm sure you broke a few laws. Maybe quite a few. Whatever you tell me now, it's not going to result in anything bad against you. You won't be arrested or charged. You have my word.'

'You have my word too, Tīmoti,' Hana says.

Tīmoti nods. Okay then.

'I drove for him. He liked to sit in the back of that big Zephyr of his. Like he was fucking King Rendall. And he got me to do stuff. We'd break into places. Burgs.* He was always on the lookout for cars to steal, to sell the parts. There was one guy who was good at the hot-wiring, he'd get the car going. Then I'd drive it back to the pad and the blow-torch guys would take it apart.'

'Do you remember, around that time, there was a big meeting at the marae?' Williams asks.

Hana had told Williams about the public meeting that happened a few days after the victim was discovered in the dunes, with maybe a hundred or so locals in attendance. Jaye was there with the other senior detective running the investigation. Hana had been there too, and she knew that Rendall hadn't been, but that Jaye had stayed around the marae for an hour or so afterwards, answering questions. That could have been when Rendall saw and recognized him.

'Yeah. I remember. We were driving past. Rendall saw all the cars in the car park, everyone inside the whare.† He told me to pull up outside, on the road.'

'Why?'

Tīmoti shuffles. He scuffs the toe of his shoe against the concrete.

'While everyone was inside, he got me and another guy to go through the cars. We nicked wallets and phones. Whatever we could find. There wasn't much. You know Tātā Bay. Not like anyone has ten cents to spare.'

---

* Burgs – burglaries.
† Whare – house (in this case, the meeting house).

'Rendall was in the car the whole time?' Williams asks. 'He never went into the meeting?'

'He stayed in the Zephyr. Then the meeting finished, people came out and started driving away. We hung around a bit and left.'

'Anything else you remember?' Williams speaks cautiously, not wanting to ask leading questions or put words in Tīmoti's mouth.

'Like what?' Tīmoti frowns, not sure what's being asked.

'Baby, your shirt,' Eyes says.

Spots of blood are showing through Tīmoti's white T-shirt at the shoulder, from the most recent tattooing. Eyes takes a tissue from her bag, lifts the fabric, dabs away blood.

'Mum,' Tīmoti says, embarrassed at being looked after in such a public way. For a moment Hana can see the elaborate lines of the tattooing on his shoulder. It's beautiful work.

'If there's anything else you can remember, Tīmoti. It could make a difference,' Williams says.

'It was like six months ago. I was drinking back then. Smoking dak. It's all a bit blurry.'

'Take your time,' Hana says. 'No rush.'

Tīmoti frowns. Thinking back. A look comes to his face.

'There was maybe something. When we got back to the Zephyr, Rendall was a bit pissed off. We'd found a couple of things in people's cars, maybe twenty bucks and a six-pack of beer. Not much of a haul. We were pulling away when he told me to stop.'

'Why?'

'I think he was watching the people coming out of the meeting.'

'Did you see who he was looking at?' Williams asks.

'I guess the cops. They were standing on the steps of the whare, talking to people. I thought, they're cops, we just broke into people's cars, why hang around with these fellas, let's gap it. But you don't tell Rendall what to do. We just sat there.'

'How did you know they were cops?'

'The woman and the man were in suits. The fella was even wearing a tie. Only undertakers or cops wear suits,' Tīmoti says with a grin. 'In Tātā Bay, anyways.'

'What happened then?' Williams asks.

'We sat there for, I dunno, a couple of minutes. Then he told me to get the fuck out of there. He was in the shittiest mood. I guess 'cos we'd only got the twenty bucks and a few beers. Back home his dog got under his feet. That ugly mongrel's the only creature Rendall ever had a soft spot for, closest thing he had to a friend. He gave it a real hard kick, and the dog ran off howling. It was limping for weeks.'

A look between Hana and Williams. Now they have confirmation. There had only been two police officers at the meeting. The female detective leading the enquiry. And Jaye. Erwin Rendall had seen him. Almost definitely recognized him, from fifteen years earlier, the realization making Rendall so furious he'd taken out his anger on his favourite dog.

'Thank you,' Williams says.

'No worries,' Tīmoti replies, still a bit perplexed, wondering what all this is about. He looks at Hana, wanting to change the subject.

'You really thinking about getting tā moko, Auntie?'

'Addison and I have talked about it. Getting something matching, something about whakapapa.* Like what you and your mum and dad have.'

'Since you asked, Auntie. Have a look.'

He pulls off his T-shirt.

Hana looks at the reddened skin from the newly inscribed tā moko. The lines of the pattern run around the joint of his shoulder, down his bicep a little way and up to the base of his neck. It's intricate: curved, unfilled koru shapes, like the curling fern fronds from the forests, and infilled, highly detailed designs running between the koru swirls – trails of intricate parallel lines, a bit like train tracks, or undulating paths over a forest floor, except the lines curve and follow the contours of Tīmoti's body.

'It's beautiful,' Hana says.

'The pattern is moko kiore. Same as Mum and Dad's.'

Hana recognizes the word. In te reo Māori, *kiore* means *rat*.

'The tā moko artist explained – for us Māori, rats aren't nasty, ugly things. They're smart as hell. They

---

* Whakapapa – ancestry, lines of descent.

figured out how to sneak onboard our canoes and stay hidden when we first came across the oceans to New Zealand. They're tricksters, man. They can get themselves out of the shittiest situations. If he's holed up under a tree, being chased by another animal, a rat will dig a trench. Just like this,' Tīmoti says, tracing his finger along one of the curving, trail-like tracks of the tattoo. And now Hana can see that the pattern is indeed like the shape of a trench.

On the footpath outside the tā moko studio, a pair of older women, Pacific Islanders, are passing by, pulling wheeled shopping bags. They raise their eyebrows at the young Māori guy with the bare chest. Tīmoti strikes a cheeky pose, a big smile on his face, like a bodybuilder in a competition.

'You can look, ladies, but you can't touch.'

The older women shoot a disapproving look at him, but as they walk on both of them giggle behind their hands.

As Tīmoti pulls his T-shirt back on, Hana puts a hand on her nephew's arm.

'You should be so proud, Tīmoti. Not just the tā moko. Everything. It's not easy to start over. You've done it.'

'I'm happy. This is how I wanna be.'

'I need you to be brave again,' Hana says, knowing that DI Williams has another question to ask.

'Dunno what else I can tell you.'

Williams takes a manilla envelope from her bag. 'I

need you to look at something.' She takes out a printed screen grab from the CCTV footage from inside the liquor shop. It's a blown-up image of the raised gun, from the moment before the trigger was pulled, and Jaye was shot in the head.

'Have you ever seen this weapon?' Williams asks.

The moment he looks at the gun in the photo, Hana sees a flash of recognition in Tīmoti's face. But he hesitates. Hana knows at once what's going through his mind: he has dragged himself free of Rendall's orbit, but that doesn't mean he's free of fear when it comes to the repercussions of narking. Tīmoti looks at his parents. His dad Matai hasn't said a thing this whole time. He still doesn't speak. He holds his son's eye. And he nods; an unspoken assurance, telling Tīmoti he has to do what's right.

The young man stands a little taller, lifts his chin a little higher.

'Yeah. I've seen a gun like that,' Tīmoti says, handing the photo back.

'Where?' Williams asks.

Tīmoti's hand goes, unconsciously, to his shoulder. His tā moko. The lines carved into his skin, his whakapapa, the connections between him and the generations of ancestors whose blood has been handed down and now runs in his veins.

'In Erwin Rendall's room. He keeps it under his bed.'

24

THE DAY BEFORE

On a screen on the eighth floor of Central Police Station, a floor-plan displays the layout of the sprawling warehouse belonging to Erwin Rendall's gang.

'The fence encircles the entire perimeter of the property. It's corrugated iron, from memory I'd say two, two and a half metres high. Barbed wire on the top.'

Hana stands near the screen, using a laser pointer to pick out areas of interest. As well as DI Williams, there are more than three dozen officers in the room, making notes as she talks, taking photos of the projected diagram. The floor-plan has been put together from the original site plans from when the place was a panel beating workshop, before it went bust and Rendall bought it for next to nothing to set up a very different operation.

'There's only the one gate in and out. I remember CCTV cameras on either side. I can't swear to it, but I think there are other cameras around the perimeter.'

Motorcycle gang-pads pretty much have a universal look, born of a common purpose and function. They are modern-day bastions, purpose-built to keep unwanted arrivals out, be they rival gang members or local hoods looking for stashes of narcotics or cash. Or cops. Fortified on all sides, the idea is to stop the enemy, or at least slow them down enough to give those inside enough time to get organized.

Enough time to get armed.

On the overhead projector, Hana marks out a pathway with the green laser pointer.

'The front roller door is probably five metres high, the same wide. There's a smaller access door to the right of it. If that's where you breach, as soon as you come through there's a big workshop area. It was full of vehicles, bikes. Bit of a rabbit warren. Lots of places for people to hide. Then there's a long narrow corridor, which takes you through the heart of the building. I remember seeing three or four sleeping areas coming off the corridor on either side.'

Hana's working from memory, from when she and Eyes walked in through the front gates, right into the heart of the gang, despite knowing they'd be outnumbered at least six to one.

That hadn't stopped them.

Clustered in the large room, the officers sit in small

groups, depending on their roles for the following day. With strong reason to expect that there will be a weapon or multiple weapons in the compound, the Armed Offenders Squad will lead the raid on the building and handle the arrest of the suspect. Once any occupants are detained, the CIB investigation team will begin the search for the suspected murder weapon. Finally, a group of uniformed police, also armed, will secure the gang-pad and the arrest location.

Hana continues her walk-through. 'The corridor takes you right to the rear of the building, where there are cooking facilities, a bar slash hang-out room, a pool table. That's as far as I've been.'

She hands the laser pointer to Williams, who uses it to pick out a series of rooms behind the area Hana pointed out, beyond the living spaces; the layout of the complex that Tīmoti described for them the day before.

'We understand there are a further series of rooms, storage areas and bathrooms back here. Erwin Rendall's room is to the very rear. That's where we believe the weapon that shot DI Hamilton may be.'

She projects the image of the gun used in the hold-up.

'As you all know, we're looking for a cut-down Alfa Carbine. We've had further information of a particular modification that will identify the specific gun we are looking for. A series of small carved notches on the butt of the firearm.'

The day before, outside the tā moko studio, Tīmoti

recalled noticing a pattern of cuts in the wooden butt of the weapon he'd seen Rendall with. 'Like he'd made neat little cuts with a knife or something,' he said. 'I think there were maybe five of them.'

In the footage from the liquor store, the handle of the gun couldn't be seen from any angle, even when it was digitally enhanced, meaning it was impossible to verify that the gun Timoti had seen was the one used in the hold-up. But if they find the gun in the gang-pad and forensically match it to the bullets that were used to shoot Jaye, they'll have what they need to put Rendall away.

Williams flicks off the projection screen. She turns to Hana.

'Thank you.'

The words are warm and genuine; everyone in the room knows that without Hana's breakthrough with the red light camera footage and her discovery of the Nokia, her connection to Timoti and the resulting inside knowledge of the gang, none of this would be happening. But this 'Thank you' is also a polite message: it's time for Hana to go. She has no further role in what is about to unfold.

Many of the cops know Hana personally, and there are handshakes and hugs as Williams walks her to the elevator.

'I'm glad what you found in that storage unit led to Erwin Rendall. And I'm glad Jaye is the man we both believe him to be.'

'Me too.'

As the elevator doors open, ordinarily it would be a brief handshake. But Williams hugs Hana, kisses her on the cheek. There's no shortage of warmth and respect between these two women.

Hana watches as Williams heads back to the briefing.

She steps into the elevator. The doors close behind her.

In the distance, the clang-clang-clang of crossing bells.

Hana walks down the cul-de-sac towards the house with the towering power pylon jutting skyward from the back yard. The plainclothes police vehicles that were stationed outside Gracie's house are gone; after Tīmoti's information confirmed Rendall as the likely shooter, the cops' urgency to find Toa disappeared. She crosses the road as the sound of the early evening commuter train passes in the distance. The front door opens before she has time to knock. In the doorway, Gracie looks tired and anxious.

'Has something happened? Is Toa okay?'

'He hasn't been found yet,' Hana tells her. 'They're still looking.'

For Gracie, every day could bring news that Toa has been located; maybe confronted by armed cops, maybe in a stand-off that has gone horribly wrong. The fact that this isn't the reason Hana is here is good news, at least. But Hana knows Gracie would much rather be told that the father of her unborn child has been found and that he's okay.

'I know you hate me,' she says. 'If I were you, I'd feel the same. I just wanted to drop this off for you. Can I put it inside?'

For the first time, Gracie registers what's in Hana's arms. It's the bassinette that Jaye kept in the storage unit, full of items from a little shopping spree Hana did that morning at a baby apparel shop: blankets, onesies, warm clothes and jackets.

Gracie steps back, silent, holding the door open. Hana hefts the bassinette, places it on a couch near the window.

'This was my daughter's. She barely used it though. And I bought a few different sizes of clothes for your baby. Should last her the first six months.'

Staring at the bassinette, Gracie's customary defensiveness shifts. She looks up from the things Hana has brought for her child, then towards the window and out onto the empty street.

'The cop cars left yesterday. Just went. I didn't know what that meant. I thought maybe you'd arrested him. Or he'd been hurt or something, and no one gave a shit about telling me.'

'Gracie, I have to let you know something. If Toa contacts you, you need to tell him things have changed.'

Gracie looks back at Hana. 'What do you mean?'

'When I talked to you last, I wasn't sure you were telling us the truth.'

The young woman's eyes narrow. 'You didn't believe a thing I was saying.'

'That's fair.'

'What's changed?'

Hana meets her gaze straight on. 'I can't speak for the cops. But for me, I'm certain it wasn't Toa who was in the liquor store.'

Gracie goes to the couch, sinks down beside the bassinette. Hana can see she's fighting the urge to sit there and cry at the relief she's feeling.

'My mum's coming down with my uncle's van, at the weekend. She wants me back. She wants me to have the baby at home. I want to go. I wanna be back there. But I just . . .'

Her hand goes unconsciously to her abdomen. 'I don't want this house to be empty. When he comes back.' She tails off, staring at the floor.

'If you hear from him,' Hana says, 'or if anyone you know hears from him, tell him what I told you. He has nothing to be afraid of now. He needs to talk to DI Williams. Or he can call me, if that feels better.'

Hana writes her phone number on a paper bag that holds a little pair of woollen baby booties.

'There's this house on my uncle's farm,' Gracie says quietly. 'Nothing flash, just four walls. Used to be for shearers to stay in, when they had sheep. Uncle told us we could come and stay, any time. Toa and me talked about painting the place, a nice light colour. I heard babies only really see light and dark for ages after they're born. We want to make the world bright for Arihia. Full of light.'

Hana reaches out. Puts her arms around the young woman.

Gracie lets herself be hugged.

Hana can feel the change in atmosphere in Jaye's room even before she comes in the door.

Looking through the window from the hospital corridor, she sees Vita, Sammie, Addison and Marissa sitting on either side of Jaye's hospital bed. They're playing Go Fish, the playing cards spread out on the blanket, his legs providing a slightly uneven playing table. Hana can hear music playing. Previously it was low key, soothing, healing. But now it's bright, cheery, sugary pop; music Hana supposes must be on either Sammie's or Vita's playlists. There are bags of chocolates and liquorice allsorts scattered around, which the younger siblings are devouring as they play cards. As Hana comes in the door, Addison is straight to her feet, throwing her arms around her mum.

'Dad's coming back!'

'Sorry?'

As Addison hugs Hana, Sammie joins in, wrapping herself around both of them. Vita watches, always more reserved and contained than her big sister. Sitting near the head of the bed, Marissa beams.

'The head of the medical team says the tests are much better than they'd hoped,' she says. 'There's minimal swelling, the pressure in his brain has reduced. She thinks Jaye's ready to be brought out of the coma.'

'When?' Hana asks, kissing Addison on the top of her head, understanding now the shift in vibe in the room.

'Tomorrow afternoon, Mum.'

It's the best news possible, of course, and Hana is every bit as delighted as everyone else in the room. And the fortuitous coincidence of the timing doesn't escape her. The day Jaye is going to be brought back from deep sedation is the same day the man she believes shot him is going to be detained for questioning.

As the remaining chocolates and sweets are consumed and the next bubblegum-pop playlist starts playing, Hana excuses herself. Marissa walks with her out into the corridor, closing the door behind them.

'The key,' Marissa says. 'Did it help?'

'Yes. It helped.' It's an understatement, Hana knows. 'It really helped.'

She waits as an orderly approaches, pushing a patient in a wheelchair.

'You asked me not to tell you anything more,' she says, carefully, as the wheelchair disappears down the corridor. 'But you should know. There's nothing in that storage unit that will make you feel any less for Jaye. The opposite.'

Marissa lets out a sigh, a heavy weight lifted.

'A day of good news, eh.'

'Uh-huh. A day of good news.'

Hana heads down the corridor. As she approaches the elevator, she hears footsteps behind her.

'Almost forgot,' Addison calls, hurrying to catch up. She is holding a colourful $2-shop My Little Pony backpack that Hana noticed sitting next to Jaye's bed. 'For the nanny you were talking about. In Tātā Bay.'

Hana's eyes instantly look up from the child's backpack she now knows is full of marijuana, scanning the ceiling. She spots the distinctive dark glass dome of a security camera.

'You could be a bit more discreet.'

'People will just think you're a middle-aged woman with really shitty taste in accessories.'

'Middle-aged?'

Addison dissolves into giggles.

'What?' Hana says with a smile, enjoying the sight of her daughter's happiness.

'You! You're more concerned about me pointing out your age than you are about doing a drug deal in a hospital corridor.'

'Jesus, Addison. Keep your voice down!'

Hana tries her very best to be stern, but it's a losing battle. After the stress and fears of the last few days, she can't stop herself from laughing along with her daughter.

'What do I owe you?'

'I got the weed cost price. Our supplier is Māori. I

told her about the nanny. She hated the idea of the old girl suffering,' Addison says, getting her laughter under control. 'We can sort out the details later. Probably not a good idea to exchange money on camera.'

Addison presses the bag into Hana's hands. She smiles again.

'Sheesh, Mum.'

'What?'

'You. You believe in the rules, until you don't. Who'd have guessed?'

She kisses Hana and turns to head back to Jaye's room.

'Love you, Māmā. Don't get pulled over.'

K Road runs almost directly east–west along the top of a ridge that looks down over the high-rise buildings of central Auckland. The sun is setting behind Hana's shoulder as she makes her way past the cafés and bars and hole-in-the-wall restaurants, noisy music coming from one of the last strip clubs left on what used to be Auckland's sex-for-sale mile. Looking at the passing K Road crowd – glowing faces, most of them marked by piercings and tatts, none of them lined by the passing of time – Hana feels suddenly out of place in a way she maybe wouldn't have an hour earlier, before her daughter described her as 'middle-aged'.

She pauses, googling the actual definition. She's

quietly relieved to find she has more than half a decade to go.

She catches a glimpse of herself in the window of the convenience store she's standing outside. It was a good feeling in the corridor of the hospital, giggling like a teen with her daughter. A feeling she hasn't had for a while. Not carefree, exactly. Just, feeling in her own skin.

Alive.

As Hana carries on down K Road, the sun sinks lower behind her. It's been strange, being heavily involved in a case again, making the frustrating little inches of progress, then the exhilarating leap of a breakthrough. And stranger still: going so far with the case, then knowing she won't be there tomorrow, strapping on tactical gear, issuing weapons, giving the statutory declaration about the conditions that justify the use of lethal force.

That's not my world anymore, Hana thinks.

Live with it.

It was also confronting, being in the house beneath the towering power pylon, feeling the pain of the young pregnant girl who just wants to know where her boyfriend is at the moment she needs him most. Williams and Hana have agreed: after Rendall is arrested, if Toa Davis is still running scared, Williams will release a statement officially announcing he's no longer a suspect in the shooting. But she can't do it before charges are laid, for fear of giving Rendall prior warning.

Hana continues down the street, passing the fish taco restaurant.

Then there was a much more welcome feeling, an hour or so earlier. Being in that room full of bouncy music and so much joy. The relief she had felt. Jaye is a good man, a man she will always be connected to because of their daughter, because of the deep ties they still share and always will, long after they stopped sharing a bed. Even so, it isn't her place to be there in the room when Jaye's eyes open.

The street lights are flickering to life. Ahead, beside the wholefoods café, now closed for the day, stands an unmarked doorway. Hana knocks on the door. Waits a few beats, then knocks again.

'Yeah?' says Sebastian, leaning out of the upstairs window of his office slash flat. It takes him a moment to register who is at his door. 'Oh. Hi.'

'Hi,' Hana says, suddenly feeling way more awkward than she'd expected.

'Stay there.' Sebastian closes the window.

As Hana waits on the footpath, she thinks again of her dad and Daisy. The things Hana has been struggling with; her father being with a woman who isn't her mum. But then seeing them so happy together. It's been a revelation to her – the extraordinary commitment Eru and Daisy have made to each other. Two people who know the road ahead will be difficult. That one day it will get painful, then maybe it will become downright awful. But both of them so certain of how they feel, and so united in facing whatever comes.

Two people taking the plunge into the unknown. Together.

Hana hears Sebastian's footsteps coming down the stairs. The door opens.

'Hi,' he says again.

It was almost an impulse, parking her car, heading down K Road, knowing where she was going but with no idea what was going to happen when she got to Sebastian's door. And maybe that was a good thing.

'I came to say, I screwed up. The stuff I said. That it was the wrong time for us to start this relationship. That I made choices because I was sad and vulnerable. It was all just bullshit.'

Hana pauses. Surprising herself by the choice of words, the speed with which she's got to the point. But there's no turning back now.

'It was me not having the courage to embrace what I feel. And what I think you feel too. I was being a coward. I'm a fuck-up and I'm sorry.'

To Hana's surprise, a smile comes to Sebastian's face.

'That's tasteful,' he says.

She follows his eyes to the My Little Pony backpack she's gripping tightly.

'I didn't want to leave it unattended in my car.'

'What's inside?'

'It's a long story.'

'Okay.'

Hana looks back the way she came. The sun has set now, leaving only distant orange streaks in the western skies, just visible above the buildings of K Road.

'I'm gonna go now.' She turns to walk away.

'Hana.'

There's a look on Sebastian's face as she turns back, and she isn't completely sure if it's discomfort, or lingering anger, or amusement.

'My grandparents told me this thing,' he says, walking towards her. 'When a tiler works on a new roof for a Korean family, they're meticulous. The way the tiles are laid, the pattern, the amount of overlap. It's an art form. The roofs are beautiful. But once the roof is finished, the tiler chooses one tile. They climb back up and they smash it. And that's the way it stays. You know why?'

'I have no idea.'

'Because only God is perfect. The rest of us are fuck-ups. Also known as human beings.'

Sebastian smiles.

'Have you eaten?' he asks.

'No.'

'Hungry?'

'Starving.'

'Fish tacos?' Sebastian asks, locking the door behind him.

'Yeah.' Hana smiles back at him. 'That would be nice.'

25

THUNDERSTRUCK

The weather can change fast in Auckland.

The severe thunderstorm warning is issued in the late morning. For a few days an ominous low-pressure zone has been steadily zeroing in on the upper part of the island from across the Tasman Sea. On land, unseasonably warm northeasterly winds have been rising all morning, whipping up whitecaps in the harbour. It's the meteorological equivalent of getting a city-sized chemical beaker and filling it with nitric acid and glycerine. The warm surface air collides with the freezing temperatures of the upper levels. The barometric pressure goes berserk. In minutes the skies darken from a pale winter blue to pitch black tinged with a scary, almost otherworldly green.

The temperatures plummet.

Then the first of the marble-sized hailstones start to fall.

'He's groggy. Disoriented. We took the respirator tube out an hour ago, and he can talk, but that doesn't mean he's going to want to. Patients say it feels like someone's been using a sandblaster on the inside of your throat.'

Addison and Marissa are with the head of the medical team, outside the ICU. The process of bringing a patient out of a medically induced coma is slow and complex. The mix of anaesthetics and muscle relaxants and pain suppressants is gradually lowered. At a certain point the patient starts to respond physically: a twitch of a hand, or the beginnings of movement behind the eyelids. Over the following several hours, sometimes days, as they are brought back to consciousness, the medical team reduce the work the ventilator is doing, and the patient starts to breathe for themselves. The final, deeply unpleasant step in this process is when they are asked to cough as hard as they can while the medical team extracts the endotracheal tube. That's the moment of truth, when the person starts breathing completely on their own. Or doesn't.

'He's breathing unassisted,' the head of the medical team tells them. 'Except for the help of an oxygen mask. It went really well.'

The family had been told that they really wouldn't

want to be in the room through the process. It can get ugly, some patients coming back to consciousness bewildered and disoriented, sometimes trying to grab at the tube in their throat, even lashing out when they're stopped from touching it. Knowing it might be a long wait, Marissa arranged for the girls to stay with friends.

'When can we see him?' Addison asks.

'How about right now?'

They're given gowns and face masks, and follow the head of the medical team into the ICU. Jaye sees them the moment they walk in the door. Even though the tube is out, he's still surrounded by paraphernalia: heart rate and oxygen and blood pressure monitors; an IV drip standing sentinel beside the bed.

Jaye's eyes are surprisingly bright as they approach, but from behind the oxygen mask his voice is like barbed wire being dragged through gravel.

'I don't know what happened. I don't understand.'

Outside, the first hailstones are starting to fall in the car park, visitors and staff members sprinting to avoid being hit by the icy shrapnel.

By the bed, Marissa strokes Jaye's hair, looking down at him.

'I'd forgotten your eyes are so blue. How can anything be that blue?'

Addison holds his hand in hers.

'It's okay, Dad. It's all okay now.'

The blue Mark III Zephyr is going way too fast as it drives through the narrow, winding forest road. The storm's been threatening for a while now, and Rendall wants to get back to Kaikākāriki Junction before all hell breaks loose.

Earlier that day he made a call about a Jeep Wrangler he'd seen advertised. Classic car, 1997, olive-green with a tan roof. Only 55,000 kms on the clock; never been driven off-road. *Probably never even been put into 4WD,* Rendall thinks. *Why buy an all-terrain car modelled on a US army vehicle if you're just going to keep it parked up in your shed?*

He called the number, told the guy he was interested and it'd be a cash sale, arranged a time for a viewing, got the address. Then he did a drive-by, checked the place out, before phoning the guy back and telling him he'd changed his mind. His girlfriend had said no way was he spending twenty thousand bucks on a car.

'Women, eh,' he told the guy, over the phone.

He'll send a few of the younger fellas to wait outside the address in a couple of days' time until the guy goes to work. Rendall had spotted the garage where he figures the jeep is kept. It looked easy enough to get into. He'll get an easy five thousand for parts, he figures.

On the radio, a new song starts. 'Thunderstruck' by AC/DC. Rendall rolls his eyes. The local classic rock radio station's idea of humour. *Ha de ha ha.*

Coming out of the next tight corner, he has to brake hard.

Ahead of him, a double-trailer truck is jackknifed,

completely blocking both lanes of the road. Maybe a blow-out, or maybe the truck rear-ended someone in the shitty weather. As Rendall slows, he looks to either side of the road, aiming to sneak round the outside and keep going, leave the loser driver to sort out his own shit. But the trees come right down to the edge of the tarmac. There's no way past.

As Rendall leans on his horn, the first hailstones start to hit his windscreen.

In Auckland harbour, all ferry movements have been cancelled. The harbour bridge is closed to high-sided vehicles, owing to the gusting winds. A Coastguard vessel has been called out; a small yacht has broken its moorings in the building storm and is threatening to run aground on the rocks on the southern side of the bridge.

With the yacht successfully wrangled and in tow, the Coastguard vessel heads back to its base. As they're passing back under the bridge, the skipper spots something bobbing among the whitecaps. Maybe a piece of wood torn from another boat in the storm, or something washed off the deck of a container vessel. Whatever it is, it looks big enough to be a hazard to shipping when the storm passes and the harbour is opened again. The skipper turns his wheel towards the floating object.

As the vessel pulls up, the first of the hailstones start to fall.

The two crew members look down, getting a closer look. It's a large suitcase. Oddly, the handles are secured with a padlock and chain.

They grab a grappling hook, and prepare to pull it aboard.

'Have I ever told you about the day you were born?' Jaye says quietly to Addison.

'Dad. They said you shouldn't be talking.'

He smiles at her.

'You cried once. Just the once. Then I picked you up and you stopped. Didn't make another sound. Just stared up at me. Ironic really. Someone with fire burning in their throat, like you. So much to say. You sure didn't come into the world that way.'

Addison rests her head against his shoulder.

'Funny thing to be thinking about,' she murmurs.

Jaye looks at Marissa. 'Something happened to me. What?'

The head of the medical team told Marissa and Addison to avoid talking about the shooting for now. Jaye needed to stay relaxed, calm. They should just be with him, for the twenty minutes or so they were allowed to be there, and make sure he didn't have any reason to get upset.

'It was an accident. I'll explain later.'

She gently puts a finger to his lips.

'They want you to rest. Shh.'

Outside, the hailstorm has passed, as quickly as it started, leaving the car park looking like someone has tipped a few tonnes of ice shavings over the tarmac. Above, dark clouds hang like curtains, an eerie greenness glowing around their edges.

From the distance, the sound of thunder. Rain starts to fall.

In the forest, Rendall leans on his horn again. And again, and again.

The hailstones taper away, leaving a mass of ice spread across the bonnet of the Mark III and the base of its windscreen. But Rendall can see that even though the hail has stopped, the dark black clouds with the weird green tinge mean there's more weather coming.

He opens the door and gets out.

'Hey!' he yells in the direction of the truck's cab. He leans back through his door, pushes down on the horn again. 'Hey, shithead. What's going on?'

No response.

Rendall slams the door. Starts towards the cab to sort this clown out. As he reaches the last trailer, the rear doors are flung open.

Five people in black uniforms stare down at him.

Large semi-automatic weapons in their hands.

Rendall spins back towards his car.

Behind the Mark III, turning the tight corner he just

emerged from, a line of half a dozen police vehicles slowly approach, two abreast, completely blocking the road. There's no going forward, no going back.

Thunder growls in the distance. Heavy raindrops begin to fall.

Rendall turns for the forest and starts to run.

On the back deck of the Coastguard vessel, the suitcase has been snagged by the grappling hook. The thing is surprisingly heavy, and it takes both crew members to pull it onto the deck. As they get the suitcase aboard, the hailstorm slows and dies, as fast as it started.

From the distance comes the sound of thunder, as one of the crew members fetches a bolt-cutter from a storage box in the wheelhouse.

Above, from the dark clouds with the strange hint of green, rain starts to pelt down on Auckland harbour.

In the ICU, Jaye's eyes are closed. Happy to just lie there, Addison's head on his shoulder, his hand in Marissa's. Listening to the steady rhythm of the rain hitting the windows.

Then he hears another sound. He opens his eyes.

Marissa is crying. Jaye looks at Addison. She's crying too.

'Why are you crying?'

Neither can answer.

He can't really move to put his arms around them. But he does his best, shuffling them closer to him. Feeling the wetness of their tears falling on his hospital gown.

And now he's silently crying too.

Outside, the rhythm of the rain hitting the hospital windows picks up.

It's about to get really bad.

Rendall sprints hard through the forest, pine branches scragging at him, stumbling over exposed roots. The rain is falling in dense sheets. He thinks for a moment that this is pretty much all he has going for him right now; it's almost pitch black among the crowded trees, and the torrential rain is making visibility even worse for the people pursuing him.

But it's shitty visibility for him too. He trips over a large fallen branch, goes head over heels. He wants to curse but he doesn't dare. He grabs at the branch to get back on his feet, not even looking behind. He's running as hard as he can, the heavy branch still in his hands in case he needs to use it as a weapon, hearing the Armed Offenders Squad officers pursuing him in the distance.

At least they don't have dogs, he thinks.

Then he hears the sound of barking.
He runs harder.

As the skipper steers his vessel through the growing whitecaps, on the rear deck one of the crew members lines up the jaws of the bolt-cutter with the curved shackle of the padlock. It takes a fair amount of effort to bite through the hardened steel, but on the third try the padlock falls free.

The other crew member undoes the handles. Together they open the suitcase.

'Jesus Christ.'

In the wheelhouse, the skipper looks back. His crew are standing, staring at the contents of the suitcase.

'Skip. You need to see this.'

As the skipper puts the vessel into idle, the rain falls onto the harbour in heavy sheets.

The crying has finished.

The head of the medical team comes to Jaye's bedside. She meets Marissa's eye. It's time to let Jaye get some decent sleep.

Addison takes another moment, her head nestled in the warmth of her father's shoulder.

'Will Dad be out of hospital by the weekend?' she

asks the senior doctor. 'We've got something happening, to celebrate Matariki.'

A smile comes to Jaye's face as the memory returns.

'Oh my god, baby, your engagement party.'

'Addison, I don't think your dad's going to be out of hospital by then,' Marissa says gently. Jaye smiles at his daughter.

'Maybe they'll let me FaceTime with you. So I can keep an eye on you and make sure no one drinks too much.'

Addison leans in, kisses him on the cheek.

'Love you, Pāpā.'

'Love you, baby.'

With an effort, Jaye turns his head towards Marissa. Her eyes are shining, her face full of light and love and joy. She kisses him gently on the lips.

'See you soon, blue eyes.'

As Marissa and Addison head for the ICU door, they can hear the sound of the rain building outside. More thunder in the distance. Then, another sound.

A violent gasp from the direction of Jaye's bed. The machines he is hooked up to start beeping urgently.

Halfway out the door, Marissa and Addison turn.

Jaye's eyes have rolled back in his head. His arms and legs are extended, rigid, like every muscle in his body has suddenly contracted.

Marissa screams his name; Addison starts running for the bed, but she doesn't get five steps before the ICU staff grab her and Marissa, hauling them out of the room.

As the door slams behind them, the medical team descends on Jaye's bed.

The AOS members move through the dense forest, close behind the handler, who is following the sound of his dog. Somewhere in the rain and the black shadows of the forest, the barking turns into a chilling, angry snarl.

'She's got him,' the handler says.

Alongside the growling of the dog, there's another sound. A human being, screaming.

Moving faster, their weapons ready, the AOS officers hurry up a rise, coming to a stop at the crest. Ahead, Rendall is sprawled flat on the forest floor where the dog has brought him down. The jaws of the German Shepherd are clamped hard on one of his buttocks, tearing a hole in his jeans. The dog has absolutely no intention of letting go. Unable to get back to his feet, Rendall is swinging at her with the branch he picked up, but she's too close, so it's hard to get leverage; half the time he's hitting his own body as much as hers. Even so, as Rendall gets in a couple of blows, the handler rushes him, using his extendable baton to smash the arm Rendall is using to wield the branch. There's a loud cracking noise, and the stick falls.

The dog handler takes a step back. His dog is still attached to Rendall's anatomy. The handler catches his breath. Happy to let his animal do its job for another moment or two.

Or three.

Then he whistles. The dog immediately releases her grip and falls in behind him.

His arm already swelling where the baton hit him, Rendall slowly rises to his feet.

As the officers handcuff him, the torrential rain washes the blood from his wounds onto the forest floor.

At the Coastguard HQ in Mechanics Bay, Hana and DI Williams head out onto the docks. The skipper had called the CIB as he was heading back to base. He'd told them what they'd found floating in the harbour.

Hana follows Williams through the downpour. She remembers hearing somewhere that when a serious storm hits Auckland there can be as much rain in a day as would normally fall in three months. This is one of those days. She pulls her jacket tighter around her as they climb the gangway to where the skipper is waiting.

'Over here.'

On the deck, a bright orange Coastguard tarpaulin has been lashed over the suitcase, to prevent any forensic evidence being washed away in the endless rain. But it's a forlorn precaution given that the suitcase and its contents were probably floating in the harbour for some time before being found.

The skipper unfastens the strapping, removes the tarpaulin.

Inside the open suitcase is a body, knees and arms folded up tight around the torso like some particularly impressive circus trick. But unlike a contortionist on stage, this person didn't willingly choose to fold themselves into this cramped space. They didn't chain and padlock the suitcase. They didn't throw themselves into Auckland harbour, in the middle of a thunderstorm.

The head of the deceased has been forced down into the top corner of the case, partially covered by the crook of one of their elbows. Hana and Williams kneel next to the suitcase, to see the face from a better angle.

'It's him,' Williams says.

Hana nods. Yes. It's him.

On the deck of the Coastguard vessel, the pelting rain falls on the lifeless face of Toa Davis.

26

CAREFUL WHAT YOU WISH FOR

The formal questioning was delayed for several hours overnight while the accused was treated under armed guard in the emergency room at Auckland Hospital. The bite wounds to his buttocks were disinfected and stitched, and X-rays revealed a fracture in his left arm, where the handler used his baton to stop Rendall assaulting his dog.

There were further delays while the accused vetted the list of three duty lawyers available that day. He finally selected a woman in her late twenties. It's mid-morning before she arrives at the holding cell in the basement of Central Police Station to meet her new client. Rendall nods as she is let into the cell. His fractured arm is in a fibreglass cast, but he has tossed away the sling. With his good arm he pats the space on the mattress-less bench, for the duty lawyer to sit beside him.

'Take a seat.'

The lawyer stays standing.

'You're saying this is me?'

In the interrogation room, screen grabs from the CCTV cameras inside the liquor store are laid out on the table in front of Rendall, alongside photos from the camera outside the shop. He picks one of the pictures up with the arm in the fibreglass cast. Looks at the figure in dark clothes and a balaclava with a dismissive sneer.

'Seriously? This is why we're here?'

DI Williams is sitting across the table from Rendall and the lawyer. The video camera is recording the interview, and, in the next room, Hana and other detectives from the team are watching the feed.

'I can see the resemblance. This guy has two legs. Feet. A head. Pretty fucking definitive.'

He holds out the photo to his lawyer. A look on his face. *Do something about this.*

In the adjacent room, Hana can see the lawyer is determined to provide a competent defence to the accused, as is her duty. But she hasn't once met her client's eyes. There's a look on her face as she speaks. Like she's swallowing a deeply unpleasant medicine.

'It would be good to understand why my client is here. What are the grounds for his arrest?'

Williams doesn't directly answer the lawyer's question. Her eyes are still fixed on Rendall.

'Here's what we think happened. You stole this vehicle. You used it to go to the liquor store. You shot DI Hamilton, twice. Then you dumped the car where it would easily be found, knowing that the evidence left inside it would point to someone else.'

Williams leans in a little, towards Rendall.

'Tell me if I have that right.'

'I saw the video on telly,' Rendall says. 'The guy runs the red light. I've never had a ticket in my life. I should be a safe-driving instructor. This goes to court, I'm going to claim . . .' He turns to the duty lawyer. 'What is it? Precedence? The guy driving that car's a fucking amateur. It's not me.'

Rendall's eyes stay locked on Williams. He leans in, as she just did. Their faces now only inches apart.

'My lawyer asked a question. What evidence do you have?'

When the duty lawyer speaks again, it's almost through gritted teeth. 'We would appreciate an answer.'

Williams knows the lawyer has been placed in a distasteful situation, defending someone she'd ordinarily cross the street to avoid. She bears no antagonism towards her for doing her job. But this is her interview room. She'll answer the question when she's good and ready.

'Do you recognize this weapon?'

Williams places another screen grab in front of Rendall. It's of the gun in the liquor store, a moment or two before it was fired.

'Alfa Carbine, eh. Every wannabe gangbanger has one. You can buy them easy as a Big Mac. And about the same price. The state of this country we find ourselves in. I despair.'

He shoves the photo back across the table.

'I know the gun. But I don't know *that* gun. Never seen it in my life.'

Williams places a new photo on the table, face down.

'Do you know these people?'

She turns it face up. Watching Rendall's reaction closely. It's the image taken from the Nokia Hana found in the storage unit. Rendall and Jaye. Rendall making Devil's horns.

He picks up the photo.

Watching from next door, Hana would kill to know what his heart rate is. Lie detectors are essentially a joke with wires; scientifically speaking they are almost completely incapable of distinguishing truth from lies. They're about as methodologically accurate as a Ouija board. But what a lie detector does have going for it is that it monitors a person's heart rate with great accuracy. Hana would love to have Rendall wired up right at this moment. She'd bet the farm that his heart rate just shot through the ceiling.

Unless he's made of stone.

'I asked you a question, Mr Rendall,' Williams says. 'Do you know these two people?'

'The one on the left is called Maffs. Least, that's what his name was when I knew him. If you don't know who the other guy is, you're even less competent than I thought.'

The duty lawyer looks more closely at the picture, realizing now that the guy with the long stringy hair on the left of the photo is Jaye Hamilton.

'So that's what this is about. Maffs is the D who got shot?' Rendall puts down the photo. 'The guy who set me up, put me away, goes and gets a bullet in him. Ergo, it was me who did it?'

He looks at the lawyer.

'Do you believe this bullshit?'

She doesn't answer the question. But she moves her chair an inch or two further away.

'I understand now,' Rendall says. 'You're a few days in, no arrest, can't find the actual guy who paid ten bucks for a popgun and completely fucked up the moment he first tried to use it. So you make up a motive for me. I get it. I empathize. But you're full of shit.'

He taps his finger on the photo of him and Jaye.

'This was what, fifteen years ago? For a long time, I wanted to kick Maffs in the teeth for what he did. But things change. If I came face to face with this fella now, you know what I'd do?'

Williams doesn't respond.

'I'd shake his hand. Maffs got into our midst the same

way a rat digs its way into someone's food pantry. Sitting there with us, working alongside us. Getting pissed with us. Doing uppers and downers and P and what have you with us. Being like a fucking brother to us. That taught me a lesson.'

He rolls up the sleeve of his police-issue sweats.

'There's only one person you can trust. And he doesn't walk down here among us.'

There's a tattoo on the bicep of the arm without the cast. A big crucifix, wrapped in barbed wire.

'I found Jesus inside. That's why I'd shake Maffs' hand. If he hadn't done what he done to me, I wouldn't be the man I am today.'

The duty lawyer isn't even trying to hide the distaste on her face now. She knows exactly the man he is. Rendall rolls his sleeve back down. Rests his arms on the table.

'Where were you on the afternoon of Friday the seventh, Mr Rendall?' Williams asks.

'The day Maffs ate some lead?'

Rendall drums his fingers, eyebrows furrowed. The look of someone searching through their memory files. Then he nods his head. Remembering.

'I was out fishing. Good haul that day, as I remember. A couple of snapper, a kahawai.* Acquired the boat recently, for a good price. A two-mast ketch. I didn't ask to see ownership papers when I bought it, so maybe I unknowingly came into possession of stolen goods.

---

* Kahawai – a breed of ocean salmon.

But I don't see how that justifies sending guys in black helmets with fucking semi-automatics after a man.'

'Was anyone with you?' Williams asks.

'I like to fish alone.'

Rendall leans back in his chair. He looks at the duty lawyer again. Over to you. She clears her throat. Really not wanting to be in this room.

'To clarify. You have a photo of Mr Rendall. And you suspect he has a gun like the one that shot Detective Inspector Hamilton.'

'Which I don't,' Rendall grunts. 'Never have.'

'Did the warrant you executed on his place of residence produce any evidence that justifies his being further detained?'

Williams stares long and hard at Rendall. There's a small smile on his face, like he knows the answer well. Finally, she shakes her head, *no*. Every inch of Rendall's compound was combed through by a specialist search team. Metal detecting equipment and mirrors on extendable handles were used to examine wall and ceiling cavities. Any freshly disturbed areas of dirt in the grounds were dug up. The dog kennels were searched, the ground underneath them examined. Toilet cisterns were opened; floorboards were ripped up.

The Alfa Carbine wasn't there.

'Are we done here?' Rendall demands of the duty lawyer.

The lawyer picks up her bag. Rendall gets up to leave. But he pauses.

'Maffs. DI Hamilton. Whatever he calls himself. We had some good times, me and Maffs. Never had a brother, but he coulda been one. Till he put a knife in my back. Is he all right? The poor fucker.'

DI Williams stares at him, her eyes hard and unflinching. She doesn't deign to reply. Rendall shrugs and walks out of the interview room.

'If the gun was in his pad, if we'd found it, we'd be in a very different position,' Williams says.

She is in a downstairs corridor in Central Police Station with Hana, speaking quietly as Rendall is processed for release in another room nearby.

'If we had the gun,' she continues, 'and if forensics tests showed it was the same one used in the liquor store, we could put him away for the rest of his life. Shooting a cop, good luck trying to ever see the light of day again.'

Hana can see Williams is as deflated as she is.

'We don't have the gun, Hana. What we do have is a photo from fifteen years ago, and testimony identifying the weapon from a seventeen-year-old kid who knows nothing about guns.'

'Erwin Rendall did it,' Hana says, her mouth dry as she says the guy's name.

'Yeah, he did it. And we'll prove it. We will. But for now, there's nothing we can do.'

Hana stares at the dull grey paintwork of the hallway.

Suddenly, being here feels a lot like being buried alive.

The door at the end of the corridor opens, and the officer processing Rendall nods at Williams.

'They're finished with him,' she tells Hana. 'They're bringing him out. Time to go.'

Hana doesn't move.

'Hana?'

'I want to look him in the eye.'

Williams signals to the officer to let Rendall out. He emerges, carrying a paper bag with the items that had been confiscated from him. The duty lawyer follows as he heads for Williams and Hana.

'I had a long talk with Miss Gentry about laying a complaint with the Police Complaints Authority. Unjustified arrest. Police violence. She dissuaded me. You should buy this lady a drink.'

Face to face with Rendall, Hana is willing herself to stay calm.

'I'm going now.' Rendall turns to the duty lawyer, puts out his hand. 'Nice doing business with you.'

The duty lawyer doesn't shake his hand.

'I really hope I never see you again, Mr Rendall.'

'Fuck, eh,' he says, amused. 'Are you supposed to talk like that?'

The lawyer looks at Williams and Hana, apologetic. Then she walks out of the station.

Williams glances at Hana. A look on her face, warning

Hana not to act on any of the things she knows Hana is feeling. The things she'd like to do to Rendall.

Hana draws a deep breath. She speaks, very quietly.
'This isn't over.'

The smile hasn't left Rendall's face.

'Be careful what you wish for,' he says.

Hana watches him leave.

Her jaw clenched, knuckles white. Barely breathing.

If she could scream, she'd scream.

But she can't.

What Erwin Rendall doesn't know – what hasn't yet been released to the media – is that while Rendall was being treated for his wounds, in an operating theatre a few floors above him, Jaye was undergoing emergency surgery. A blood clot had developed in his chest; an undetected post-operative complication. The clot had dislodged soon after he was brought back to consciousness, causing a massive and catastrophic pulmonary embolism when it hit his heart.

The surgery was unsuccessful.

Detective Inspector Jaye Hamilton died on the operating table at 3:35am that morning.

27

IT STAYS LOST

Two very different farewells.

Two very different occasions.

So many shattered lives.

At the little wharenui on the hillside where Hana went to speak to Toa's family, she and DI Williams have returned to pay their respects on behalf of the police. Addison has come too. She really wanted to be there, but she wasn't sure if that's what Gracie would want. But when Hana called ahead, Gracie said that Addison would be more than welcome.

'It's not her fault,' Gracie told Hana over the phone. 'None of this is her fault.'

Three days earlier, after Addison had called in the middle of the night, distraught, telling her that Jaye had passed, Hana went to be with her daughter and Marissa and the girls in the hospital chapel. She stayed there until Williams called to let her know there was a crisis meeting with the Asian Organised Crime unit, about Toa Davis' murder. As the sun rose outside the windows of the eighth floor, Hana listened to a conversation that was pretty much identical to the one she'd later have with DI Williams when she had to release Rendall.

Everything about Toa's murder points back to Moon Lake Bistro and Lounge. Just like everything about the execution of Jaye Hamilton points back to Erwin Rendall. But knowing something is true and being able to prove it beyond reasonable doubt: those are two very different things.

Toa's casket lies in front of the third pou* on the right-hand side of the meeting house.

DI Williams lays flowers beside the casket. Addison holds a big bunch of peace lilies as she walks hand in hand with her mother. Following behind Hana and DI Williams, she places the bouquet beside the other flowers, then kisses Toa on the cheek and embraces the family members who hold the places on the mattresses closest to the casket.

When she kisses Gracie, Gracie takes her hand.

'I don't have a voice like yours. But can we sing together, for your dad, and for Toa?'

Standing at the foot of the casket, the two young Māori women sing, arm in arm.

---

* Pou – ornately carved pole or support beam depicting an ancestor.

Te aroha
Te whakapono
Me te rangimarie
Tātou tātou e.*

Afterwards, Gracie walks with them back to their car.

'Toa's brother is pretty messed up.'

Hana had seen, on the other side of the casket, the older brother Kura sitting close by Toa, staring at his face, eyes red.

'He stood up the first night, when Toa was first brought on. I didn't know what he was going to say. Could've been ugly, you know. I thought maybe Kura would call him all the names he'd called him when he was alive. But he just started to cry, couldn't stop. He talked to Toa, lying there in the casket. Begged for forgiveness. Said he'd look after my little one like she was his own. He means it. My family too. She's gonna be the best-loved kid ever born.'

Gracie rests her hand on her abdomen as she looks between DI Williams and Hana.

'Be honest with me. Whoever did this to Toa. They're probably gonna get away with it, eh?'

'I hope that's not true,' Hana says.

DI Williams retrieves an envelope from the back seat of the car.

'I'm sorry to have to ask this of you right now,' she

---

* 'Love, belief, and peace, be the things that bring us all together.'

says to Gracie, taking a photo of Erwin Rendall from the envelope. 'But it's important. Do you know this man?'

Hana can see Gracie recognizes the face immediately.

'That piece of shit. Toa used to deliver stuff to him. Out of town somewhere. One time the guy came and picked up the gear from our place. I'd just got out of the shower, had a towel round me. He looked at me like I was a piece of raw meat. Toa saw him staring, shoved him out the door, told him to fuck off. The guy looked like he wanted to rip off Toa's head.'

She hands the photo back, like she doesn't want the taint of it on her hands.

'He came to the house you're at now?' DI Williams clarifies. 'He knew where you lived?'

Gracie frowns, reading between the lines.

'It was him? You think he was the one who stole Toa's car? He's the guy who did all this, who set Toa up? Have you got him?'

Neither Hana nor DI Williams respond. But Gracie knows the answer.

She looks back to the wharenui, where Toa is lying in the casket.

'The father of my child. He wouldn't have got justice if he'd lived. He's not gonna get justice now he's dead.' There's anger in Gracie's eyes, but she manages to hold it in. This isn't the place or the time.

'I hope you get the person responsible. But I'm not holding my breath.'

Eden Park is the mecca of rugby in New Zealand, the home of the all-conquering national team, the All Blacks. The ground occupies the same Everest-like sporting stratosphere as Wembley Stadium, say, or the Melbourne Cricket Ground, or Dodger Stadium.

In the middle of the playing field stands a large gleaming hearse. Inside, Jaye's coffin is draped in the flag of the New Zealand police force.

Tens of thousands of people are in the stadium. Much of the New Zealand police force is there, in full ceremonial uniform, along with uniformed members of the army, air force and navy. But by far the majority of those gathered are ordinary citizens, drawn to pay tribute to Jaye. The police commissioner speaks, followed by the paramount chief of the local iwi,* Ngāti Whātua ki Orakei. Finally the prime minister speaks with emotion about the debt the government and the country owes Jaye.

At the end of the service, the police commissioner takes the flag from the casket, folds it into the shape of a triangle and hands it to Marissa.

As the coffin is driven slowly through the sea of uniformed officers, Marissa and her two daughters walk behind the hearse. Exhausted and numb. Unable to comprehend living through this cruel nightmare a

---

* Iwi – tribe.

second time. Hana follows, her arms wrapped around her own daughter as Addison weeps, trying hard not to fall apart herself and barely winning the battle. PLUS 1 holds Addison's other arm, Eru and Daisy walking behind them. The entire police contingent join in a haka, the symbol of the highest respect and honour.

Sebastian is somewhere in the middle of the surging emotions, Hana knows; alongside the other members of the public in the stadium, joining in with the haka as the stamping feet and screaming voices echo around Eden Park.

As the hearse leaves the stadium, a regiment of the army fires a twenty-one-gun salute. Smoke fills the air. As Hana follows the vehicle through the access tunnel beneath the main stand, the final gunshots echo around the now hushed stadium.

Out in the parking lot, as the others get into cars to join the funeral convoy, she sees two figures waiting for her. Her cousin Eyes, and Tīmoti.

Hana can see in Tīmoti's face that there's something wrong.

'Can you two go with Grandpa and Daisy?' she asks Addison and PLUS 1. Hana kisses her daughter on the forehead, wiping away tears from Addison's eyes, trying to keep her voice from cracking. 'I'll be there soon, baby.'

'The other day. When you came to the tā moko place, Auntie, you and the cop woman. I didn't know what you were asking, exactly.' Tīmoti is with Hana and Eyes in the access tunnel, where Hana had taken them to speak privately. 'But when we heard that thing on the news about the Māori kid they found in the harbour, I understood.'

After Toa's body had been recovered, and following Rendall's interview, the police issued a media statement clearing Toa of any involvement in the shooting in the liquor store. Hana knew the news brought little consolation for Gracie, or for Toa's family.

'The stuff you were asking about Rendall,' Tīmoti continues. 'You think he did this? You think it was Rendall who shot Jaye?'

'That's what I believe,' Hana says.

'My boy said he had to see you. That it was important,' Eyes tells Hana. 'He hasn't told me what it's about.'

'You can talk to me, Tīmoti.'

Tīmoti's eyes are fixed on the concrete floor of the tunnel. The young man's coping mechanism when he's feeling a crippling level of stress or confusion.

'If Rendall finds out I said something. I dunno what might happen.'

'Whatever you tell me, I promise you, he won't know it's come from you.'

Tīmoti's eyes rise to look out towards the field, where uniformed officers and members of the armed forces are embracing each other, no one even trying to hide their emotions.

'Jaye was a good fella. He brought down that cop car and let us have a drive. He's Addison's dad. He has people who love him. Makes me fucking sick.'

'Me too,' Hana says. 'I need your help to put this right.'

'When you went to the gangpad. Did you find the gun?' he asks.

'There was nothing there.'

Tīmoti's head nods slightly.

'We did this burg one time. A break-and-enter, some fancy war museum place. Rendall heard war medals could be worth heaps to sell to collectors. We got all these display cases full of old medals. Then he heard from another gang that the cops had an idea it was Rendall who'd done it, and they were on the way to ask questions.'

Eyes takes Tīmoti by the arm, squeezing his hand tight.

'Keep going, son. Kia kaha,* my love.'

'When he knew the cops were coming, he sent a few of us off with all the stuff we'd nicked. There's this place, a bridge over the Kaikākāriki River. The river from there on down is like six kilometres of insane rocks and rapids. Really fast water. No one goes in there, not even those crazy kayak people, it's too dangerous. We went and threw everything off that bridge.'

---

* Kia kaha – be strong.

Tīmoti's shoulders relax a little. Like he's been able to get rid of a weight threatening to crush him. When he speaks again, his voice is very quiet.

'Rendall told us: "You lose something in that river, it stays lost."'

28

TOO BROKEN

Stan is pounding the biggest of the hanging bags, the seventy-kilogram. There's no style. No stance. He's smashing the hard, heavy leather like he wants to punch his fist through one side and out the other.

'Bro, what's going on?'

Stan wasn't booked in for a session with his usual trainer; he just turned up with his gloves, walked into the middle of the gym and started attacking the big bag.

'You're going to break a wrist or something,' Dax says, genuinely worried.

But Stan's not hearing anything.

That day, he waited until the end of work. There was a desperate sadness across the whole building. Jaye's passing had hit the whole workforce like a tidal wave.

And the guy who'd almost certainly pulled the trigger, Erwin Rendall, had walked free.

After the rest of the team on the third floor had headed home, Stan opened the report on the death of Toa Davis. He looked at the forensic photos. The suitcase on the boat, opened, lying on its side. The body scrunched up inside, looking more like a broken mannequin from a second-hand shop than a human being. He pulled up the photos from the mortuary. Toa's skinny brown body, lying on the cold steel of the pathologist's table. He read the pathologist's report. It had been impossible to determine the cause of death, but it was very likely asphyxiation. *Hopefully he was dead before they put him in the water*, Stan thought. Hopefully he didn't know the terror of being forced into the suitcase, hearing the chains wrap around it and the padlock close, being dropped into the wild storm waters, feeling the ocean filling the suitcase. Not being able to move or escape. Then not being able to breathe.

In the gym, Stan is punctuating each punch now, with words spat out under his breath.

'The bastards.' *Slam*. 'The bastards.' *Slam*. 'The bastards.'

Heads are turning.

'Bro, you're making people uncomfortable,' Dax says.

Stan keeps pounding the bag. Not even hearing Dax. His mind is somewhere else.

The cul-de-sac. Knocking at the door. Seeing Toa running off down the pedestrian alleyway. Grabbing him before he got over the fence. Beating the shit out of him and seeing the raw fear in his eyes. If they'd never knocked on that door, Stan thinks, pounding the bag harder still; if he'd told Addison he couldn't help her with her crazy idea of hunting down the house near the railway tracks.

If he'd said no, maybe Toa Davis wouldn't be in those forensic photos on Stan's computer.

'The bastards.' Stan keeps slamming the bag. The words spilling out of his mouth, a messy, angry, bitter rhythm. 'The bastards. The fucking bastards.'

Stan had turned up at Addison's place early on the morning she went to pay her respects to Toa Davis.

'I keep thinking about Toa in that alleyway,' he told her. 'Me laying into him. Punching the shit out of him. Thinking I was giving payback for what he'd done to Jaye. And he had nothing to do with it. He was just a fucking kid.'

His voice cracked as he spoke. Addison could see that Stan was right on the edge.

'I'm worried about you, bro.'

For a moment his jaw tightened. Then he burst into tears.

'I'm so sorry about your dad.'

Stan crying only made Addison cry, again. They held each other for a long time.

Everyone else in the gym has stopped working out now. They're all staring at Stan.

'The bastards.' *Slam. Slam. Slam.*

It's not about any one thing, not even about any one

person. It's everything. It's everyone. It's Erwin Rendall: what he did to Jaye, how he set up Toa Davis. It's Moon Lake Bistro and Lounge. It's a young Māori kid who just wanted to be a good dad, but who ended up floating in Auckland harbour. It's the flash of light Stan sees behind his eyes every night, just as he's almost asleep; a hundred times brighter than looking at the sun. The impact of the eardrum-bursting explosion, then the rush of heat, until all that's left is staring up and counting shipping containers.

'The bastards.' *Slam*.

And the thing that has broken Stan once and for all. Before he left the office that day, he took the elevator to the eighth floor. Found an excuse to lurk at the door, to listen in to the evening status meeting for the team investigating Toa Davis' murder: a combined task force of the Asian Organised Crime Unit and the CIB. There were photos projected on the wall of Gold Brother and Hàoyŭ. DI Williams was adamant, the team had to try everything they could to penetrate the fortress of silence surrounding the Moon Lake syndicate. To gain some kind of leverage; to get someone on the inside of the organization to talk; to work on the competing syndicates to find out if anyone had heard anything. But she was realistic.

'These guys know how to cover their tracks. We'll need a miracle.'

Stan knew what that was code for. Work your arses off. But prepare for the worst. They're almost certain to get away with it.

'The bastards. The bastards. The bastards.'

Inside Stan's gloves, the skin on a couple of his knuckles has torn, the wet warmth of blood dripping down his wrists. He only hits the bag harder.

'The *bastards*.'

The door of the office swings open and the owner of Delaney's gym comes out, looking around his place, seeing all his clientele standing staring at the guy with the artificial leg going crazy on the big bag. He pushes his way through, grabs hold of Stan, shoves him up against the nearest mirror.

'What the hell?'

Stan tries to pull free, but the owner's an ex-boxer; he's in his sixties now, but he's never lost his fitness or his strength. He leans into Stan with all his weight, pinning him against the floor-to-ceiling mirror. The older man takes in the wild look in Stan's eyes. His flushed skin. The bulging muscles trembling with barely controlled rage. Recognizing the telltale signs, he grabs one of the sleeves of Stan's sweatshirt and pulls it up, exposing the inside of his arm. He looks at the puncture marks in the skin. He throws Stan against the mirror again, hard.

'Get out of my gym. Don't come back.'

Dax watches as Stan snatches his bag, knocking over a bench in the process, then storms out of the gym, kicking open the front door, none of his fury dissipated.

Just the opposite.

Hàoyǔ is sitting in the private lounge with a couple of new young language students who have been recruited to work the slot machines. He's going over the routines. The kinds of clothes they should wear. Something decent, so they don't get turned away at the door. But not too flashy.

'You want to look like nobody.'

'Do we pay for the clothes ourselves?' the male student asks.

'What do you think?' Hàoyǔ isn't as harsh as he could have been. The young man is in his early twenties. He reminds him a little of his own son.

This isn't Hàoyǔ's favourite job. Babysitting, he calls it. He explains the routines, the fee paid for working the slot machines. He tells the students in detail how to check the bags of cash they're given, before they exchange them for chips.

'If the banknotes smell mouldy, or if they're cold, it's a red flag. The casino will think the money's been stored somewhere damp, or that it's been buried. The person selling the chips is legally obliged to make a suspicious transaction report. It'll probably go nowhere; the banks and the real estate agents and the casino make hundreds of reports every week. All the same, you'll be in the system. Then you're no use to us.'

As Hàoyǔ continues, the front door of the restaurant bangs open. Stan strides in. He shoves past the waiter who goes to greet him, heading straight through the tables, his eyes searching for the person he's after.

He spots three people out in the private room. He recognizes Hàoyǔ from the organized crime profiles. He walks faster through the tables, rips the gold braided cord aside; before Hàoyǔ can even look up, Stan swings his fist into his face. Stunned, Hàoyǔ tries to bring his hands up to defend himself, but Stan swings again, hard, feeling a welcome crunch of cartilage as he connects flush with Hàoyǔ's nose, screaming in his face as he punches a third time.

'Bastard! You fucking murderer!'

The two language students watch, terrified. This wasn't what they were expecting when they were offered a cushy job playing pokie machines.

'STAN!'

Hana comes running from the front door, DI Williams a step behind her, both of them barrelling into the private lounge. Then they're one on each arm, hauling Stan off Hàoyǔ, restraining him from throwing any more punches.

As two uniformed cops follow them and take over restraining Stan, the entire waiting staff are gathering to watch.

Hàoyǔ shakes himself, clearing his head. He looks down at his shirt. It's covered in blood from his badly broken nose. His wife had just bought the shirt for him. Ruined. He looks at Stan. Ice in his eyes.

'Who the fuck are you?'

The female language student helpfully translates.

'Get him the hell out of here,' Williams says to the

uniformed cops. Stan is putting up no resistance now, the explosion of fury and pain done, leaving him shattered, an empty shell.

As the officers take Stan away through the gathered staff and customers, Hàoyǔ's eyes meet Williams'. A cold smile of recognition comes to his face. He takes the edge of the tablecloth and wipes away blood from his chin.

'You. Again. This is a law-abiding business being repeatedly targeted and victimized by the police.' He looks over to where Stan is being escorted out the door. 'Now I'm attacked by some insane man, in front of you. And I'll bet good money he's not going to be locked up.'

As the young language student translates his words, Hàoyǔ takes a step closer to Williams. His voice quiet and soft, and all the more dangerous because of it.

'We've done nothing wrong.'

Williams stands her ground. Undaunted.

'We both know that's not true. We both know exactly what you've done.'

For a moment, a stand-off. Hana comes to Williams' side. Finally, Hàoyǔ nods at the restaurant staff who have gathered. The semi-circle at the entrance to the lounge behind the two women opens.

As they walk out of the restaurant, Williams glances back over her shoulder. Hàoyǔ is still watching them, every step of the way.

It's dark on the back deck of Stan's house. Hana is there, with Stan's sister Melody, PLUS 1 and Addison.

'I know I said I wouldn't tell Mum,' Addison says. 'I'm sorry. I had to break my promise.'

'It's okay,' Stan says. 'You know what? I'm glad you told her.'

Earlier that day Dax had called Addison, telling her what had happened in the gym.

'I'm sorry to put this on you right now. I know you're going through a lot. But the guy's ready to explode, bro. You gotta do something.'

Addison immediately phoned her mother, telling her what she'd sworn not to, about how there were enough pills in Stan's bathroom cupboard to stock a chemist shop. About how Stan was losing it in the gym, cursing out someone.

'The bastards, the bastards.'

Hana knew immediately who Stan was talking about, and where he was going.

Back at the police car where the uniformed cops had taken Stan after dragging him out of Moon Lake Bistro and Lounge, Williams released Stan into Hana's care. 'This is a mental health issue,' she told Hana and the other officers. 'I'm not laying any charges.'

She took a moment to speak quietly to Stan. 'You fucked up. I understand why, but you still fucked up. I know you were a good cop. I know you'll be a good cop again. This is your one free pass. Get yourself sorted.'

When Hana arrived with Stan back at the flat he

shares with his sister, Addison and PLUS 1 were already there, waiting, worried sick. Hana told Stan to call Melody, that she needed to know what was happening. Hearing the distress in her brother's voice on the phone, she finished work early and came straight home.

'Show us,' Hana says. 'You have to show us what's been going on, Stan. What you've been taking.'

Stan goes inside, into the bathroom. After a couple of minutes he re-emerges onto the deck. His arms are full of sleeping pills, anti-depressants, unlabelled bottles of steroids. He puts everything down on the BBQ table, then slumps down on the top step, his head in his hands.

All of the rage and wild energy long gone now.

Empty.

'Oh, big brother.'

His sister comes to sit at his side, putting her arms around him.

'You've been trying to patch yourself up with this stuff. But you're too broken.'

Melody starts to cry quietly. Stan looks out at the obstacle course that replicates the one he was to take the following week, to get back into the cops.

'The PCT test. I would have nailed it next week. I'm so ready.'

'You have to fix yourself, Stan,' his sister says, sobbing. 'You have to.'

Stan rests his head on her shoulder. His voice hoarse and shaky. Tears falling.

'I need help.'

29

SALUTE

If he was being completely honest, he would admit it was his own fault. He was meticulous, a planner. He always thought ahead, always covered all the angles. Until he didn't.

He let his guard down with Maffs.

The clues were all there. Like that one time he and Maffs went to beat up some young shitheads who hadn't paid up for their eccies. Fucking MDMA users. In love with being in love. Not so in love with paying for their drugs. He noticed, when they were dealing to the kids, Maffs seemed to be pulling his punches. Maybe he'd damaged his knuckles or something, he thought at the time, stepping in and doing the job himself.

That was his mistake. Giving Maffs the benefit of the doubt. All that time he'd spent hiding in plain sight, and his eyes weren't open the one time someone else was doing the same.

Then the doors got kicked in.

Maffs disappeared, like a puff of smoke from a glass pipe.

Never to be seen again.

That is, until he saw him, again.

Never say never.

Doing the thing he decided he was going to do to Maffs; it wasn't going to be any kind of easy job.

Turns out, the guy had become a somebody.

In the years between them taking the Devil's horns selfie and them crossing paths again at a distance in Tātā Bay, Maffs had become a big deal. A cop, and not just any cop. Well-known. Top of the pile. When Maffs hit the floor, it was gonna make a hell of a noise.

It was going to be a challenge.

Which made it all the more exciting.

That first time, on the cliffs in Sydney, after the sun went down, he'd sat on the bench, watching the passersby. Looking at each face as they passed, working out who was going to draw the short straw. He thought long and hard about a young woman in tight Lycra and a headscarf, swinging her arms as she power-walked up the hill towards him. There was no one else around. He had the rock in his hand, his fingers tight around its hard, jagged edges.

Getting ready. He could always see things vividly in the little movie screen in his head, and as she drew closer, he pictured how it would go. Her hair was a messy knot of bleached tresses under the scarf. He imagined the short, sharp thud of the rock against her temple, the hiss of air as she gasped her last breath. A flood of pinky red spreading fast and sticky through her blonde hair.

Perhaps a splinter or two of cranial bone, fallen, on her green headscarf.

He imagined the rush of adrenaline, the surge in his loins. As she got closer, he could already feel the hormones moving through his blood.

But then he realized how small she was. A hundred and ten pounds at most. She had earphones in. She wouldn't even hear him coming. He'd bring the rock down once; that's all it would take. He probably wouldn't even have to swing very hard. She'd be dead before she hit the ground.

The tendons of his fingers relaxed, then. He slipped the rock back onto the bench by his thigh. She wasn't the one. She smiled as she passed, meeting his eye. He nodded in return, thinking she'd just won a lottery she didn't even know she had a ticket for.

He likes a challenge.

The girl in the headscarf and Lycra would have been no challenge.

The man Maffs had become: he was.

But it was more than that. It was so much more than that.

Maffs, raising his eyebrows. *That* was the straw that broke the camel's back.

He remembers the night the door got kicked in. A sea of cops in black uniforms flooded in, like someone had opened a dam. He was pushed face-first down on the ground, a knee hard in his spine, another cop wrenching his hands behind his back, the metal of the handcuffs biting his wrists. All through the gang-pad, the air was ringing with cursing and threats. The cop who cuffed him told him to stay on the ground.

Don't fucking move an inch.

He moved an inch.

He turned his head far enough to see the shattered door the cops had smashed with the battering ram. Beyond the door, now hanging from its hinges, unmarked police vehicles. Moving his head just a little further, he could see someone being led from the gang-pad towards a matt-black Armed Offenders Squad vehicle.

The guy wore the same patch as the men lying face down on the floor. But no one was pointing a gun at him. He wasn't wearing handcuffs. The cop who helped him up into the vehicle had a look on her face, like she was in the presence of a hero. As he climbed into the AOS vehicle, Maffs looked back for a moment.

Their eyes met, through the splintered remains of the door.

Maffs raised his eyebrows. The bro salute. Like he was just heading out to get a crate of beers. Then he disappeared into the vehicle, and it sped away.

He'd had to teach himself every emotion. Except one. Anger was the only one that came naturally.

In the liquor store, in the moment before he fired the gun the first time, he thought about Maffs raising his eyebrows. Then before he pulled the trigger the second time, another memory came, unbidden. Being in the garden shed. Trying not to listen to the sounds his uncle was making. Seeing the rat watching from the shadows.

His mind is a sticky place. Like the glue-soaked fly ribbons you hang from the ceiling. Nothing escapes.

He fired the gun, twice.

One for Maffs raising his eyebrows.

One for his uncle in the shed.

He took the money from the till, put it in the bag with the video game logo. He looked down at the red of Maffs' blood mingling with the faintly fizzing bubbles from the broken champagne bottle on the floor. The cop's eyes were open, but it seemed unlikely he was seeing anything.

He didn't give a shit if Maffs saw or not.

There was something he had to do.

He raised his eyebrows. The bro salute.

Then he stepped over Maffs, and walked out the door.

30

NOW WE KNOW WHO YOU ARE

Redoubt Bridge is a one-lane bridge that traverses a tectonic split in a vast shelf of prehistoric schist. Carved into the hard rock by millennia of relentlessly rushing water, the canyon that it crosses is quite narrow. You could throw a tennis ball from one side to the other.

The river upstream of the bridge is wide and deep, and the waters run slowly. But as the current hits the narrower cleft in the rock, they start to rush and become turbulent. There's a sudden drop in the height of the river, and downstream from the bridge the waters turn white and treacherous, rushing past huge boulders, turning into torrential waterfalls. A frenzied, unpredictable and deadly waterway that continues on for a good six kilometres.

It's pretty much exactly the way Tīmoti described it, Hana thinks, as she looks down from the bridge at the tempest below.

Rendall was right, when he was interviewed. There's no hard evidence that links him to Jaye's shooting. According to Tīmoti's statement, Rendall almost certainly clocked Jaye at the meeting at the marae in Tātā Bay; he recognized the cop who had put him in prison for almost a decade. Rendall had a gun of the same type as the one that was used to shoot Jaye. He knew Toa; he had been to Toa's house, from where the Corolla had been stolen. Rendall had motive – to get revenge. And he had means and opportunity, a history of foresight and planning and the skills needed to steal Toa's car and frame him. Every part fits the scenario that Hana and DI Williams have built. What they don't have is the only piece of the equation that actually matters: the physical evidence needed for a conviction.

The weapon that shot Jaye.

Without the gun, they might as well have nothing.

There's a rock shelf just below the bridge into which its foundations have been sunk. On the jutting section of smooth schist, two dozen members of the police national dive team are gathered in the freezing winter air. They've been given intensive safety briefings, and all the divers will be diving in pairs and working velcroed together with surfer-style leg ropes that can easily break away if anything goes wrong, so they won't drag each other down. In the most treacherous sections of white water, the pairs will be tethered to two watchers on land.

The divers know what they're looking for.

A cut-down Alfa Carbine. With a series of small notches carved into the base of the handle.

'It's not going to be fun down there. We wouldn't send you into these kinds of conditions if we didn't have to.'

DI Williams is standing on the shelf of rock below the bridge, addressing the dive team. The strain of the investigation is starting to show in Williams' face, Hana can see, but her voice is firm and steady above the rushing waters, keeping the divers focused on the task at hand.

'I have to ask you to go the extra mile. This is now a homicide. It is about a dead cop. The death of a fellow officer.'

The dive teams nod. They're ready. They move out, heading towards the first sections of the river to be searched. It's going to be slow and painstaking. Hazardous. Dangerously low temperatures. Eddies and crevasses. Hidden openings on the bottom of the riverbed. Spaces beneath rocks where things could get lost and stay lost. It will be a very long process, and everyone knows there is no guarantee of success.

As the dive teams move into the water, Hana and Williams climb back up to where the vehicles are parked on the road.

'See you back in town,' Hana says, heading for her car.

She doesn't notice a flicker of movement on the hillside

high above the bridge. Looming over the rushing river is a promontory that was the location of a British army outpost in the nineteenth century, during their battles with the local tribe – the stronghold that gave Redoubt Bridge its name. Hidden in the shadows of its trees, a lone figure is watching as the grey wetsuits enter the water.

As Hana gets into her car and starts the engine, the figure shifts, turning in her direction.

Erwin Rendall's eyes rise from the river, watching Hana's car drive away.

'You're a cop, right?'

'Well. Not really. But kind of.'

'Kind of a cop. Okay.'

Hana is at the house of Maia's grandmother, Nanny Niki, who she met at the celebration sausage sizzle for the young people who had earned their drivers' licenses. It was only a few days ago, but it feels like years have passed since then. The old woman is sitting in her garden, surrounded by a sea of bright rhododendrons and camellias. While Maia makes them a cup of tea, Hana sits with the My Little Pony backpack that Addison gave her on her knee.

'It's nice out here in the mornings. I try and get some sun in my bones. If it's a day when I'm moving okay, I do a bit of work in the garden. Sorry it's such a mess.'

'It's beautiful,' Hana says. 'I'm a gardener. I always

seem to go for ferns and natives. This feels so happy. Maybe I should loosen up. Try a bit more colour.'

The old woman's eyes are on Hana, curious.

'So, you're a cop. Kind of. And you drove down here with a couple of kilos of weed in a kid's backpack to give to a stranger. No offence. But that's not exactly normal behaviour.'

Hana has to smile. She thinks back to earlier, standing with the group of police divers by the river, alongside one of the highest-ranking cops in the Auckland district. All the while very aware of what she had stashed in the back of her car. She'd been relieved to see there were no sniffer dogs as part of the search.

'Why are you doing this?' Nanny Niki asks.

As Maia brings out the tea, Hana looks across the sea of flowers, considering the question. She remembers what Gracie said outside the uncarved meeting house, that Toa would likely never have justice, in life or death. She thinks about Stan at the Moon Lake Bistro and Lounge, his fury that no one would answer for how the young man had died. She thinks about her absolute certainty that Erwin Rendall shot Jaye, and the real possibility that it will never be proved. She sips her tea, thinking about what Addison said in the hospital corridor.

'You believe in the rules, until you don't. Who'd have guessed?'

Maybe that's how it works, she thinks. *Maybe, sometimes, doing the right thing isn't the same as doing what's in the rulebook.*

She doesn't reply to the question, and Nanny Niki doesn't push her. Hana takes another sip of tea. Leaves the My Little Pony backpack on the seat where she was sitting.

'I better get going. Nice to see you, Maia.'

As Maia gives Hana a hug, the older woman looks at her.

'What do I owe you, dear?'

'Nothing. Just take care of yourself.'

The road from Tātā Bay back to Auckland leads through a long, twisting gorge. The sides of the gorge are steep, with long falls to the river below; sometimes, over the winter months after heavy rains, slips can close the road entirely, which means a diversion through an alternative route that adds an hour on to the trip. So far this winter, the route has stayed open.

As Hana drives the winding road, something is eating at her. That morning, as the dive team started in the river, DI Williams took her aside.

'This has to stay between us.'

Now that all eyes were on Rendall, Williams told Hana, the police data forensics team were digging into his historic movements, to see if there was any way to arrest him in connection with other criminal activity and get him off the street. They'd uncovered some interesting points of intersection on his timeline. Rendall had shown up on a longlist of persons of interest in an infamous missing persons case: a young, just-married German couple who'd been on their honeymoon in New Zealand. They'd disappeared while camping in a national park area twenty years ago; their bodies had never been found.

'Rendall was in the vicinity of the area when the Köhlers went missing. He was questioned twice,' Williams told Hana.

It was difficult building a thoroughgoing timeline of Rendall's movements, as he'd drifted between a number of different motorcycle gangs over the years, moving from one branch to another, or shifting allegiances to rival gangs when it had suited him. But as the data sweep built a picture, other blips came up on the radar.

An unsolved hit-and-run in 2002 in rural Waikato. A home invasion of an isolated South Island farmhouse that ended in a fatal shooting. For a couple of years, Rendall had been connected to a gang in a district two hundred kilometres away; not close enough to make him a focus at the time, but of interest when looked at retrospectively, with a possible pattern forming.

'There's another connection. This one's bizarre,' Williams continued.

Rendall had only left the country once, flying to Sydney when he was nineteen years old. He'd been in the city less than a day, and during that time there had been an unexplained homicide. A Fijian rugby league player, attacked from behind and shoved off the cliffs at

South Head, to his death. The only witness was a woman who had been power-walking in the area in the minutes before the assault, who'd described someone hanging around nearby. A man who fitted Rendall's description at that time.

Hana takes it slowly through a hairpin curve. The engine works hard as the car starts the climb up through the steepest part of the gorge.

'The links are paper-thin,' Williams admitted. 'We've got zero substantive evidence, nothing that shifts the dial, nothing that could lead to an arrest. If you look hard enough, you could very probably connect most people to being in the vicinity of a homicide at some point in their lives.'

But being in the vicinity of five killings? Hana thought. *On five separate occasions?*

'At this stage it's just data points,' Williams continued. 'The kind of intersections that a good defence KC will call coincidence, not correlation. Still. There's a point where unlucky starts to look careless. Finding that gun is our very best way to get this bastard.'

There was something else unsaid, that both women were thinking. Hana gave it voice.

'Elisa. Tīmoti said it looked like there were five notches in the wooden butt of the gun in Rendall's room.'

Williams nodded. She turned back to look at the dive teams making their way down the river.

There's a knot in Hana's gut, and it's not down to the rollercoaster turns and switchbacks of the road.

CARVED IN BLOOD

She's never believed in the concept of inherent evil. She knows most people who come to the attention of the justice system are shaped by so many things beyond their control: socioeconomics, emotional or physical abuse, intergenerational trauma, brain injuries, sheer desperation to feed the ones they love. Then there are the narcissists; those who fit somewhere on the very wide spectrum of sociopathology. There's a wiring problem at play for sure: for those individuals at this end of the continuum, the interconnectedness of their neurons leads them to see themselves as the centre of the universe, with everyone else only there to be used in some way or another.

Objects. Playthings. Disposable.

A movement in her rear-view mirror draws Hana's eyes for a moment. She catches a glimpse of a vehicle behind her, maybe half a kilometre back, rounding one of the tight corners she's just passed through. Then it's gone.

Evil is an idea, a musing, a philosophical slash religious concept. Whether it exists or not isn't a question any cop has much time for, let alone an ex-cop who has walked away from the justice system. But Hana knows, offenders out at the far end of the sociopathic continuum occupy very dark, very scary terrain. If even a part of the suspicions DI Williams is harbouring is true, Erwin Rendall could be a kind of offender that neither Hana, nor Elisa, nor anyone in the history of New Zealand policing has encountered before.

Erwin Rendall is uncharted territory.

Another movement in her peripheral vision takes Hana's eyes back to the rear-view mirror.

A glimpse of blue. Then the vehicle disappears behind the intervening curve in the road.

You're going way too fast, Hana thinks, looking for a place to pull in and let the driver pass, before remembering that the road stays this narrow for at least another ten minutes.

Coming out of the next hairpin curve, she realizes.

Erwin Rendall's car is blue.

The thought has barely landed when the car behind her comes into view again, its tyres squealing round the hairpin bend she's just passed. Hana glances in the mirror. Just for a moment. But it's enough to see she was right.

A blue Mark III Zephyr.

It's closing fast.

Hana pushes the pedal a little harder. The last thing she wants is to be rear-ended, to lose control and risk smashing through the protective barriers. But then, trying to out-run the other car is just as bad an option: meeting an oncoming vehicle at speed on this narrow road would be an unthinkable mess.

In the mirror, the Zephyr is closing in.

Hana looks for longer this time – long enough to confirm it's Rendall, and that he's alone in the car.

As she rounds the next corner, her eyes go to the speedometer. She's going way faster than is safe now.

She glances at the passenger seat, under which she keeps the tyre iron, rather than in the boot next to the spare tyre. A habit formed after many years of driving alone through night-time streets and rural roads.

She exits the next corner. Ahead is a section of straight road the length of a couple of rugby fields. Behind, Rendall is closing in, faster and faster, only twenty yards behind now. All her options are bad, Hana knows, but in a matter of moments she'll have no options left, and she'll only be dealing with the consequences of what Erwin Rendall decides to do.

'Fuck that,' Hana says, surprising herself that she's said the thought out loud.

She slams her foot down hard on the brakes.

The grill of the Zephyr smashes into her car, sending the rear bumper flying into the air.

Hana pushes down harder still on the pedal.

The hundred and fifty yards of straight road ahead shrinks to one hundred yards, then ninety yards. Her car is still going way too fast, pushed from behind, the engine of the Mark III screaming. Rendall hasn't taken his foot off the accelerator, and the length of the runway is getting shorter by the moment. Hana feels the interlocked vehicles start to jackknife towards the edge of the road on her right, and corrects the steering wheel into the arc of the turn, forcing the two cars to straighten again. Her foot is losing feeling from the sheer force she's exerting on the brake pedal, as though she wants to push it straight through the floor.

Fifty yards.

Forty yards.

For a moment Hana's eyes drop to the speedo. The car is slowing, fast.

But is it enough?

Thirty yards.

Her gaze lands on the metal safety rail on the outside of the tight right-hand curve ahead.

Twenty yards.

If she had another half a rugby field, they'd come to a complete halt.

She doesn't have half a rugby field.

Ten yards.

Hana feels her torso slam against her seat belt, the explosive sound of metal smashing into metal filling her car as it hits the safety barrier. The impact instantly smashes apart the heavy bolted connection between one length of the barrier and the next length. The two sections of metal railing cleave apart and out, nuts and bolts erupting into the air like bullets, before tumbling the hundred-metre sheer drop to the rocky river edge below.

Hana's car has pushed partway through the mangled railings, like a cowboy stopped mid-stride, halfway through a swinging saloon double-door in an old western movie.

The two now-separated sections of the safety barrier have been bent back violently.

But they hold.

She tentatively touches her chest. Her ribs throb; the bruising is going to be a hell of a sight. But nothing feels broken.

In the mirror, she sees the door of the Zephyr opening.

She grabs the tyre iron, pushes herself out of her door, turns to face the other car.

As Rendall approaches, Hana expects a clenched jaw, pupils opened wide from adrenaline, a body readying to explode with the same brutality just inflicted on her car. But in his face, as he walks towards her, there is none of this. If she had to describe his expression, the word she'd use would be *nothing*. There's nothing there. She recognizes the emptiness in his eyes. She's seen it before.

The mako shark that circled her in the ocean.

Rendall's eyes are exactly like the shark's.

Cold. Emotionless. Watching.

He stops, an arm's length away, and looks at the tyre iron gripped in Hana's hand. When he speaks, his voice is calm. Quiet.

'You wanna use that thing, don't you? Take the law into your own hands.'

He takes another step forward. Hana moves backwards, keeping the same distance between them, but now she feels the rear of her car behind her, stopping her from going any further.

'Go, Rendall. Get back in your car and go.'

'Or what, Sheriff?'

There's no mocking tone in his nickname for her, the

word coming out as flat and empty as his eyes. Her grip around the tyre iron tightens. Ready to use it.

In truth, she'd welcome the chance.

'I know what you did,' Hana says. Keeping her own voice calm, despite the utter rage flooding through her as she stares at the man she knows killed Jaye. 'I can't prove it. Not yet. But I'm going to. I'm gonna put you in prison. You're going to fucking die there.'

Rendall moves again.

Hana takes a short, sharp breath. Raises the tyre iron, ready to strike.

But he walks straight past her.

She turns, as she turned with the circling shark, watching as he goes to the edge of the road, moving into the yawning gap between the two sections of the destroyed safety barrier. He stands right at the jagged lip where the tarmac ends. In front of him, nothing but air.

Then a long, sheer fall to the hard rocks far below.

'You can't prove a thing. You're not even a pig anymore.'

Rendall turns back to face her. He slowly spreads his arms.

'Do it.'

Hana stares.

'Do it. You can say it was to defend yourself.'

In her mind, a flurry of images. Stan walking into Moon Lake, trying to take justice into his own hands. Jaye on life support in hospital. Toa lying in a small, simply painted meeting house in his pine casket. DI

Williams describing the shopping list of horrific crimes Rendall could be connected to. Addison weeping in her arms as they followed the hearse holding her dad's casket.

Hana takes a step forward. Another step. Another. Closing in on the man who did all this. Who fucked up so many lives.

Standing in the gap between the tortured, twisted metal, Rendall doesn't move. One arm in its fibreglass cast to one side, his good arm to the other. Making no attempt to protect himself. Another step, and Hana is within a yard of being able to strike, to send him and all the things he has done and all the pain he has caused tumbling down into the abyss.

Falling.

To the justice he'll never otherwise face.

Hana stops. The tyre iron still raised.

Her heart beating hard against the heavy bruising on her ribs.

Ready to strike.

Wanting to strike.

But she doesn't.

From somewhere far above, Hana hears the screeching call of a hawk circling, its powerful eyes searching for carrion. Ready to fold back its wings and dive, to drop through the sky like a rock, and feast. It's an eerie sound. The hawk's cry echoes around the rocky walls of the gorge, gradually fading away into the chill air.

Rendall lowers his arms.

'You were going to do it,' he says. 'It was there, in your eyes. *You wanted to do it.*'

He walks forward, towards her, past her. Hana tries to keep herself from recoiling as his arm brushes hers. 'Now we both know who you really are,' Rendall says quietly as he passes.

He gets back into his car, reversing hard, untangling the twisted metal where the two vehicles became locked together, the sickening graunch like metal fingernails on a metal chalkboard.

Without looking back, he drives away.

31

FLAMES AND WATER

The search has covered just over half of the six-kilometre stretch of the river where the police believe the gun could be. It's a slow grind, not helped by the fact that it's almost the shortest day of the year, and there's less than ten hours of usable daylight in which to safely search. The water at this time of year is brutally cold, and even with the best wetsuits and insulated gloves and boots, it's tough, exhausting work.

Beneath a ten-metre waterfall, the conditions are particularly difficult, the water a sea of swirling bubbles, pitch black at the bottom of the basin. The duo working their way around this area consist of a senior member of the police dive team, Constable Heggie, and her search partner, a young recently joined member of the squad named Greer Finlayson. It's taken Heggie and

Finlayson a good hour to methodically make their way around the fifty-metre circumference of the base of the waterfall, using their head lanterns and torches to search the floor and the indentations in the rock walls, kicking hard with their fins to fight against the wild currents.

As they reach the farthest bank, the end of this search grid, they come across a large, heavy section of tree trunk wedged hard against the rocky wall at the very deepest point. They both move around it, examining it from all angles. Where the tree trunk has washed up against the rock wall, it is covering the opening to what looks like a small cave. There's a gap of a few inches that debris could tumble through, but the space isn't big enough for the divers to get their bodies in, and with the light of their torch beams they can only see a little way into the darkness beyond.

Heggie signals; both divers kick to the surface. They take off their breathing regulators.

'If we both wedge ourselves against the rock wall and push together, we might be able to shift the thing,' Finlayson says. Heggie smiles. With new divers, there are two ways they might go about their work. Nervous and deferential, waiting to be told what to do. Or full of beans and enterprise, ready to do the hard yards, no matter how challenging and dangerous the underwater environment. It's pretty clear to Heggie which kind of diver Finlayson is.

On the bank, their spotter calls down to them.

'The boss is here. Morning debrief when everyone's out.'

Heggie looks downstream to where EZ-up tents have been erected. DI Williams is already there, talking to the head of the dive teams.

'If we both give it a try, I reckon we'll get it,' Finlayson continues, itching to get back under the water.

Constable Heggie signals to the spotter. *We're going back down.*

The two divers put their mouthpieces in and descend back into the darkness.

As Marissa paints and polishes her nails, Hana helps with her hair.

Marissa's hair is naturally long and wavy, bordering on unruly if she lets it go. She doesn't like to let it go. There aren't that many vets who spend twenty minutes straightening their hair before they go to work in the morning, but that's what Marissa does. 'I don't care if it's just bull terriers and cats with broken legs who see me,' she'd tell Jaye when he'd complain about how long she was taking in the bathroom. 'I want to look decent.'

That morning, Eru and Daisy had come at dawn. The family said karakia together around Jaye's casket. They all said their final goodbyes. Marissa was the last to kiss him. Together they carefully put the lid on the casket. Each of them twisted one of the screws into place.

The cremation is happening late morning. Daisy has taken Eru back to the motel they're staying at for a rest.

Addison and the girls and Marissa have been sleeping in the lounge the last few nights, on mattresses alongside Jaye's casket, and that's where they're all getting ready. Addison is doing the girls' hair, the long, tight matching pigtail plaits both Sammie and Vita love.

No one has said much at all since the casket was sealed. There's an understandable heaviness in the air. But as Hana moves on to the last section of Marissa's hair, Marissa puts down her nail polish.

'You know what? Let's not do it like this.'

She goes to the kitchen, comes back with the girls' Bluetooth speaker. She puts it beside Jaye's casket, takes her phone, opens her music app, finds the song she's after. Music fills the room. The goofy country slash hip-hop number about cowboys and roping steers and riding across the prairie.

Marissa sits back down by Hana. As Hana starts in again with the hair straightener, Addison and Sammie start to smile. Addison begins singing along to the words, Sammie doing some of the moves. *Chasing-the-runaway-horse. Heel-tap* to *toe-tap*, back to *heel-tap* again.

Vita is the only one not joining in.

'Baby. Come here,' Marissa says.

Vita folds herself into Marissa's arms, quiet and sad, letting herself be held.

The very bottom of the basin beneath the waterfall is a field of small rocks rounded and polished by the constant movement of water over the centuries. There's a rhythmic sound of clacking as they shift and knock against each other in the eddying currents.

Heggie and Finlayson are back down at the tree trunk, their headlamps on, working hard with their fins as they look at what they're dealing with. The tree trunk is big, the size of a small car, battered and branchless from its violent descent during one of the flooding events that hit the area once or twice a year. On land you'd need maybe a half dozen people to try to shift something this size. With the buoyancy of water, two strong people might be able to dislodge it.

Maybe. Then again, maybe not. After all, it is the size of a small car.

Using hand signals, the two divers make a plan of attack. Heggie goes to one end of the log, Finlayson to the other. They both wedge their fins against the rock shelf, grabbing hold of whatever part of the trunk they can get most purchase on. Heggie makes a signal, and they push hard in unison. The tree trunk moves a little, the gap opening an inch or so, but when the two divers ease off the pressure, it slips right back into the same spot.

The divers adjust their leg positions, trying to get better leverage. They push again, a half inch more opening up this time, but when they ease off, the heavy tree trunk slips back into place once again.

Finlayson kicks closer to Heggie, gesturing with her arms, a motion like rocking a baby. Heggie nods in agreement. They retake their places, but this time, rather than a single, long, hard, brute-force, energy-sapping push, they shove hard, gaining an inch or two, then release the pressure. As the log subsides back against the rock wall, they use the slight bounce to push off in unison again, the gap opening an inch more this time. They do this again and again, rocking the tree trunk back and forth, building momentum. Each time, the huge log moves a little further, until finally Heggie signals for one last big shove.

The massive tree trunk tips free, its weight rolling it away from the schist wall and down the incline into the bottom of the basin. Constable Heggie grins at Finlayson through her mask, *good work*. They turn back to the wall, their headlamps picking out the shadowy indent that has been revealed in the base of the rock. It runs deeper than they thought, stretching back under the shelf for a good ten yards, but the gap from the ceiling to the floor of the small cave is narrow, and to push into the tight gap, they'd have to shimmy-kick their way in sideways, to stop their oxygen tanks being wedged against the roof.

Finlayson is the smaller of the two, and she manages to squeeze furthest into the narrow space. She looks to and fro in the darkness, the beam from her headtorch picking out shapes deeper in the cave. There's a lot of debris — small sticks and branches washed through the gap between where the tree trunk once sat and the opening behind it – but no sign of the gun. Then Finlayson feels an urgent tap on her leg. Behind her, Constable Heggie is indicating something she's seen in the far corner of the cave. Finlayson turns in that direction.

Something metallic flashes in the beam of her headlamp.

Finlayson squeezes forward, twisting her body as much as she can to avoid her tank getting stuck. Whatever is reflecting her torch beam, it's still half an arm's length away, and she's already feeling like she's shoved herself in as far as she can possibly go, the sides of her torso wedged hard between the top and base of the narrow opening.

This would be a nightmare if I had claustrophobia, Finlayson thinks.

But people with that particular fear don't tend to be drawn to this job.

She adjusts her headlamp. Looks again.

It's so close.

She glances back at Heggie. Makes a signal. *I'll try one more thing.*

Finlayson takes a big, deep breath from her tank. She exhales slowly, emptying her lungs, stretching herself out long and straight. Making herself as thin as possible, trying to imagine herself as a freshwater eel or a sea snake, rather than a fully equipped diver with a hell of a lot of breathing apparatus strapped around her torso. She pushes herself forward again, as hard as she dares, making another inch of progress, and another half inch. But it's diminishing returns now. For a moment, it goes through Finlayson's mind that this would be a really shitty time for an earthquake to happen, under all this brittle ancient rock. This isn't where you'd want to get stuck under two tonnes of fallen schist. She gets rid of the thought and pushes again – another half inch – her gloved fingers extended.

The object reflecting the beam of her headtorch is still just beyond her reach.

She grits her teeth. A little half twist to gain a tiny bit more wriggle room; another hard push, her fingers straining to their maximum length. Even as she is thinking that it's going to be such a bummer if it's just a Coke can, Finlayson makes one last, long, final stretch.

Her fingers wrap around something hard and metallic.

It's not a Coke can.

The hearse holding Jaye's casket turns off the main road, towards the crematorium.

Hana is driving Marissa's car, following behind. As they approach where Eru and Daisy are waiting for them, in the back of the car Marissa kisses Vita gently on the forehead.

'You okay, love?'

Vita looks at her sister, on the other side of Marissa. She looks at Addison in the front seat. All of them worried at how hard this is hitting the younger daughter. Finally, Vita tips a pretend cowboy hat. Both sisters, and Addison, and Marissa, call out the same thing in perfect unison.

'Yee-ha!'

When Eru opens the door, everyone in the car is laughing.

At the EZ-up tent just down from the waterfall, DI Williams is laying out the takeaway noodles she picked up from a place in a neighbouring town, slipping the owners a couple of fifties to open a few hours early so there'd be hot food for the team on the cold winter morning. As she talks with the search team co-ordinator about the likelihood of getting to the end of the next search grid before sunset, there's a sound from up by the waterfall.

A whistle.

Along the river, everyone stops. All eyes turn towards the source.

At the base of the waterfall, Constable Heggie has surfaced. Every diver has a whistle attached to their wetsuit. There are two prearranged signals. Two short blasts repeating means diver in trouble. One long blast repeating: we've found something.

Heggie blows a long blast. Then another long blast. And then again.

Everyone starts to run. DI Williams clambers down the rock bank. As she reaches the side of the river, out in the middle of the water Finlayson is surfacing. She holds something up in the air.

A handgun.

As Heggie and Finlayson kick into shore, Williams wades waist-deep into the water to help them out. She carefully takes the gun from Finlayson. It's an Alfa Carbine. The gun that's become the weapon of choice for much of the New Zealand underworld. The same type and calibre as the weapon used to shoot Jaye. Williams turns the gun to look at its stock. The part Tīmoti described in detail; the thing that had struck him about Rendall's gun when he saw it.

'Five little cuts, carved into the wood, at the very bottom,' Tīmoti told them. And there are five old, weathered cuts in the stock. Just as he described. Williams looks around the team.

'It's Rendall's gun.'

The divers whoop and cheer, embracing and high-fiving. But Williams stays where she is, ignoring the biting cold of the swirling winter waters. Her eyes are fixed on the stock of the weapon. Alongside the five cuts that Tīmoti described, there's something else.

Another cut. The colour of the wood in the sixth notch is lighter than in the others.

The sixth cut is new.

CARVED IN BLOOD

A convoy of four matt-black Armed Offenders Squad Land Cruisers races through Kaikākāriki Junction. There's a single-pump local gas station on the main street of the tiny town. The owner comes out to watch as the vehicles speed through. On the other side of the street, a small, understocked convenience store is the only other retail premises in the neighbourhood. The owner comes to her front door, mesmerized by the commotion.

From their houses, other locals emerge, drawn out by the screaming sirens, the flashing lights, the chop of the blades of the police helicopter passing overhead. They watch as the AOS vehicles and the Eagle chopper disappear into the distance.

The town's been down on its luck for a few years now, since the meat company that had a processing plant there shuttered the business. All the locals know well enough where the vehicles are headed. Whatever is happening now, if it means Erwin Rendall and his hangers-on might be gone at last, it will be one of the few pieces of good news the locals have had in a very long time.

It's another five minutes from the town to the corrugated iron front gate of Rendall's compound. Flying ahead of the Land Cruisers, the helicopter radios back to the convoy.

'The whole place is burning.'

In the passenger seat of the lead vehicle, Williams is readying her protective gear.

'Any signs of movement?'

'Negative.'

The tyres of the Land Cruisers squeal as they speed around the final corner. Ahead, black smoke is rising into the air. Williams gives the order and the lead vehicle accelerates, the bull bars smashing through the gate, the cruiser braking to a halt in the weed-covered forecourt.

Williams gets out, her weapon in her hand.

'Get fire services out here,' she calls into her handset, knowing even as she says it that the nearest staffed fire station is more than half an hour away, and with the amount of smoke already coming from the buildings, there will likely be very little left to save by the time they get there.

'Stay where you are,' Williams orders the AOS team as she hurries towards the main entrance. She goes in as far as she can, to the main area where she knows the stolen cars are dismantled, but already the heat is too intense to go any further. Whatever accelerant has been used to fuel the blaze has been spread throughout the building. The fire has been burning for some time now, and the flames are everywhere. Williams manages to get to the beginning of the corridor that leads to the living quarters. She kicks the door in.

Behind it, an inferno rages. No way to get in there.

She hurries back out to the AOS vehicles, maintaining a safe distance from the possible explosion of welding cylinders or fuel containers. Williams turns back to look at the front wall of the burning building. She can just make out three letters through the thickening smoke, each one as tall as a human being, painted on the corrugated iron.

The same three letters as the largest tattoo on Rendall's right arm.

FTW.

Fuck The World.

As Williams and the team of AOS officers watch, the flames continue to rise. The painted letters bubble and melt in the increasingly fierce heat.

The steel door of the cremation chamber closes behind the casket.

The pre-heated furnace is already around eight hundred degrees Celsius. With the door shut, the effect is almost instantaneous. The lacquered finish of the casket ignites, flames surrounding it, the wood immediately bursting into fire.

The night before, as the others lay asleep around Jaye's casket, Marissa sat on the mattress beside him. As everyone else slept, she wrote on the top sheet of one of her daughters' notebooks. A last message for Jaye, to send with him. She knew exactly what she wanted to say.

She carefully folded the note, tucking it into the breast pocket of Jaye's dress uniform.

Inside the chamber, the fabric of Jaye's uniform pocket catches fire. For one microsecond, the piece of paper holding Marissa's final message for him floats upwards, lifted on the currents of swirling, super-heated air.

See you soon, blue eyes.

Then the paper ignites, the words becoming fire and smoke.

In the crematorium, as the muffled sound of flames rises from behind the steel door, Eru looks at Marissa.

'It's a nice day outside. Why don't we go wait in the garden?'

Addison takes the two younger girls by the hand, leading them out into the sunshine. Eru walks with Marissa, his arm around her shoulder, Daisy following them. Hana pauses in the doorway, and as the others carry on into the garden, lets the door close in front of her.

She subsides against the wall, needing a moment to process the last twenty-four hours. Coming face to face with Erwin Rendall on the narrow road beside the cliff. The pure fury she felt, translated into her hand grasping the tyre iron like a club. Rendall had been right. She had been ready to use the thing, to bring it down on the man she knows killed Jaye. The tsunami of hate and anger she felt in that moment terrified her.

That's not who I am, Hana thinks, leaning against the crematorium wall. *That's not me. What right does that piece of shit have, murdering the father of my child, in cold blood. Then almost turning me into someone I don't recognize?*

She looks back towards the reinforced door of the

cremation furnace. Takes a long, slow breath. She feels moisture on the fingers of one of her hands, and she doesn't have to look to know that it's her own tears.

Her phone buzzes in her pocket.

She finds a tissue. Dries her eyes. If it's a text from Sebastian, she'll give him a call straight away. It would be good to hear him; in fact, right now, his voice is the best thing she can imagine. She opens her phone.

The text isn't from Sebastian.

Rendall has disappeared. He's gone.

Hana stares at the message from Elisa Williams. A sick, empty, angry feeling deep in her gut.

But there's nothing she can do about it.

There's nothing she can do.

She pockets her phone, takes a deep breath. Goes out to join the others.

32

A NET FULL OF SOULS

Above, in the heavens, the skies are clear. The tempestuous mid-winter weather has settled.

Below, the crying is done.

A fire burns on the sands beneath the headland that offers the best vantage point from which to watch the rising of the sacred stars.

That morning, back in Auckland city, Addison and Hana went with Stan and his sister Melody to Odyssey House, the residential clinic where Stan was going to be supported to address his untreated PTSD, and his addiction to anabolic steroids. Stan had committed to a 24/7 plan with the head of counselling services; Melody and Addison and Hana were all signatories and designated support people for the tough times ahead in his treatment. They had pledged to be there for Stan whenever he might need them.

'We're in this together,' Hana told him as they left. 'Every step of the way.'

Stan couldn't hide his tears as his primary counsellor took him into what would become his home for the next several months, until he was well again.

Afterwards PLUS 1 and Addison drove down to Tātā Bay and spent the rest of the day collecting driftwood from up and down the beach. There's enough to keep the flames alive until well into the small hours of the morning, when Matariki will rise above the horizon.

The sun set a few hours ago, and now Vita and Sammie are wrapped up in twin sleeping bags near the fire. They had fallen asleep as Sebastian sang a song for the engagement, a Korean love song his parents had taught him when he was at school. Daisy played guitar and harmonized as he sang. They all shared a few bottles of the champagne that Jaye had chosen, the one with the red diagonal sash, and they sang and spoke quietly as the heavens slowly turned.

Earlier that day, Marissa and Addison and Hana had gone to the tā moko studio where Tīmoti had been tattooed. The artist had given them kirituhi.* While tā moko is only given to those of Māori descent, and incorporates traditional symbols that reflect individuals' particular tribal heritage, kirituhi can also be worn by non-Māori. The patterns are still deeply

---

* Kirituhi – a form of tattooing, literally meaning 'skin art'.

symbolic, and to honour Jaye, Eru had designed matching images of a pou – a foundation pole, for instance the centre pole of a meeting house – for each of their forearms. A symbol of what Jaye was and will always be to them.

A tribute, carved in blood.

The last of the driftwood has just been put on the fire when Eru sees them, out over the ocean to the north-east.

'Welcome back, old friends,' he says in te reo.

Marissa wakes the younger girls. Despite insisting long and loudly that they be woken when the stars rise, Sammie and Vita grumble as their mother folds up their sleeping bags and helps them climb the slope. At the top of the headland, everyone looks out towards the horizon. The stars glimmer gently, a delicate glow in the surrounding darkness.

'If you look just a wee bit to the side, use your peripheral vision, you can see them better,' PLUS 1 whispers to Marissa's girls.

Eru takes off his battered old hat, holding it in his hands.

'When I was small, one of our kuia* told me that the nine stars form the prow of a waka. A canoe, just like the ones that brought our ancestors here. But the job of this waka is to carry us to our real home. All year long the navigator of the canoe collects the souls of those who have passed in a net. Then the waka disappears, and

---

* Kuia – older woman and elder.

when it emerges again, the souls are released. And they become the new stars.'

They stand there, together, until it is too cold to stay any longer.

Walking back along the beach to her grandpa's house, holding PLUS 1's hand, Addison speaks quietly. 'I want to try to be as good a person as Dad.'

Hana slips her arm through Eru's. 'I want to be half the person my father is.'

Eru's fingers are laced with Daisy's. To Hana, her father usually seems to have the energy of a man half his age. But tonight, she sees a deep weariness in his eyes.

'I want to live long enough to see the man who killed Jaye answer for what he did,' he says.

Hana's eyes fall. Seeing the sadness in her father's face is just too much. She wants the same thing as Eru. More than anything in the world she wants Rendall brought to justice while her father can still remember it.

It shatters her heart to think this may not happen.

As the others carry on, Hana pauses, waiting for Sebastian, who is carrying Daisy's guitar. They stand face to face on the beach together. Hana takes Sebastian's free hand, raises it to her face and kisses it. Then she rests her head against his neck.

Her eyes find the north-east horizon.

She looks to the skies.

To the gentle twinkling of the distant sacred constellation.

The souls of those who have passed, now stars.

Two days later, Hana drives back to the city.

She takes the elevator up to the eighth floor of Central Police Station, heading to the office that until recently was Jaye's. She hands back her certification as a temporary constable of the New Zealand police force, and DI Elisa Williams reluctantly accepts it.

'It was a privilege to finally work with you,' she tells Hana.

'My ID,' Hana says. 'Did Jaye really keep it?'

Williams goes to the top drawer of the large desk, retrieves the lanyard photo ID Hana had when she was Detective Senior Sergeant Westerman. She comes back to face Hana, holding the swing-tag in her hand.

'What do you want me to do with this?' she asks.

An unwelcome memory comes to Hana's mind.

Erwin Rendall, standing in the gap between the two lengths of twisted metal railings. His eyes. Emotionless. Cold. Watching. And another memory. The mako, circling her in the water. Once. Twice. Three times. The shark's eyes never leaving hers, before it turned away and disappeared into the darkness of the ocean.

Hana takes her ID from DI Williams' hands. She has made her decision.

'I'm coming back,' she says, pulling the lanyard over her head.

'I have unfinished business.'

33

BLEACH

He walks along narrow, twisting alleys formed from crates stacked to the height of two men, laden with fruit and dried fish and sacks of rice and live turtles ready to be traded to the city's restaurants. This area of the port is where the local fishermen dock, and the small coastal trading boats. The air is heavy with diesel smoke and raised voices.

A handcart hurries towards him, laden with durian, the porcupine-like fruit the size of a basketball that is so treasured in Indonesian cuisine. In the hectic lanes of commerce of Jakarta's main trading harbour, pedestrians are neither welcome nor made concessions for, and he has to quickly duck between two crates of building bricks to avoid being run down. *It would be ironic*, he thinks as the handcart races past, *to have safely navigated five thousand nautical miles of winter ocean, only to be killed by a barrow of spiky tropical fruit.*

Rusting metal cranes unload steel containers from the larger ocean-crossing cargo vessels that occupy the far end of the port. He follows the train tracks that lead out from the warehouses and loading docks, past the brightly painted red and blue food carts that feed the area's workforce. In the distance, the lights of the skyscrapers of central Jakarta are flickering to life. He continues on towards a collection of makeshift dwellings and shanties wedged between the polluted, slow-running waters of two rivers. Many of the buildings are little more than corrugated metal walls and tarpaulin roofs. Outside a row of identical plywood-walled rooms, each holding one sad bed and little else, working girls sitting on boxes watch him pass, some calling out invitations to the foreigner to spend a little time with them.

He keeps walking.

It's hard to overstate the utility of a bottle of household bleach.

He was at sea nearly six weeks. Fortunately, what would prove to be the biggest tropical cyclone of the winter had already passed over the Tasman Sea. He isn't about to forget that storm. In the middle of the deluge, he was attacked by a police dog and bitten so badly he needed twenty-five stitches in his arse. His arm fractured by a baton.

How could he forget that?

But the terrible weather was done by the time he set sail. His two-mast ketch, which would have struggled in really big waves, had much smoother conditions in which to operate. A couple of days after he'd set out from his anchorage, in a cove just south of Tātā Bay, he took scissors to his bushy, full, black-grey beard, then shaved the stubble with the cut-throat razor he always carried with him. It was the first time he'd been clean-shaven in more than two decades, and he was certain there wasn't a single photo taken of him in the whole of his adult life where he was without a beard.

That's a good thing, he thought, looking in the mirror.

Sailing up the eastern seaboard of Australia, about the time he decided his arm had healed enough for him to toss the fibreglass cast overboard, he trimmed six inches off his long, straggly hair. Then he tried the bleach. It came out a little disappointing the first time, more of a jaundice yellow than the lived-in, light, sandy colour he was hoping for. Over the next few weeks, as he rounded the north-eastern tip of Australia and headed west along the northern coastline, he carefully repeated the process several times, using well-diluted mixtures of bleach, so that the changes in hue were incremental. He wasn't aiming for platinum blond. Nothing showy, nothing that would draw attention, nothing that would stand out in a crowd.

Exactly the opposite.

As the boat sailed west along the islands of the Indonesian archipelago towards Java, he settled on a shade that looked real, natural. It was a colour he'd describe as mousey blond, if he was in the habit of describing hair colours. He carefully snipped and trimmed the hair into a style that didn't look particularly cared for but at the same time wasn't pudding-bowl brutal. A very feasible look for a guy who spent his life on a boat and cut his own hair. He recorded the dilutions of hydrogen peroxide that he'd used to get the right shade, so he could do it again, and again. As he sailed into port in Jakarta, he took a last look in the mirror, assessing his work.

I don't recognize myself, he thought.

Which was exactly the point.

Past the rows of sad one-room brothels, the train lines head into a more brightly lit area. It's not downtown Jakarta; it's not the area where the well-heeled business crowd from the financial district go to drink Dom Perignon and mojitos; it's not the leafy, hilly part of the city where the gated embassy compounds are located. Far from it. But it's the part of town that has the thing he's looking for. Bright neon signs. Bars with loud music. Cheap restaurants. Milling crowds of locals and tourists.

Tattoo parlours.

He works his way through a half dozen tattoo places before he finds one that feels right. Lots of sterilization equipment. All the staff wearing gloves and masks. He's here to get a job done, but he really doesn't want to contract hepatitis in the process.

Do you do laser removal of tattoos?

The middle-aged woman in a hijab who owns the place asks him to roll up his sleeves. She raises her eyebrows at the sea of inelegant body art.

Just this one will take maybe half a day, she says, indicating the biggest tattoo. The one that says FTW.

Can you do the job? Get rid of all of them?

Yes. Anything is possible, she tells him. But it's going to take a while.

Erwin Rendall nods.

I'm in no hurry, he says.

Acknowledgements

This book is dedicated to my beloved brothers, Mark and Bruce.

In October last year, aboard the great waka with its prow formed by the nine stars of Matariki, the navigator threw out his net, and he picked up my oldest brother Mark. Less than four months later, my next oldest brother Bruce joined Mark in that same net full of souls.

It warms my heart, even in the sadness, to picture my brothers together aboard that waka in the skies.

They're both in the styliest outfits either ever owned; the turtlenecks and matching super-cool herringbone jackets that they wore in their caskets. On the waka, Mark is wearing one of his dozen pairs of designer reflective sunglasses. Bruce has his $20 off-the-shelf reading glasses. They're a tenth the cost of optometrist prescription specs, but just as effective. Mark and Bruce are smiling their big 10,000 watt smiles, they're laughing like little kids. Telling all the old stories. Brothers and best mates in life; now riding the great waka through the heavens, side by side. Then a few months later, in June, the waka will emerge from its long journey through the darkness. Just above the horizon, out to the north-east, the stars of Matariki will once again rise.

The navigator will empty his net into the night.

And Bruce and Mark will become the new stars in the sky.

Moe mai rā, Maaka. Moe mai rā, Bruce. Haere, haere, haere atu rā.

Fly. Soar. Shine.

To Katherine Armstrong, my wonderful, insightful and generous editor, ngā mihi aroha. To George Gibson, my US publisher, my endless gratitude for your endless belief and support. Ngā mihi nui to Craig Sisterson; you are so much more than an agent. To Tim Worrall (Ngāi Tūhoe), the cultural advisor on this series of books, thank you for your wisdom and aroha. To the Pou Matua of this book, Te Aranga o Otene Kane Hopa (Ngāpuhi, Ngāti Whātua, Waikato); ngā mihi for your tautoko.

Simon & Schuster are one of the great publishing houses; they are also a warm, generous, embracing family. Thank you especially to Georgina Leighton, project manager, who often seems even more passionate and invested in Hana and Addison and their fates than me. Ngā mihi to Sian Wilson for another cover that deserves to be framed and hung on the wall. He mihi nui to the Simon & Schuster rights team, to Rich Vlietstra and Lily Searstone in Marketing, to Joe Christie in Publicity, and to the sales, production and digital teams. Ngā mihi to Maddy Hamey-Thomas, the copy editor, and to Gillian Hamnett, the proofreader. My gratitude to the publishers and editors and translators and narrators who are taking this book into other languages, and other forms of media.

My daughter Māhina Bennett once again gave the gift of her beautiful Māori designs for the cover and throughout the book.

My thanks and love to the friends and family who have my back and who have held me up in so many generous ways in the writing of this book – Jared Savage, Steve Brewer, Miriama McDowell, Cian Elyse White, Jane Wilkinson, Greer Finlayson, Carys Finlayson, Rachael (Ra On) Kim, Krissi Holtz, Herb Holtz, Sandra Noakes and everyone on the team at Harper Collins NZ, Niki Bennett, Detective Constable Turi Bennett, Harriet Crampton.

Creative New Zealand, the Arts Council of New Zealand Toi Aotearoa, is an extraordinary body without whom so many artists simply could not do the work we do. The writing of this book was possible because of their generosity.

Whānau is a small word, just two syllables. But it means something taller than the sky. To Jane, to Tīhema, to Māhina, to Matariki – you are the twinkling sacred constellation that holds and guides me. To my mum and dad, to my siblings, to Kath, to every beautiful gossamer thread of the vast wonderful spiderweb of our whānau – ngā mihi aroha. These books are about a whole bunch of stuff: crime, suspense, social justice, the collision of good and bad, fate, destiny and redemption. But always these stories circle back to the only two things which truly matter, ever – love, and family.
Michael Bennett
February 2025